The Big Eye of Summer

by

I.H.M. Smart

Papyngay Press

First published 2004
Papyngay Press
Tualatin, OR U.S.A

ISBN 0-9755749-2-2

Contents

Preface

None of these stories were written for publication outside the pages of the Scottish Mountaineering Club Journal. Over the years, the different Editors of the Journal have always been tolerant souls, so I have written about things that happened to interest me without regard to whether they interested anyone else. I did not have any readership in mind beyond half a dozen friends who I hoped would find them an interesting read. Although the Club has about four hundred members, only a handful actually get round to reading the Journal. A handful is more than enough. And it is to this fan club (who can be counted without taking off more than one shoe) that this anthology is dedicated. Most stories concern Scotland, a land that has given me deep roots in a fertile soil. The others relate to the empty quarter of Northeast Greenland with which I have had an affair for fifty years.

This anthology would not have happened at all if my friend Phillip Todd had not founded Papyngay Press. He set up this idiosyncratic but commendable enterprise for publishing 'obscure literature which I believe should be available.' He continued, 'In the case of your writings, my motive is mainly selfish: I'd like to have a book of them myself. If there is a large potential market for such a book, then we are certainly not the publishers that can reach it; however, I'm sure there is a niche market, and we can address that totally inefficiently.'

This attitude is compellingly eccentric. Previously, I saw no point in cluttering up the world with yet another book but I find the policy of Papingay Press and its Director too civilized and congenial to resist. A niche without commercial razzmatazz is the ideal repository for quiet thoughts for a limited audience.

I am very grateful to him for the trouble he has taken in organizing the production of this collection. The stories are presented more or less in the order and form in which they appeared in the Journal.

Some of them have been altered slightly to remove arcane references of no interest outside the penumbra of the Club. I hope you enjoy at least some of these stories.

Preface to the Second Edition

In the 9 years since the first edition of this book was published, Papyngay Press has managed to squeeze a few more stories out of I.H.M. Smart. As the editor for the new second edition, I had the pleasure of reading and integrating these new stories into the previously-existing collection, a task which was both interesting and delightful. This edition contains more stories of a fantastical nature, which Smart is particularly adept at telling. His tales weave you through time, space, and philosophy. As I sailed, climbed, walked, and convened with other-worldly characters, I found myself itching to go outside. Of all the things the author is able to do with these stories, the most striking is his ability to install the exciting into the mundane. Though the hero of the stories goes as far as rambling around exotic bits of Greenland, he is still able to remind me that a walk behind my backyard can be thrilling and magical.

The Big Eye of Summer

In the High Arctic, there are long periods of summer when the weather is calm and cloudless. At such times, the silence, clear light, and brilliant reflections make previous experience unreliable. The detail visible on distant hills is such that twenty miles seem nearer two. The fjord waters mirror the stone hills and icebergs so exactly, that seaplanes coming in to land cannot distinguish the essential interface between reflection and reality. A cry in the lowlands vanishes into the air as disconcertingly as a stone disappearing into water without a splash or ripple, while a shout among the hills comes back from the planes of rock in multiple echoes of varying intonation whose loudness is often unrelated to their sequence of return.

The familiar sun, however, remains above the horizon all day tracing an easily verifiable circle in the sky. This most reassuring fact is said to be an illusion; many believe it is the moving sun that is stationary while the solid earth rotates. Be all that as it may, once during a period of settled weather, our small boat crossed the inner reaches of Scoresby Sound, threading its way along the narrow sea lanes between the hundreds and thousands of icebergs which are a feature of this area - mansions, palaces and cathedrals of crystalline splendour daring and original in design and each meticulously repeated by its reflection in the still water, a silent white city fifteen miles across, the Summer Capital of the Winter King built like others from the resources of its hinterland.

I was left on the shore near the mouth of the Schuichart River while the boat returned; vanishing Lethe-wards among the reflections. For reasons that need not distract us here, I had to be 125 miles away as quickly as possible. This was no hardship; a man who finds himself to be healthy, alone, and free to travel lightly laden in the still emptiness of the High Arctic has been granted a high privilege.

The first leg of the journey lay across the level floor of the broad Schuichert Valley. My initial target was a point clearly visible five miles away through cotton grass haloed against the low sun. Such uncomplicated terrain induces a liberating tranquillity. There are no navigational problems and the mind is free to join the landscape. The mechanism of progress can be left to the spinal cord, which enjoys an autonomy it has not had since the introduction of cephalisation.

After a succession of these five-mile stretches, the route left the valley floor and climbed up to the broad saddle leading to Orsted's Dal and the sea. Here I stopped for a few hours' rest while the sun hung low over the northern horizon. The shadow of night lay far to the south with its edge over Scotland. In Greenland, however, it was the time of the union of opposites when there is no today and time hangs between the brocaded richness of yesterday's evening and the clear light of tomorrow's dawn.

I was sitting opposite the terminal moraines of the broad Roslin Glacier. A dozen years before, the youthful Slesser and I made the first crossing of the unknown Southern Stauning Alps and emerged down this mighty glacier after days of crevassed uncertainty and windy camps in the much-serrated interior of the range. I remembered reaching the mouth of the glacier on an evening as serene as the present. We had, with growing confidence, separated. Slesser had wandered off by himself, and a mile of flat glacier lay between us, but such were the acoustics that we could still argue distinctly by slow shouts. I remember the final shout 'C-a-l-l-y-o-u-r-s-e-l-f-a-b-l-o-o-d-y-e-x-p-l-o-r-e-r'. It echoed and re-echoed from the ranks of broken buttresses of bracken-brown granite, returning again and again in the glory of the golden evening, sometimes clear, sometimes fragmented; a scene where only man was vile and he was a mile off the route, too.

A decade later, another expedition fought its way up the same glacier through the deep melting snow of early summer. After three days of heavy-laden struggle they reached their base camp in the promised land of an unknown side glacier deep in some inner sanctum of the range. Four prospectors were already there sitting round a table of playing cards in front of a large, well-appointed tent with a helicopter parked suburbanly by its side. They offered these travellers from an antique ideology cups of coffee and kind smiles, fresh rolls and the latest news.

The route now wandered through a pleasant landscape of green meadows and blue lochans. Herds of muskoxen safely grazed among the poppies and sun-caught cotton grass. Skeins of well-rehearsed geese peter-scotted across the dawn sky. Legs given their head moved effortlessly, rhythmically, feet rattling against the yellow and white Draba flowers. The soul was free to take down interesting thoughts from the well-stocked shelves of the mind, throw them up in the air and watch them sparkle in the clear morning light. This exhilaration stemmed from confidence in one's physical and mental ability to travel in empty lands, the perfectly tuned mind in the perfectly tuned body in an aesthetically perfect environment.

This lasted until noon. Time for a short nap. It was then I noticed an impulse to crawl headfirst into my sleeping bag, easily resisted but an odd desire, nevertheless. After a few hours rest I descended into the middle reaches of Orsted's Dal. But something had changed. The landscape seemed to be taking note. The hills hemming in the valley were no longer mounds of indifferent stone to be patronisingly measured by the mind as being shapely or ugly, but seemed to have usurped the initiative and were taking cross bearings on my slow progress down the long valley. This feeling of being watched grew all afternoon. Every pebble stood out sparkling and crystalline in the clear light, each a cell in the great compound eye of the landscape. If only a tent were available to crawl into to reduce the visibility, or a cave to provide some privacy and an escape from the singing breezes. You can't lie down to sleep in a whispering shop window or a room walled with one-way mirrors.

Towards evening the native hills drew back to leave a plane ten miles across. The golden light filled the early autumnal landscape up to the blue shadow of the northern hills. It would soon be time for supper and a relaxing dram before enjoying the surrounding grandeur as one dropped off to sleep, tired by an unforgettable day's walk. The mind tried to board up the windows with the old familiar clichés but they kept falling off. Maybe it would be better to cross the Pingo Dal river first, a few miles further on and nearer the hills. It would be easier to relax with this obstacle behind. It was reached effortlessly, passing on the way the gaze of a bright-eyed lochan surrounded by blue eye-bright and the Argus-eyed inflorescences of the Arctic Primrose, the latter a rare plant in these parts.

The river was bigger than I had expected. Its braided tresses sang in the sunlight and the far bank lay in cold shadow. Still it would go with care, and a safe route could be picked out among the gravel banks. The crossing was in fact easy until an irreversible commitment had been made to the last stretch, which turned out to be deep and fast. The sunlight shimmered on the dazzling, dancing, trilling water which seemed so much more attractive than the cold gloom of the approaching opposite bank. It would be so reasonable, so interesting, to yield to the eager insisting pressure of the thrilling, lifting water and discover the origin of all the excitement. Experienced legs, however, kept moving ahead, gripping the riverbed, unmoved by the heady firewater. Then into the shadow: the jewels turned to lead, and the seductive laughter to splashing grey water.

After the trembling and the cold sweat had passed and the hair on the nape of the neck lay flat, I sat in the shadow of the valley, back against a boulder, in the protection of a sleeping bag, looking southward to where the warm brown moorland of Orsted's Dal lay combing its golden hair in the sunshine. To the left crouched the lowering pack-ice with its wandering bears and unpredictable ways. Behind and to the right the dark and drublie hills still lacked their usual indifference as if they sensed the action had gone wrong. Nearer at hand, clumps of Saxifraga Stellaris starred the dark tundra - a tenuous link with the past, for they also grew light years away at home. Time to take stock - the clichés were beginning to run out.

The Big Eye is a well-known phenomenon in the arctic, characterised by sleeplessness and the feeling of being constantly watched. The mind usually does a good job in protecting its owner from the pressure of surrounding things: the unknown is efficiently silvered over to give comfortable reflections of the familiar. In lonely open places without the constricting resonance of a companion or any sign of human artefact, the expected reflections return only weakly. The silvering begins to dissolve, and bright undefined things come through and create a debatable land of possessor and possessed. The searing nakedness of that which is there becomes too much for eye and mind. Exploration of this territory is an unchancy business, and in moments of emergency survival depends on the immeasurably greater experience of sub-cerebral reflexes. It is no time to have a beginner in the driver's seat.

After a six-hour rest, the journey continued through a range of Torridon-type mountains into the next broad valley turning red and gold under the first frosts of autumn. Then another night passed in a gloomy pass, but controlled this time with the frontier better defined. Another day in the silent land, and I was safely back in the Danish weather station at Mestersvig, back in the kindergarten again with the old familiar pictures on the wall. The walk seemed to have taken a long time, but measured by the schoolroom clock it had lasted half an hour under three days.

I.H.M. Smart

Three Immoderate Mountains

The Halls of Dis

'. . . . et rebus nox abstulit atra colorem'

'. . . . and the rest of Aeneid Bk. VI.

My memory of this story begins on the top of a remote peak in East Greenland that had not yet divulged its name to mapmakers. We had climbed it by an interesting ridge of red granite, and I remember a bull musk ox (no mean climber itself) ambling away from the summit as we approached - a gesture on its part that allowed us to complete the first recorded ascent by bipeds. It was moreover a finely focused High Arctic day of silence and clear air; the sort of weather through which you could see far into the interior without any aberration. Under such circumstances, the contemplation of mountain and rolling tundra required a high order of attention, and it was several hours before we descended by thrilling glissades down a gully of granular snow. The valley below led to the sea along a five-mile carpet of low plants hugging the ground in the height of their autumn colour. We stopped half way for coffee amid a patchwork of wine-dark blaeberry and scarlet-leaved bearberry as black as the apples of the underworld. While extracting the minimum of dry twigs for a fire, a branch of willow had come away; it was too green to burn and its yellow leaves too beautiful to leave, so it was thrust through the top of my rucksack where it made a rather attractive pennant against the blue sky.

Further down the valley the fine focus of the day faded, and the landscape returned to normal. As we approached the sea, a film of cloud moved high across the sky, the rich evening colours drained away and something came to brood over a colour-forsaken land. As is well known, there are places on the earth in some way haunted and unhappy, where a man will not willingly linger. This place was such, and in spite of weariness we kept moving along the shore. The situation was not improved by the rising of the moon like a grey hole in the gloaming, through which light from the other side ebbed and flowed. And so we travelled onward under the shade of the lonely night through the empty halls of Dis and his ghostly kingdom, finding our way by the grudging light of an inconstant moon. It really was a bit like that.

There were two cruxes on the night's journey along the shore: first a passage through the cold, grey streams of a many-fingered river delta that searched us for our credentials; and then the horror of stumbling on the low grass-grown walls of a long-abandoned Inuit house with a skull in a recess where a light should have been.

Some hours later, we were able to strike inland again. After the labour of steep snow and the toil of unstable scree, we reached the upper air and crossed a pass back into the interior. By dawn, the shadow had passed, and we had our morning coffee amid the crisp autumn colours with the details of distant hills enhanced once again, and the sweet wood-smoke rising straight into the air. In its way, this penetrating clarity was every bit as disturbing as the myth-laden gloom of the previous night.

The Palace of the Winter Queen

'The Dark Goddess and the White endure the cold together,
Rivals in elegance amid the frost on the moon.'
Li Shang-Yin

The hill behind our house is of no great height and its summit has been attained by numerous sheep and rabbits. Last January, however, under a spell of cold, clear weather, two feet of powder snow and a full moon, its homely slopes and woodlands were transformed into an unfamiliar land basking in all the colours of the moonbow from shining white to luminous dark. I cannot recall any experience so aesthetically rewarding as the first midnight ski descent from the silver summit of glittering Soracte to the river below the house: first down the winking snow of the upper slopes leaving a trail of diamond dust so fine you could see it floating and sparkling in the moonlight as you turned; movement through the air-filled snow was so near to levitation that the mind easily bridged the difference, then through the little glen with the lone pine, followed by a skating waltz across the dancing floor of the frozen lochan, for the moon plays an exhilarating tune when she keeps her finger off the back lil, then past the Sitka spruce trees with their backs straight in the moonlight though their arms sagged full of diamonds, next past my house with the yellow lamplight shining faintly through from the other world where copious drams were awaiting release from magic bottles, finally a schuss through the open birchwood, a palace encrusted everywhere with jewels of frost and hung about with ice crystal chandeliers. Here a shadow concealed a natural ski jump and a period of true levitation followed, then the joy of grabbing a passing chandelier of frost-candled pendular birch and swinging to a halt still upright, amid a pile of tinkling ice crystals, a life-long ambition to swing from a chandelier accomplished without its intrinsic vulgarity - this was after all a magic night. The speed from the rest of the slope carried the skis across the silver haugh to the old ford and its guardian, an ancient twisted, white-robed larch. Here to pause a while in wonder and watch the moonbeams quiver on the ice-bound river.

Beyond the Dreams of Avarice

'An t-or is fearr air bith

- the best gold of any'

Salm xix, 10

The western slopes of the Colorado Rocky Mountains have spectacular Fall colourings. Predominant is the bright yellow of the aspen poplar. This tree is tall slender-stemmed with a terminal canopy of trembling leaves that turn their colours on and off in the breeze. We had climbed a shapely mountain somewhere in the San

Juan Range which gave a circumferential view of these realms of gold. Near the top, I remember, was a last isolated thicket of low juniper. Here, under a bough were traces of a twig couch and a very modest fire where some discriminating citizen had passed the night. Had we had the foresight to bring food into this Midas land we would have done the same. Our improvidence forced us off the top in the late afternoon and the rocks and screes funnelled us towards a steep slope stalked and shared with aspen saplings fifteen feet high. Their thin, whippy stems were ideal for cushioning the descent. I can remember brachiating down the golden brae swinging from trunk to pliant trunk through the wake of currency shaken from the trees by my spendthrift companion. The air was filled with coin of the realm raining down from the blue sky: sovereigns, doubloons, guineas, Kruger rands and gold moidores floated in the air shining as they hit the sunlight full-face and disappearing when they turned edge on. This was copious, innocent wealth you could revel in with a clear conscience - a cloud off gold a hundred yards long you could run through whooping and yodelling and shouting, 'Rich beyond the dreams of avarice!' There were banks of it on the ground and as you could kick it back up into the air again to join the gold leaf raining down from heaven. I have always wanted to order a pile of sovereigns from the Bank and kick them up into the air while the tellers showered me with gold moidores: It was every bit as enjoyable as I supposed.

This experience is clearly recorded somewhere in my mind and I often re-run the episode during boring committee meetings. Up till now it has always been played silently and without movement but I suppose one time I will forget and start kicking the order papers up in the air, whooping and yodelling the while. Such behaviour will no doubt arouse criticism.

A Tree for Each Season

'...the best fantasies are based on a sound notion of reality'

Andrew Greig; 'Men on Ice'

Here are four stories about climbs that seemed to reach their main conclusions under trees. They are four beads strung on the thread provided by the introductory quotation.

Spring

'The great wood in motion.

Fresh in its spirit;'

Sorley Maclean; 'Woods of Raasay'

This tree was a Scots pine great in the number of its branches. I received its hospitality one memorable March night when I couldn't get back to my car because of a swollen burn. The day had begun well enough skiing across the twinkling snowfields in clear still weather. Under such conditions you can travel effortlessly for miles. At the end of the morning, alas, a weather front moved in bearing cloud and rain on a warm wind. The expected exhilarating ten-mile return run in the evening glory became a slow trudge through grey porridge with a visibility of yards. Eventually the burn appeared; it had been miniscule in the morning but was now huge and frothing at the mouth, tugging at the chain holding it to the hill. There was no way past this man-eater burning white in its cave of gathering darkness. Fortunately some shelter lay nearby in a gloomy forest of the night, a wood of feral pine trees framed unexpectedly in fearful asymmetry against the last of the gloaming. The chief tree, the many-armed warrior mentioned in the opening sentence, offered the only escape from the soggy ground. The lowest branch was easily accessible and broad enough to give a perch of reasonable security. It's interesting how these old knacks come back again so easily after millennia of disuse.

Through the long night the overflowing burns roared from the corries. The winter kingdom of a few hours ago had been so peaceful. Now the old regime had collapsed and the restlessness of a new dispensation was in the air. There was life in the warmth of this disturbing wind; things were moving, not least this mighty tree that was taking the brunt of the wind.

Hours later the rain stopped and the cloud started to break, shreds passing from time to time across the moon. Then, moon and clouds stood still and the trees started a headlong rush through the night. It was a misconception of course; the mistake you make when you think the other train is stationary and you are moving when it is actually the reverse. Well, either you correct this impression and spend a boring night back home in a damp wind-buffeted tree or, more enterprisingly, you enter into the spirit of the thing. And so we galloped down the glen, hair streaming moonlit in the wind, gathering reinforcements from the scattered remains of the old forest until we reached the stockaded plantation of sheep-like spruce trees, the dull usurpers that had driven the unprofitable natives into the upper glen. These boring trees we ravaged, putting them to the blunt axe of the wind.

It can't all have been imagination because the next morning a lot of them lay flat on the ground.

Summer

'Bacchum in remotis carmina rupibus
Vidi docentem ......'

This tree was a birch arching gracefully over a patch of greensward by a purring burn tumbling itself over and over into bright waterfalls and brown pools. I encountered this spot on a sunny day of high summer after the first of the only two very severe rock climbs I have ever led in my life. It was therefore a very long time ago but, nevertheless, clearly remembered. The climb had been delicate and exposed, cruxing in a holdless corner, a veritable diedre of the sorrows with each move more dreadful than the last. In those days we climbed these routes raw; we were too thick to think of using protection, so ascents were unnecessarily complicated by the cold breath of impending dissolution.

Leaving the hill afterwards the descent was lightened by the glow of survivor's joy; that feeling of suspended gravitas you get when your appointment with the Great Dentist in the room next door is suddenly cancelled. It was then I encountered the patch of birch-shaded greensward. What an opportunity! The others were away ahead, too far to be consulted. Without thinking further I was down there supine on the grass, head pillowed on my rucksack. The ambience was too good to obliterate in serious slumber; it was better to hover on the brink aware of the smell of the warm earth, the trill of water and the green canopy of the tree seen through half shut eyes flickering in the breeze as heliographing leaves deflected little bits of sunshine into the restful shade. Then came the powerful sensation of a presence and the sound of something like distant singing coming from some hinterland of reality. Whatever this strong and disturbing land may be, it is usually kept hidden by a protective screen of suitably opaque metaphors. My old pagan friend Quintus Horatius Flaccus who saw round many an odd corner of reality recorded the sensation pretty accurately in Book II, Ode xix, the introductory lines of which head this section. (Bacchus, by the way was originally a more general nature God before he took up drink.)

It's all physiological of course. The effects of falling adrenalin levels and the release of dear knows how many curious neurotransmitters, neuromodulators and endorphins by an alarmed nervous system make it relax its guard. Flickering light and the melodious trill of water in this case confused it even further and generated a bit of a wobble in the perceived world. Some thing similar happened after the second climb of that standard I led, so ever since I have stuck to easier routes which produce a lesser effect. Some people I know can climb at extreme standards all day and every day and find it pleasantly stimulating. These are hard men with pieces of fencing wire for fuses in their nervous system. You have to be suitably deferential in their presence; some of them can even construe Horace and must know all about distant singing in rocky places.

Autumn

'Sunt lacrymae rerum et mentem mortalia tangunt.'

Virgil

This was a sad sort of autumn day - dark, damp and edgily disagreeable. I left my rucksack under the ghost of a birch tree, a grey stem ascending into a cloud of leaves drained of colour. The path then led past an abandoned shieling mouldering under a pall of grey nettles and dun bracken. The reason for treading this depressing place was the crag above. It had looked attractive when first seen weeks ago. A scramble on its rocks had seemed a good way of spending a poor day. This, however, was an unusually poor day. There were tears for things in general and mortal things in particular touched the heart. However, the rock seemed good and in spite of the psychological burden of pervading melancholy the pitch went well. Thirty feet up after an irreversible move the horizon started to move or, more correctly, although it seemed to take quite a time for the mind to work this out, the slab bearing the crucial holds toppled over and fell. A hand, one of mine as it happened, clutched at a passing hold and swung me away from the executing crunch of the descending megalithic axe which then bounded on downwards chopping grey scree and sombre bracken with each blow against the passing hillside. It all happened quickly and the avoiding action was calculated and carried out by an efficient subconscious organisation without, it seemed, much help from one's own dulled persona. This fits what is known about the evolution of the nervous system. Very little is discarded: primeval circuits are maintained and underpin the new accretions acquired during slow evolutionary time. In the old days the survival reflexes could get on with their job without extraneous input from higher centres given over to contemplating such absurd notions as lacrymae rerum. In an emergency these ancient survival routines are still able to wriggle out within milliseconds from under a burden of blunting subjectivity and camsteerie logic to look after their owner's immediate interests - otherwise we wouldn't be here. As a bonus the higher centres after a near miss seem to celebrate their reprieve by being particularly sensitive to the colour and depth of the world around. This became apparent a little later when the weather turned for the better. In the improving light a colourful landscape of near and far emerged from the flatness. Searchlights of sun came through the moving clouds and scanned the hillsides, picking out from time to time autumnal birch trees, bright against the dark heather, including for one exhilarating moment as I retrieved my rucksack, the silver stem and golden crown of the one that had earlier been a grey ghost with colourless leaves.

Winter

Dispel the cold with amber fire
From logs laid timber dry upon the hearth
And pour the twelve year old Glenlivet
In generous drams from its earthen jar.
Horace Ode I, ix.

I made camp early in the morning at the head of the Glen among the trees of the old forest. The rest of the day was spent on the ridges above in an uncompromising land of winter where rock and snow were abraded by spindrift driven by searing wind. Travel in this dead land at the edge of survival was exhilarating for a while but as the day waned and the shadows grew it sharpened a hunger for living things. The last mile back to the camp was made in dying light with the growing loneliness of seeming to be the last man left alive on a dead earth. Usually you have to grit your teeth a little before entering a wood in the twilight. The additional darkness is not easily accepted. This time, however the old forest offered company and protection from the callous wind and the hard glitter of the stars. As the fire flared up a comfortable room was fashioned from the darkness. Its floor was sheltered and the cold light of only a few stars penetrated the pillared walls and vaulted ceiling. Relaxing after dinner with half a bottle of malt in a comfortable fireside armchair provided hospitably by the thrust out roots of a particularly noble tree was as pleasant an experience as I can remember. The trees gathered round the fire and we communed together in a companionable way in spite of the vast differences in our ages and the divergent paths we had followed in the course of evolution. I thought of other Scots pines I had bivouacked under - in Rothiemurchus and the Derry, around Rannoch, in lonely Barrisdale and over the sea in Norway; then of more distant relations - a piñón pine in Utah which had shaded me from quiet moonlight and a most ancient bristle-coned pine I had snoozed beneath in sunny Arizona. While we went through all this family gossip the greater darkness waited indifferently outside; in time it would reabsorb tree, man and earth alike and recycle us all into, and maybe beyond, the hadrons and leptons of an indeterminate universe. Meanwhile we living things gathered round a common hearth, preserved for a time in an amber bubble of firelight, purring contentedly together and enjoying each others' company.

An Encounter with Gramsci

I first heard the name Gramsci at Ben Alder Cottage in April 1944. My friend and I were both fourteen at the time. There was a war on. The Highlands were empty; the roads were narrow and bereft of traffic. We had walked from Rannoch Station on a sombre, windless afternoon. Heavy cloud darkened Ben Alder and Loch Ericht lay black and filled with shadow. We were very young and unsophisticated for fourteen as was the custom at that time; the result of living protected lives in a rigidly conventional, straight-laced town and attending a school that drove us along intellectual tramlines. We walked through the ambient gloom in frank awe and apprehension, aware of our psychological vulnerability as unsupervised town dwellers in a wilderness devoid of the familiar artefacts of the urban world.

We saw the cottage from the edge of the primeval wood. I can remember being aware of the awesome emptiness of the surrounding landscape and of a burn whispering from the back of a great cave of silence. A column of smoke rose straight from the cottage chimney. This disconcerted us. We thought the cottage would be deserted. A keeper must be in residence. We knocked timidly at the door which had fishing rods propped up against the wall on each side. The buzz of conversation inside stopped. Eventually a man opened the door. He was large. His shirt was stretched over an ample abdomen so that diamond shaped gaps opened up between the buttons. Through one of these his umbilicus stared at us like the eye of Polyphemus after Odysseus had stirred it around a bit.

'Aye?', he enquired without warmth.

'We.... we forgot to bring a tent.... we wondered if we could sleep in your outhouse?'

'Where youse fae?', he demanded in a Glasgow accent.

'Edinburgh.'

'Edinburry? Jeeziz Christ', he opined with unconcealed scorn, looking up into the sky so that this high authority could join him in his displeasure.

'Away in there', he said at last, indicating the room to the right.

We entered an unfurnished room with some blankets folded on a pile of heather in one corner. We heard the Cyclopean keeper return to the other room and announce cheerfully,

'It's twa wee Edinburry shites.'

The buzz of conversation next door resumed.

We lit a small fire in the grate and started to cook. Soon a visitor from next door appeared, a small, dark man with a sensitive face, also very Glasgow. He looked with some interest at the two spoonfuls of reconstituted dried egg on a piece of bread and margarine that formed our main course. He questioned us about our background, what our parents did, where we went to school, why we were here and so on. He went away and soon came back with two large trout, gutted and headed and about a pound a piece, indicating that they were for immediate consumption.

'It must be grand being a keeper', we said.

He looked at us in disbelief. Thereafter he talked to us in the kindly tones that Glaswegians use when talking to the mentally retarded or people with a weak grip on reality among whom of course are Edinburgians of the more harmless kind such as we obviously were. We ate our fill of poached trout. The first time in our lives we had eaten a whole pound of first class protein in one go.

That evening in the other room there was conversation and laughter , also singing of songs both rousing and sad. There was a mouth organ backing and occasional, expertly played chanter solos.

It was quite a party; we were not invited in. Late in the night some men came through, slumped out on the heather and snored loudly.

We left early the next morning, driven out by the cold. Sleeping bags we had of course heard about but never seen; we would have considered them fit only for well-to-do cissies. We had slept on the floor wrapped in a couple of blankets discarded as no longer fit for home use. Our clothes were in a similar sub-terminal condition. Wearing anything else would have been unthinkable; clothes were in any case strictly rationed. However we did not feel 'deprived'. We had probably never even heard the word used in this modern sense. We were just the same as everyone else. To be hungry and cold we regarded as normal; all our reading indicated that this was an integral part of travel on the edge of the known world.

We climbed Ben Alder in a bitter black wind which tore the clouds apart and blew them in bits across the sky so that sunlight and shower patterned a moving landscape. At this time we were in our Central Asian phase and the grey-green snow-dappled Grampians we looked over were in our minds the wild rolling plateau lands of Tibet. We returned to the cottage bubbling with success, naively prattling about the view and how it looked like Central Asia. We carried very little intellectual baggage and were able to hop around exuberantly within our minds light-footed and free. The bloom, as Tom Weir would say was still on the grapes of adventure.

The occupants of the other room were a bit bemused by all this untutored enthusiasm and invited us in. A pot of stew simmered beside an ample fire. A dismembered deer lay on newspapers on the floor. A plate of big trout shared the table with a sten gun and clips of ammunition. Another gun hung from a nail on the wall. To civilians so much naked protein on display was like entering an Aladdin's cave of gastronomic riches. We were told to help ourselves. They taught us to boil the venison a bit and then fry it in its own fat. We even saw how black pudding is really made. Compared to dried egg this was a man's diet.

Gradually people drifted in from the hill or lochside until about a dozen were gathered together. Our claim to have climbed Ben Alder was confirmed as we had been seen on the top and we were more or less accepted into the group in spite of our dubious background. They were soldiers on embarkation leave and we were proud to be of their company. It was a memorable night for boys avid to escape from the tram rails. The talk was of strange mountains with strange, evocative names in parts of Scotland we had not even heard about. Remember in those days most mountaineering lore was transmitted orally. Its acquisition was gradual and you were only told things if you were deemed worthy that is if you were 'sib'. The secret corners of Scotland had yet to be sterilised by the fluorescent glare from glossy magazines and there were no guide books of the modern razor-sharp kind that shave the face of the land bare of mystery.

The songs that night were strange Scots songs sung in an idiom unfamiliar to us which our school would have described as 'unrefined'. Many were political. The cyclopean 'keeper' sang one about Spain where he had fought. We were informed that after the war there would be a Labour Government and as Labour was the party of Home Rule, Scotland would rise from the ashes of the past: a new educational system would liberate the working class from whom a new generation of engineers, teachers, doctors, lawyers, artists and writers, not to mention mountaineers would arise. There was a great deal of learned discussion with quotes from Marx and Lenin and many others, including John Maclean and Gramsci. I remember these two because I thought it odd to have a name like MacLean mentioned in the same breath as Lenin and Gramsci was the sort of name an anarchist would have in a comic paper.

The party went on until the small hours. There was firelight on faces, the booty of hunter and fisherman on the table, the glint of guns on the wall. This was indeed an escape from our prissy school. We seemed to be living in the main stream of events. All over Europe partisan bands in mountain hide-outs just like this were heroically fighting for a great ideal. The war, inter alia, was for the right of small nations to exist. Scotland it appeared was to be one of them and a refreshing new Scotland of high standards and high endeavour at that. We were converted. Glasgow in our minds became Stalingrad and Edinburgh akin to Vichy, as I suppose it remains to this day.

The following morning we climbed Ben Bheoil and spent the afternoon vainly scouring its flanks for signs of Cluny's Cage. We were also under the influence of Stevenson's 'Kidnapped' and had our own theories about the location of this romantic refuge of the dispossessed. When we got back in the evening the cottage was empty and cleared up to the satisfaction of even the most stringent of hostel wardens; the fire was set and ample wood was neatly stacked by the hearth. Since our heroes had such high standards when our turn came to leave we could have no less.

The next time I visited the cottage was one Hogmanay years later. I was with a group of fellow students. We climbed a winter gully in the great coire of Ben Alder; we had a great meet. My mind was too full of the rich present to think much, if at all, about my former heroes. I was now part of another dispensation; their influence had faded.

Several decades later, approaching from the south we encountered a notice warning us of the danger of being shot by high velocity rifles. Then we met a Range Rover filled with nice enough people who languidly knotted the air with triphthonged vowels. The cottage we found to be full of poor souls from the nether-British twilight. One of them was the leader of some sort of 'public' school party. He spoke with authority from the back of his throat. He knew everything about everything but didn't seem to know anything at all about anything else. There was no humour here. There were no shadows in this man's world. His belly button would never have peered at us gallusly from a gap between his shirt buttons. That night we slept out on the side of Ben Alder like Cluny MacPherson before us.

What happened to the bold mountaineers of 1944 and their dreams of a native renaissance? This is where Gramsci comes in. I looked him up in a Biographical Dictionary after writing the draft of this story. Gramsci was a political philosopher who tried to explain to the Marxists why the established system would not in fact collapse under its internal contradictions as predicted. It must be first be infiltrated, he said, by bearers of a new enlightenment until all the key positions had been occupied. He then went on to acknowledge that the system was so strong that successful infiltrators would be strung along until they eventually forgot why they were there. So this may well be what happened to the men of 1944 unless, of course, they were eliminated in the war. In either case there was never any danger of a brave native resurgence led by intellectual mountaineers.

However, they do say that Ben Alder cottage is haunted. I am sure it is. It is highly probable that on certain April nights the sound of Scots voices can be heard earnestly discussing the way forward to better things. But do not be afraid. The weight of Gramsci's chains (you may even hear them give a comforting rattle) will keep these ghosts from breaking through into the present world. You will be quite safe to go on lying snug in a warm sleeping bag on a state-of-the-art camping mat, dreaming short-sightedly of tomorrow's climb. What else can you do? The more distant future will make you cooperate with it whether you want to or not.

Dalwhinnie

Dalwhinnie, even now, can be a dour place to wait for something to happen. Two of the following stories tell of waiting there for lifts in the days of long ago, and the third is an update.

The Days of Innocence

In April 1945, we put up our cotton tent in the wood at the Loch Ericht turnoff. We lay for interminable hours wrapped in our blankets, waiting for some vehicle to pass. The roof, with its camouflage pattern, flapped monotonously in the grey wind. It was painted thus because of wartime regulations. A white tent would have attracted enemy bombers.

We were on our way back from an expedition into the fastnesses of Rothiemurchus, penetrating beyond the remote village of Coylum Bridge, along the pot-holed cart track to uninhabited Loch Morlich and then by the narrow footpath through the primeval forest to the Clach Bharraig bothy. We spent the night in this legendary, now-vanished howff, whose presence we had known about through the oral tradition. The next day we climbed Cairngorm and felt we had accomplished a great feat. We really were that naive. Then we camped in the woods over by the mouth of the Lairig, and had a little fire under the stars, intimidated by the old trees that loured darkly around us.

On our second day by the bleak roadside we heard an engine, not a bomber but a military vehicle of some kind. Usually army lorries did not stop, as it was against regulations to pick up civilians. We had been hoping for a commercial traveller - the only civilians who made long journeys by road in these years. We hurriedly packed up just in case. A long flat-bedded lorry lumbered up with a ruined aircraft on board. We thumbed it despondently. It stopped! The driver, a genial soul, told us to hop on the back, but to lie down out of sight if he blew the horn, as this would mean the approach of other military traffic. We climbed aboard and found half a dozen people already there. There was a dignified, fine-featured woman with two windswept children; they were from Glen Fruin and spoke Gaelic. We gathered her husband had been killed in the Western Desert. The highlands were still largely inhabited by Highlanders at that time. It would be strange today, but then it was quite normal. They were, however, already unprofitable anachronisms, the Scottish equivalent of Red Indians. We did not understand that after the war they would be surplus to requirements, and would have to go. We, in our innocence, treated them with deference; we felt we were visitors to their inalienable native heath. The other passengers were three dishevelled civilian men who looked down on their luck. They were very old, maybe even in their forties. We all crouched together under the wreckage in what little shelter we could get from the slipstream.

The Highland family got off at Dalvine, the rest of us at Dunkeld. Nearer to Perth the road got busy, maybe a car an hour, and our driver didn't want to chance his luck any further. We thanked him and started to walk south into a hard gloaming. We reached Birnam where there was a Youth Hostel in the old school, now levelled to the ground. There was no resident warden, and it was a cold draughty place with a high ceiling. We had a whole tin of beans left, also some dog biscuits. (Food was rationed at the time, and we were quite rightly never allowed to take our ration books away from home: besides, financial constraints were such that the less you ate, the longer you could stay away). After supper round a smoky coal-burning grate that shed heat grudgingly, we retired to the bunks and lay under a heap of blankets, converting our beans and dog biscuits into heat by shivering. We thought that this was the normal way of doing things. I can remember being aware of the luxury of finally feeling warm and the blessing of shelter from the night wind that was making the rafters creak. There were no lights in the darkness outside; the war had another month to go.

End of the Line

Later in the same year, we were once again becalmed on the north-south traffic watershed at Dalwhinnie, this time on the return from our first trip beyond the Great Glen, until then a closed area requiring a military pass to enter. We had seen the fabled country to the north, reached the remote Cuillins and climbed the Window Buttress and the easy side of the Inaccessible Pinnacle with a borrowed rope. I think we thought we had really made it into the first rank as rock climbers; we were obviously still very naive, but then we had only read books on the craft, had no friends who were rock-climbers. Youth leaders had yet to be conceived.

As petrol was rationed, traffic was sparse. But then so were hitchhikers, and most vehicles would pick you up; there was still a sort of camaraderie in the air. After a few hours, something approached from the north. It emitted black smoke and rode the undulations of the old road like a well-found vessel, for this is what it was, a steam-driven ship of the road, probably one of the last of the puffing billies. It clanked to a halt smoking and hissing. Three black faces with bright shining smiles beamed down us. 'If youse come wi us, ye'll hae tae pass us coal fae the back', said Para Handy, indicating room beside the coal on the back platform. MacPhail and Sunny Jim beamed down in confirmation. We gratefully accepted. Steam lorries even then were archaic vehicles; this might be the last possibility of riding a live and working dinosaur and a paradoxically early carboniferous one at that. *Vitalsparkosaurus rex* weighed anchor and set course for its home port of Inverkeithing. I can't remember much about the journey but we must have steamed our way all day along a rambling archaic version of the A9. I can remember climbing the narrow winding road up Glen Farg, because we had to stop at the Bien Inn to do something mysterious to the engine. The crew made a brew over the fire in blackened syrup tins with wire handles. They generously decanted some of the creosote into our mugs. At Inverkeithing, the ship of the road berthed and the crew disbanded. 'Ye'll be in Embro the nicht', they said, waving farewell. We too were now the colour of the crew, and undeniably proletarian. Thus promoted, we got friendly greetings from passers-by in the street and were addressed as equals by the lassie in the chip shop as she wrapped up our suppers. Like ship-wrecked mariners, we trudged to the Queen's Ferry, signed up for the passage and managed to reach home in douce, bourgeois old Embro that evening. I remember my mother saying, 'Thank goodness you arrived after dark.'

Selling the Pass

Recently, I spent an August day exploring the mysterious territory around Gaick, and was returning in the late afternoon to my car near the old Dalwhinnie road end. From the heights of Carn na Caim, I could see the great new road crowded with traffic streaming north out of Atholl and skailing bumper to bumper into Badenoch and Strath Spey (or the Spey Valley as the new owners now call it). It was some sort of holiday in the dark south, and a major population shift was taking place. Cars and caravans trying to make the best time they could mingled with lorries and vans bent on maximising their speed. None of these vehicles were dangerously ramshackle, rusty and bald-tired like so many cars of the frugal fifties: they all had heaters and radios and cassette players and did not need to rely on hand signals. I had sufficient recall of the elder days to realise the magnitude of the new wealth blessing the land and the inordinate increase in happiness that must surely have accompanied it. However, the memory suddenly came of a postcard I once bought in Tombstone City, Arizona. It was a photograph of the great Apache chief Cochise. It depicted a man with a noble demeanour. His visage was intelligent and dignified, but nevertheless wore a deeply puzzled expression; probably the same look he wore when he sat on his horse watching yet another covered wagon train appearing over the eastern horizon. No matter how many palefaces his Apaches killed, replacements arrived in increasing numbers. On such an occasion, he was heard to remark with weary incomprehension, 'Is there no end to these people?' The norms of his world had collapsed. An alien population explosion could no longer be controlled by the tomahawk. Yet, had he but realised it, these people coming over the horizon were mobile profit, potential customers rather than potential scalps. With a good lawyer he might have negotiated the Arizona Big Mac franchise for himself and scholarships to West Point and the Harvard Business School for his sons. He could have become a real Big Mac, that is, a Highland instead of a Red Indian Chief.

And so I stood with my arms across my chest, tried to look noble, watched the covered wagons rolling endlessly over the southern horizon, muttered, 'Is there no end to these people?', and then tried to realise that these were not really people but customers, profit on the hoof, a source of wealth. Dignified surrender may be all very well for making tragic postcards but has no real biological future. After all, even we in the SMC, toffee-nosed elitists though we are, make efforts to increase the numbers of customers who stay in our huts and buy our guide books in order to increase our own cash flow. I could feel my belay taking the strain as my expression started to become streetwise and speculative.

I.H.M. Smart

The Sinister Coast

Shortly after our arrival at the Inuit settlement of Scoresby Sound on the north side of the biggest fiord in the world, an immaculately dressed Eskimo with an expensive single-lens reflex camera slung round his neck came up to us and, with some amusement, took a photograph of the well-known explorer Dr Slesser as he was prising open the lid of a tea chest with an ice axe. Taking no further notice of his celebrated visitor, he chatted urbanely with a fellow citizen, and then departed on a more important errand, leaving Dr Slesser breathing heavily. This episode was the highlight of our attempt to climb Mount Mikkelsen, a 10,800 foot peak situated inland from a particularly inaccessible part of the East Greenland coast 200 miles to the south of us and half way to the next habitation. The 'sinister' Blosseville Coast, as one of the early accounts described it, has seldom been visited even in recent years because of its barrier of unpredictably moving pack-ice. The plan was to navigate southwards with a small party in a small boat using small shore leads to bypass ice-jammed bays and headlands. With good luck, the return journey including the 25 mile march inland to Mount Mikkelsen could be done in 30 days or so. We carried two month's food in case we had to abandon the boat and travel back on foot as far as Cape Brewster and survive there until the sea froze over and we could walk across to the main settlement on the north side of the Sound.

We had a sixteen foot clinker-built wooden boat with a 5hp engine and a smaller back-up engine. We towed behind us a ten foot inflatable, the kind without floor boards that shoogled like a jelly. The leader of this powerful argosy was, of course, the perfunctorily photographed Dr Slesser alluded to in the opening paragraph. He is a man who can assess risk realistically and make bold, yet competent decisions. The expedition was his concept, and he had done the entire organisation of this complex exercise. It was no easy task to assemble such a lot of equipment at such a remote spot. Second in command was Carlos Ziebell, a Dane with long years of experience in the sledge patrol, a remarkable character and fine companion. Allan Pettit, a trendy dentist from Brechin, and myself formed the crew. We did what we were told and were frequently upbraided for minor displays of initiative. Pettit took refuge in prolonged sleep, and I became a keen botanist.

The Sound is twenty miles wide at the place we crossed, twice the breadth of the Minch from Uig to Scalpay. (It is confusingly called a Sound because the celebrated whaler William Scoresby had surmised that it extended right across Greenland to the west coast, when in fact it only goes west for a couple of hundred miles.) Our first careless rapture rapidly petered out. We were delayed frustratingly at Cape Stewart, still on the north side, because of the wind and the waves and the intimidating gloom. Far away across the Sound, we could see its southern shore, the Inhospitable Volquart Boone's Coast, its black mountains striped with grey snow, following the description of 'inhospitable' to the letter. The black sea between us and this uninviting destination was strewn with ice floes moving with the tide, grey in the gloomy light of noon and even more dismal at dim midnight when the sun should have been shining. It was also raining.

In the end, we set out. We had to; we were getting short of time. The days were passing by. We started to cross, slipping from the lee of one ice floe to the next. Half way, the wind really got up, and grey horses charged across our path and jumped occasionally into the boats. Now comes the interesting bit. Ice floes derived from the polar pack are in fact miniature continents. They have a coastline with harbours and an interior of mountains and rivers. It was deemed necessary to seek haven in one of these. Remarkably, within a harbour the size of a drawing room on the lee side of an acre-sized floe, all was calm. We unloaded the boats, pulled them up on the ice, and pitched our tents, being careful to return half our supplies and equipment to the boats in case the floe should undergo a sudden catastrophic fracture and we had to abandon it à toute vitesse.

Malcolm and Carlos exuded confidence, they knew all about this from years of experience. The crew was impressed and relaxed in the presence of such manifest competence. Later, it transpired that neither had actually camped before on an icefloe in a wild sea. Their savoir-faire was based on book-learning and the intuitive understanding that the floes were big and massive enough to support the comparatively small mass of men and equipment that we imposed on their tonnes and tonnes of frozen water. We were safe, even if we were mere passengers moving to the destination of the icefloe, wherever that was. We brewed up in the tent, dosed intermittently, and in between times read books and engaged in urbane conversation.

In the end everything gets boring, even being the frightened guests of a sullen icefloe in a wild sea ten miles from land while engaging in bizarrely intellectual conversation. So we set off once more towards the Inhospitable Volquart Boone's Coast. The pack thickened. The rain got heavier. So, we entered a harbour on a massive continental floe. It had its own miniature mountain ranges with rivers of meltwater flowing down through flood planes and miniature grand canyons to the sea. The trouble was, this big floe was beset with smaller floes and was continentally-drifting out into the wild East Greenland Sea. Camping was again suggested until we saw that we were being carried by the tide past the Greenlanders' houses on the south side of the Sound, now visible about a mile away into the open coast at a speed of five knots or so. We had to get off, and only just made it to more open water before the smaller floes ground against each other like a zip-fastener closing behind us. If we had stayed with the continental floe, we might have made one of the great journeys of the decade because in the wide sea outside Scoresby Sound, it would have entered the East Greenland current, which proceeds southward at six to eight knots. We might have made it to Cape Farewell in more senses than one. Maybe we lacked something. Maybe, like J. Alfred Prufrock, we had seen the moment of our greatness flicker, we had heard the eternal footman hold our coat and snicker - in short, we were afraid.

And so we beat westwards against wind and tide back into the Sound for a few hours, looking for a gap in the pack to make a landing. We finally landed on an arm of shingle, which formed a small natural harbour below the steep moraines of glaciers discharging into the sea on either side. It rained for two more days. Icebergs hovered occasionally into and out of the mist, and thousands of black and white little-auks flew to and from their nesting colonies in the cliffs and screes above us. The troll-like crooning from these buttresses added a final touch to the superb melancholy.

Eventually, the sun came back and we left on a morning of unflawed calm and brilliance. We passed an hour with the Greenlanders and then rounded the cliffs of Cape Brewster in a spanking breeze, only to be storm-bound on a rocky peninsula for days while the wind battered us unceasingly. The tents collapsed at intervals. Flowers were blown from the botanist's hand, and had to be pursued at a gallop. Seawards, the pack lurked several miles offshore, a thin line edging the wind-dark sea; southwards, blue headlands receded into an unknown distance. 'We are getting weak', announced Carlos one day, 'We need fresh meat.' Wandering the wind-swept plateaus behind the camp, gun on shoulder, eventually produced a hare, which Carlos stewed to perfection.

Perhaps a week later, the wind dropped and we got underway and made about fifty miles of southing. At one time, we encountered a walrus snoozing on a piece of ice. Carlos, who had shot many walrus, ordered us straight for it. The rest of us who had read about the ill-nature of these creatures wished to go full astern. There were a few minutes of heated discussion, not to say shouting, while the boat zig-zagged, unsure of its direction, but attracted ever nearer to the unattractive creature. Before we got too close, the walrus lurched down and swam off disdainfully to a part of the coast less frequented by trippers, where it could sleep in peace. Carlos upbraided us for our lack of moral fibre in a photographically interesting situation. Towards the end of this day of movement, our progress was stopped by an ice jam between the mountainous Turner Island and the mainland. We tried to go round the outside of the island but were again stopped by ice, which had moved in silently from the sea. We camped in a troll-haunted valley half way down Turner Sound, and next day moved round the island along a series of shore-leads until stopped again by dense pack whose only weakness was some seductive leads running for an inadequate distance into the 15 miles of ice which lay between us and the frowning coasts opposite. We climbed onto a ledge on the cliff above us, while the ice breathed gently against the shore. 'If you wish to reach Cape Dalton you must follow these leads', declared Carlos. 'But Carlos, how do we get back?' 'BACK?' queried Carlos, baffled by such a suggestion from men who, in spite of the walrus episode, he had believed to be as steadfast as himself. We dithered a little, posturing on the rocks pizarro-like, gazing to the distant Cape Dalton where the real unknown began. The pack held its breath. Carlos leant against a rock, smoking and looking southwards over the expectant ice. For a party that did not wish to risk wintering or worse, there was nothing to do but return. The pack sighed. We went back to the protected waters of Turner Channel to await developments, disturbing once more the enraged walrus, this time asleep on a sandbank.

We spent the next three days travelling light and fast on an expedition ten miles into the interior to climb a mediocre mountain in an abrasive wind. The indifference of the immense inland glaciers contrasted well with the sinister shiftiness of the pack ice.

We arrived back on the third day to find ice everywhere. Next morning, we were awakened by the sound of Carlos roaring, 'Slesser, you are sleeping again!' Carlos, who shared a tent with Malcolm had a habit of waking early and entertaining his tent-mate with long tales of derring-do for a couple of hours before breakfast, and found the inability of his companion to keep his eyelids from drooping very irritating. An early rise was justified, for that day was fine and we managed to make a few miles south into Romer Fjord, which turned out to be a place of charm, the daffodil among the skulls. On a sunlit flower-covered promontory lay a few stone huts, left by some long-extinct Inuit. Further on, hot springs bubbled improbably from the ground. Mosses and vascular plants grew in water uncomfortably hot for the hand. In the moss close by grew a dozen of the most northerly orchids in the world.

Heavy ice still blocked the outer coast. We now had to extricate ourselves from the trap. At a touching ceremony by the shore of the arctic sea, the expedition was renamed the 'Romer Fjord Expedition' and thus became one hundred per cent successful. Mount Mikkelsen can be reached by this route, but it requires good weather and good luck as well as a willingness to trust the uneasy, unpredictable ice which measures time in a way unfamiliar to the visitor from our urban jungles.

Four days later, we reached Cape Brewster again after an encounter with two (some say three) polar bears, one of which was uncharacteristically climbing a hill. Once round the Cape, spirits rose, the last whisky was drunk, and Carlos sang wild Jutlandic songs as he stood in the stern, foot bracing the tiller, his habitual pose. Within half an hour of our arrival at the Greenlanders' houses a four-day blizzard struck. Life with the Greenlanders over this time was very pleasant. Our host shot any bird that happened to pass by the window, which was kept open specially for such opportunist snap shots. When sufficient assorted wild fowl had accumulated his wife undid their gift wrapping and boiled them with some rice and onion. We all sat round the common pot and fished for our supper.

After the blizzard had passed through, we dodged across Scoresby Sound before the weather noticed, said goodbye to Carlos, who returned to Denmark by sea, and started on the final hundred mile boat journey into the inner Scoresby Sound. On the first day, we headed into driving snow, and on the next we sailed between the bergs in bright sunshine over a mirror smooth sea while the primus purred on the fore-deck and a pot of soup sent up clouds of steam just like a real liner. Leaving the boat in the inner fjord for next year's expedition, we wound up with a walk of hundred mile or so to the airstrip at Mestersvig and returned to Scotland after an absence of forty two days.

Pushing out the Boat

This addendum to the Sinister Coast was written over thirty years later with the wisdom of hindsight

One of the problems of being a slow thinker is that you are still trying to figure out what really happened in adventures that took place long ago. This is why I am returning to an event that occurred on the 1969 expedition to the Sinister Blosseville Coast. A particular episode from that journey keeps resurfacing as a troubling memory. I hope I shall be able to articulate my problem in the next few paragraphs so that, with your help, I can exorcise the memory that lingers on, and hang it up tidily on a hook at the back of the cupboard of the past, never to trouble me again.

You may remember that back in 1969, at the beginning of the expedition, we were camped on the north side of Scoresby Sound, the entrance to a great system of branching fjords on the east coast of Greenland. We were on our way to climb Mount Mikkelsen some hundred or so miles to the south, and were under the impression that we would gain some kind of merit if we reached its summit. A day after setting out, the expedition had come to a halt. The Sound was in a bad mood. There was wind and rain and low cloud, and we were very prudently going nowhere until the weather improved. We were, however, gradually becoming gloomy, possibly even morose. We were short of time. The sullen weather showed no sign of improving. Something had to be done. Soon. We had to push out the boat. And, of course, in the end we did.

Immediately, our fragile argosy cast off morale improved. We were going somewhere at last. Exhilaration set in. Hours later towards the end of our eventful crossing, when we were trying to get through the final stretch of coastal icepack to reach the Inhospitable Volquart Boon's Coast, the episode I would like to exorcise occurred. We had entered a lead. After half a mile, it ended. On our retreat, we found that a fifty metre high iceberg had drifted across our return path, churning up the surrounding ice floes. Under the effects of wind and tide and the laws of its own buoyancy, it began to teeter and metronome across our line of retreat. In its own slow heaving time, the berg worked out the possibilities for its future and for ours. Fortunately, its centre of gravity remained lower than its grim sense of humour, and it remained upright and proceeded on its way. At the time, I remember watching it carry out the requisite mathematical calculations with interest while making contingency plans for surviving a worst-case scenario. Also in the back of my mind was the question, 'What are we doing here?' The feature I found so bizarre about the whole enterprise was that the four of us were family breadwinners and parents of a number of young children. At home, we had good, secure, interesting jobs, and very adequate life styles. Why were we motivated to launch ourselves into this completely unnecessary and risky exercise? Why were we actually paying to be here? Neither law nor duty drove us to this desolate part of the earth's surface. Where was the boundary between constructive boldness and destructive folly?

Now, what I want to discuss with you is the wild exhilaration you get when you push out the boat into the unknown, when you make the irreversible decision to go on. Once you make it, you are possessed by a wild, fearful delight, a deep exhilarating satisfaction, a feeling of optimistic dread, a perverse sense of fulfilment in presenting your intellectual, emotional and physical endowment for an unknown examination by an examiner who judges dispassionately and seldom allows resits. If you fail, you are edited out of the book of life.

Nevertheless, at the actual time you would rather be there with all its irrational, unnecessary danger than walking under the stars with a dusky beauty with fireflies in her hair along some moonlit tropic beach towards your reward under a palm tree. In saner moments, I often wonder why I didn't choose this option instead of ending up on the grim shores of the Inhospitable Volquart Boone's Coast and its equally minatory southern extension the Sinister Blosseville Shore. It's too late now, of course. However, if I ever get the chance in some future incarnation, I am going to go for the dusky maiden with fireflies in her blue-black hair and the aroma of cloves and cinnamon on her breath.

However, back at the problem we are dealing with in the here and now of the present incarnation, I believe the sort of behaviour I am describing is the result of the way our brains are configured. They seem to like exploring the edge of their envelope of possibilities. Some of us have worse brains than others in this respect. We are not content to bask comfortably in the middle of our span of capabilities. We have to find out our physical and mental limits. In biological terms this behaviour no doubt has survival value. The species is merely using individuals as expendable probes to find the boundaries of its range. The individual thinks he is being bold and enterprising because he thinks that he is making voluntary decisions and is unaware that he is being used by the lump of jelly in his head which, in its turn, is being used by the species to discover the limits of its physical and conceptual possibilities. Life has to send out emissaries. Those who do not return supply important negative feedback; they tell where the dead ends are.

At the risk of embarrassing you, can I end by quoting a few lines from Yeats, which rationalise the mental state of those embarking voluntarily on missions where the outcome is in doubt?

> I balanced all, brought all to mind,
> The years to come seemed waste of breath,
> A waste of breath the years behind
> In balance with this life, this death.'

There, now I have got that out of my system. Thank you for your help. The species can now get on as best it can without me. I'm off to buy a ticket on a slow boat to some island in the sun to explore a more delightful mystery redolent of cloves and cinnamon, maybe even a touch of vanilla, and lit by fireflies glowing among lustrous blue-black tresses.

A Hero's Welcome

This is a story about a climb long ago when, in Sorley Maclean's immortal line, we were 'young and light-stepping without the heartbreak of the tale', or at least the tale was just beginning. Our foray began at the Linn of Dee on a clear, windless May morning. We set off soon after sunrise light-stepping through the sun-striped woodlands of Glen Lui, scattering the gleaming dew drops from the grass and knocking off a fortune in diamonds from the bejewelled spiders' webs. This was the morning of what was obviously going to be a day of days! Bliss was it on this dawn to be alive, but to be young and on the way to do a mighty climb was very heaven! In the open strath beyond, skylarks were singing their crunluath a-mach, tremulous dotted quavers high above in the Van Allen belt of song. With our spirits doing something similar, we crossed through the Clais Fhearnaig to the old wood of Glen Quoich where the trees are always so alert and watchful, then we climbed the broad shoulder of Beinn a'Bhuird and so on to the summit plateau, where colourful burns rising from the ashes of the winter snow frolicked off with the gravity pulling them seawards. For us such boring laws of physics were temporarily suspended, and the imprisoned psyche was able to soar a little above the law-abiding land. Bright words bubbled out of the springs of the mind and ran about twinkling on top of our thoughts like grace notes ornamenting a happy tune. Duncan Ban MacIntyre must have felt like this when he was on Beinn Dobhrain with his trusty gun Nic Coiseam on his shoulder, the one with the eight-sided barrel he bought in Glen Lochay. Oh, to be able to sing a similar song about Beinn a'Bhuird or even, in my case, Moladh Beinn Dobhrain in tune.

More to the point, we now descended into Glen Avon and to the foot of the Mitre Ridge, which we climbed. No need to describe the technicalities here; this has already been done in excellent guide books. The route, I remember, was serious and about as hard as I would ever wish to climb, but it went well. The lot of the waiting second was alleviated by the views to the north, always the horizon that draws the most, for over it are mid-night sunny tundras, lonely unclimbed mountains and mysterious fjordlands, fraught with wandering, unpredictable bears. Then there was the occasional sight of the heroic leader silhouetted against the blue sky with a fair weather cumulus cloud on his shoulder. And when it was your turn the adrenaline release brought the world into fine focus; the crystals in the rocks twinkled more brightly and the mountains sharpened up their edges.

On the summit ridge we celebrated our own crunluath a- mach, the crown of dexterity; then, levitating with survivor's joy, we returned over the grey-green mossy horizons of the eponymous table land, down the Alltan na Bienne and through the woods of green-helmeted pines where the trees froze their muscular arms in mid-gesture while we passed. By the bright pebbled waters of the singing Quoich, we lay for a while under the whispering tresses of a slender silver birch, revelling in the smell of the good clean earth and the heavy pagan incense of thyme. It must surely have been under a tree of such loose-girdled grace that True Thomas of Ercildoune fell asleep. Lesser men than we would have succumbed to the sweet seduction that hung in the soft, expectant air and elected to slumber beneath this sensuous enchantress for seven years of murmuring summer playing with the tangles of a wood nymph's hair. Alas, strength of character, a curse we both carry undiminished to this very day, drove us on. We proceeded with cat-like tread, springy-stepping our way homeward in the purring warmth of the late afternoon.

At some point my companion, Malcolm (for who else could it have been but he) remarked 'Never mind, when we get back home we'll get a Hero's Welcome.' A Hero's Welcome! I have only had such a thing once in my life. It was in the old Empire Theatre in

Edinburgh when the Covent Garden Company were putting on the Grand Opera 'Aïda'. We had been hired as extras and were dressed in the full regalia of the Pharaonic army as depicted in the better sort of Eighteenth Dynasty tomb. We were returning from a victorious war against Abyssinia and marched across the stage be-strung with bows and a-quiver with arrows to the rousing strains of the Grand March while the chorus girls sang our praises and showered us with paper rose petals. I have always looked back wistfully on this occasion; it was the summit of my military career. Now the omniscient Slesser had prophesied a similar welcome, the real thing from our own proud families. Come to think of it, they had given us a fairly civil send off; there could have been an orchestra playing as we drove away, and perhaps a shout or two of 'Ritorno vincator!' - it was hard to remember, so much had been happening of late. When we did eventually arrive home in Glen Shee, it was indeed latish and long, languorous shadows were reclining over the mellow countryside as the day, replete with events, relaxed into the quiet mystery of a luminous May night. It was a gloriously theatrical finale to a memorable day.

Oddly, no delegation emerged from the house to greet us. Inside, some sort of civil war was in progress. One wifely participant broke off to say,

'Where in the hell have you two been? You were supposed to be back hours ago.'

'We have just done the Mitre Ridge.' said Malcolm bracing himself to receive the expected applause.

'Walking all the way from Linn of Dee.', I added so that the full magnitude of our achievement should be evident and the praise correspondingly unstinted.

'Well, you certainly took your time. Here, you go and see what the children are doing next door. They're breaking something. And you, for goodness sake go and sort that tricycle. The wheel has been falling off all day. You said you'd do it before you left.'

Later, as we sat supping the soup of anti-climax, we heard about the real struggle that had been taking place that day. Hero status for us, it seemed, was out of the question, not even a subject for serious discussion. Perhaps if, like Ramides, we had brought back the gold of a defeated empire we might have got some favourable mention of our absence, but to return from a foray bearing a story about a pointless rock climb and a long-tressed birch tree, useless metaphors both, instead of a fat roebuck slung between us on a pole or even a small rabbit hanging from our belt - did we really expect a Hero's Welcome for that?

We had obviously misunderstood our role models. Donnachadh Ban nan Oran would have brought back to Mairi Bhan Og not only a fine song but an antlered stag from the Coire Raineach as well: he would have deserved a Hero's Welcome.

The rousing strains of the Grand March faded from our minds, drowned out by the brain-numbing, but biologically imperious music of domesticity. We were deflated and puzzled. Somehow we had fallen off ingloriously at the crux. Yet the guidebook had said that the crux was on the first pitch, and we had done that well enough. Guidebooks obviously knew nothing about real life. Neither did we at the time; we were still young and light stepping without the heartbreak of the tale, and only dimly aware of the triune nature of women.

Disobeying the Rules

The Scottish Mountaineering Club owns a hut high on Ben Nevis. It is a privileged refuge in a unique position for climbing on the north face of the big bad Ben. Although a private hut, the Club runs it for the benefit of all mountaineers. But such is the pressure for accommodation that rules governing its use are very, very strict. The Custodian, originally a gentle man, after years of disillusion with the thoughtlessness and even frank delinquency of both legal and illegal clientele, has become fierce and uncompromising. One rule that must never ever be broken is that no one, whether member or not, should ever on any account whatsoever use the hut without informing him. Keys are only issued after searching negotiation. There is also a system of passwords so that different parties sharing the hut can verify that the others are legitimate. Only the President has his personal key during his time of office. But this is only an ornament. The President, like everyone else has, to obtain the permission of the Custodian before he dare use his key and set foot in the hut. This is not bloody mindedness; it is the result of many and bitter disillusionments in dealing with gross humanity. The other rule is that even authorised visitors cannot bring in more people than they have booked for. This is to prevent someone booking a number of places and then bringing in extra people so causing overcrowding and bad feeling among the other legitimate users. During my time as President, I once abused my privilege and broke both these rules. I had a good excuse. I was free at short notice; and he didn't answer his phone. As it turned out, it was quite an occasion. The Custodian fortunately never found out, and sufficient time has now passed to make it safe for me to tell you what happened on that memorable night.

I left the car park in brilliant winter sunshine with the great white Ben a-twinkle. I climbed with the slow pace of a senior citizen carrying a heavy rucksack, and did not reach the hut until the late afternoon. During the last hour, the weather had of course deteriorated, reducing progress to the usual slog through the whirlwind and blizzard, freezing the marrow and the gizzard as the Club Song puts it so well. Once inside the hut with the lights lit and the place warmed up, the scene became warm and genial. I sat relaxing with a coffee and a substantial dram, purring quietly in front of the fire, enjoying the thrill of being alone in a golden pocket of comfort beneath the big bad winter Ben. I was hardly settled when there was a thumping at the door, which of course, I ignored. The noise continued, and so reluctantly I went to investigate, hardening my heart as I went; someone was going to get a flea in their lug. Immediately after I opened the door, a figure walked in out of the knock-you-off-your-feet wind without waiting for an invitation. I pushed the door shut against the accompanying cloud of snowflakes surging in from the outer darkness. As the flakes settled to the floor, the visitor removed its bone-dome, shook out a shock of golden hair, and said in a pleasant Scots voice, obviously female, 'Thank God for that. You must be deaf.'

'What's the problem,' I said trying to look dour and unwelcoming, a difficult task when confronting what was emerging as some sort of radiant Storm Goddess.

'The problem,' she said genially sitting on the bench of the antechamber and taking off her crampons, 'Is, I've left three loonies up there on the Orion Face. I thought I'd better tell someone important, like a member of the SMC.' She said this with well-modulated irony. 'Besides I need a coffee.'

She wanted a coffee! She wanted in! I ran about inside my mind trying to find the manual for dealing with this emergency. What would the Custodian expect me to do? Should I ask her if she had booked and if so what the secret password of the week was? Should I point to the door like a Victorian father in a cartoon? I rather liked that scenario. However my sense of self-preservation saved me. Instead I heard my voice saying,

'Come away in then, lassie.'

After all, I was the President and had a certain authority. Not that that would stand at my trial as anything but an irrelevant technicality, a despicable cry for special treatment requiring a harsher sentence.

I made her a coffee and rather overdid the welcome by pouring her a substantial dram.

'Oh good, Bruichladaich', she said. 'My home island. 'S ann an Ile rughadh mi, 'S ann an Ile bhoidhich'', she sang in a simple thrilling voice.

I was entranced. Obviously a character. She had now emerged from her outer clothing as a girl in, I would have guessed, her mid twenties. She had the mischievous, intelligent face of an intellectual gamine.

'So what happened up there on Orion ?'

'I'm not sure', she said, looking puzzled, 'I met this trio in a pub in the Fort last night. Two men and a girl; they wanted to do the Orion Face, and asked me to make a fourth so we could climb more quickly as two parties of two. I had been let down by my boyfriend (whom I've now discarded) so I joined them. We left when the bar closed and bivvied in our cars at the golf club car park. It was fine this morning. They moved fast, knew what they were doing, and I thought we were going to make it in record time. From the start, however, there had been an 'atmosphere' between the other three. The girl and her boyfriend were tense. The spare man who I climbed with, on the other hand, was a bit laid-back. He was the real leader, and I felt he was trying to calm the emotional tension all the time. Anyway, they could all climb fast and well, even though they kept arguing. It came to an end, as far as I was concerned, with an incomprehensible stushie at the end of the third pitch. The boyfriend, Harry by name, suddenly wanted to re-arrange the ropes so he could climb with Michael, that's the name of the laid back character I was roped to. And then he wanted me and Maggie, the girlfriend, to climb together as the first rope--something about giving the girls a chance. The climb was well within our capabilities; we were all leading through without difficulty. It would have suited me fine; I like the view from the front. Mike or Michael or whatever he was called, stopped being laid back and would have none of it. They started to shout at each other. You don't stay with an emotionally unstable party on high grade ice in deteriorating weather, if you want to live. I had made a mistake, so I bailed out. I tried to get Maggie to come with me but she wouldn't leave Harry. So I just abseiled off, leaving them shouting at each other.

'You abseiled off - alone - in this wind ? '

'Why not? The wind's only really got up in the last hour. Abseiling isn't all that difficult, you know - would you like a lesson?', she said impishly. Before I could say, 'Yes please, any time you're free', she continued, 'I had to leave three ice screws behind. Thirty quid, but cheap to escape from that accident waiting to happen. There are times you have to be decisive. Anyway, I thought I would warn the people in the hut here. I'll tell the mountain rescue in the Fort when I go down that there's probably going to be trouble.' Then added matter of factly, 'You know, tell them where they should start looking for the bodies.' I was reminded of Tom Patey's observation: 'It pays to be realistic on these occasions.'

'Why not wait a while, they may make it and pass this way coming down from Coire Leis', I heard myself saying.

'Can't say I want to see them again. Well, okay, I'll have another coffee and then go down. I don't want to hang around. I've things to do.'

From then on we got on very well. Her father was a man of Islay and her mother from Deeside, from the next parish to my own as it happened. She was a native Gaelic speaker and familiar with the present literary revival, which she talked about brilliantly. I had minimal learning on the topic but nevertheless enough to join in an adult conversation and benefit from the poems, stories and general enthusiasm prevailing in her accounts. After a third Bruichladaich I heard myself saying, 'Why not stay for supper? I have a nice bottle of Mouton Cadet and enough steak for two.' In the back of my mind I knew that, if discovered, I would now be banned from the hut for life without the possibility of appeal, but that seemed a trivial inconvenience compared to corrieneuchin cosily with a Storm Goddess over dinner.

'Okay, I'll do the soup' she declared cheerfully; 'You do the steak.'

We had a very pleasant little party during which the conversation became incandescent. (At one stage I surreally agreed to meet her two weekends hence to do Point Five Gully.) She was completing a Ph.D. in the social anthropology of some third world country. Her basic findings seemed to be that in any run-down, declining community, it was the men who failed first; any residual intellectual and emotional strength resided in the women who intuitively understood the realities of long-term community survival. True for Scotland, too, she declared. It was the women who were realising that you can't treat the communal home as just another saleable commodity to be frittered away. Scots men she dismissed by singing a few lines from Michael Marra's 'Hermless' in a voice appropriately flat and sardonic, followed by some hilarious imitations of well-known figures that, if delivered in public or in print, would have been actionable. The Renaissance in Scotland, she declared, if it comes at all, will come appropriately enough from women. I valiantly tried to defend us men as equally aware, and was just getting into my stride when there was a banging at the door. Naturally I tried to ignore it. She was more charitable.

'Surely you're going to open it? It may be "them". They may need help.'

I tried to explain about the hut rules and the fierceness of the Custodian. I had already endangered my standing by letting her in. She said something in Gaelic which sounded withering. When I looked it up later in the dictionary I found out that it translated, roughly, as 'pusillanimous creep'; Gaelic is an expressive language; however this is not the place for a digression into semantics. Stung by her body language, I went to the door, resolved to deal firmly with the situation. I donned a flinty expression and cautiously unsnecked the door, meaning to conduct a conversation through a crack. Such was the wind pressure I couldn't hold the door back, and it forced itself open. Three people blundered into the porch while I was engaged in heaving the armour-plated door shut again against the wind, snow, and darkness billowing in from the outside. It was indeed 'them'. 'Can we come in - my boy friend is in a bad way.', said a worried female voice. 'I suppose so,' I said reluctantly. What else could I do? They were in point of fact already in. Apart from ruining a pleasant evening discussing important matters concerning the future of Scotland with a well-informed fellow Scot and part-time Storm Goddess, here was the further Infringement of the Rules. If this sort of thing went on, I could end up being the first President to be expelled from the Club while still in office. The trio decramponed, dumped their gear, and helped the casualty into the inner room. I crept after them pusillanimously. The situation was getting out of hand.

The casualty was Harry, the boy friend, a nice looking young chap about, say, twenty-five. He was indeed in a state of collapse. Maggie, the girl friend had dark hair, dark eyes - a real stunner. I would have put her in her early thirties. She was in a state of high anxiety. Mike seemed a detached, slightly bored bystander,

'He's suddenly become quite irrational.' continued the dark lady once inside, 'He's had at least one fit. I think he's got a *brain tumour* or something. He's got to *see a doctor* quickly.' She somehow very attractively inflected her voice so you knew when she was using italics, an interesting trick. She reminded me of Ursula Cairnwhapple only in a much minor key. We installed Harry in a bunk where he lay on his face moaning and twitching. He seemed in a bad way. We tried to contact someone on the radio but it either wouldn't work or we lacked the technical aptitude to coax it into activity.

'Well I'm going down *now*; he needs a doctor quickly,' the dark-eyed Maggie repeated, ' I've *never* seen him like this before.'

I remembered that once upon a time, I had been a doctor, and offered to take a look. I got Harry onto his back and examined him with my head torch. I took his pulse and managed to see that his pupils were equal and reacted to light.

'It's that bastard Mike', he moaned. 'I wanted to fall off and take him with me.'

Whatever was wrong with him it wasn't a brain tumour.

'He seems to be having some sort of anxiety neurosis or maybe a hysterical episode', I said delivering a likely diagnosis to the surrounding circle of waiting laity.

'Nonsense!', said the girlfriend contemptuously, 'He's *not* the type.'

I was never very convincing as a doctor; I didn't seem to have lost my touch.

'I'm going down *now* to get help. A helicopter with a *proper doctor* must come up first thing in the morning.' She said this firmly in an authoritative boarding-school accent. Everyone tried to dissuade her, but she was neither to hold nor to bind. She snatched a cup of coffee prior to departure and sat by Harry keeping an affectionate hand on him.

'You can't go down the glen alone in a night like this', declared the Storm Goddess. 'I'm going with you.'

'Why can't Mike here go with her, it's *his* responsibility.' I said desperately, lapsing inadvertently into italics myself at the thought of losing the company of the Storm Goddess.

Michael, however, declared quite emphatically that he didn't think it necessary.

'I think the Doctor here is right. Harry'll be all right after a rest. Go down if you want to. I'll stay with him here until he gets a grip of himself.'

The Storm Goddess went off to get booted and spurred. When she came back she quickly pencilled her telephone number on a piece of paper torn from a Ryvita wrapper that lay on the table. She handed it to me with a ravishing smile saying, 'Give me a ring to confirm arrangements for Point Five',

I saw the two of them to the door. At the threshold, the Goddess and I spontaneously struck the palms of our upraised hands together as if we were Pavarotti and Placido Domingo changing places on centre stage. 'Hang in there', she said mischievously nodding her head towards the inner room where Michael-the-laid-back and Harry-the-recumbent had remained. She vanished into the swirling snow from whence she had come, leaving a void behind her. The flame in my heart became a bonfire.

So there I was left with these two unwelcome men. I sat down and started to read without trying to hide my ill-temper. Michael, a handsome bastard who might be pushing thirty, if that, sat there pleasantly minding his own business with a sort of regal equanimity. An occasional moan came from Harry. After about half an hour my sense of hospitality returned. They were, after all, strangers and it was a dark and stormy night. I really ought to offer the honours due to unfortunate travellers. In spite of the hut regulations. Bob might never find out. You never knew your luck.

'How about some soup and beans on toast. It's all I've left.'

'Okay', he said pleasantly, 'I'll give a hand. I have some brandy if you have three glasses.' He got a commendably large, matt-black flask out of his sack and poured three substantial shots. It was a very, very fine brandy indeed with a rich complex bouquet redolent of Flora and the country green. While I reconstituted some soup and heated up the beans, he cut the bread and made toast. We conversed easily and he dispelled my smouldering resentment. He had a civilised manner, spoke a curiously correct English with pleasant Scottish vowels and unblurred consonants with maybe a hint of an Australian vowel shift. He easily opened me out. He found out that my mother came from Deeside. His mother, he averred, came from Donside, and his father from Ettrickdale in the Borders. Anyone who was anyone in the hut tonight seemed to have Aberdeenshire connections. From then on, I noticed he developed a pleasant Aberdeenshire intonation with an occasional unforced use of Doric. 'I suppose Harry comes from Aberdeenshire too', I said to fill a hole in the conversation. 'Yes, as a matter of fact, on his father's side he's from the Howe of Alford and his mother is from Caithness with Orcadian grandparents; the family were neighbours of mine in Alford. Maggie is from one of the big hooses near Auchterless (she's supposed to be descended from the trumpeter of Fyvie - although it's not talked about in the family) and her father's from the Stewartry, or maybe next door in Galloway. I can't remember which. So we are all a bit of a mixture.'

Michael went over to the bunk, shook the twitching Harry and said impatiently, 'Come on Harry, snap out of it. Supper's ready.' He heaved Harry from the bunk, draped him over a bowl of soup, and made him sip some brandy. The patient gradually cheered up, and hoovered up his share of the soup and beans. My diagnosis about him must have been right; he had been having a hysterical episode. The number of correct diagnoses I have made in my professional lifetime was beginning to approach double figures.

The rest of the evening passed very pleasantly as the seemingly bottomless bottle of aromatic brandy circulated. The pair of them worked for some international conglomerate. He wouldn't say which for 'security reasons' - you had to be careful - industrial espionage and all that. 'Economics is war by other means to paraphrase one of our directors', said Michael. They were very well informed about international affairs with fascinating and very plausible stories about what was really happening in the world with an impressive historical perspective. I kept my end up as best I could, but was completely out-classed by both of them. Their historical knowledge seemed encyclopaedic. They appeared to have met anyone who was anyone in the last couple of hundred years. Under the influence of the mellow, aromatic brandy we became more and more relaxed. Michael authenticated his Aberdeenshire connections by singing 'The Burning of Auchindoun' and the original version of the Jolly Beggar. He gave an interesting first-hand account of how Byron picked up this ancient ballad in some inn near Aboyne and respectabilised it into, 'We'll go no more a-roving by the light of the moon'.

I tried to keep my end up by singing 'The Soutar's Feast', but during the first verse I saw Harry and Mike exchanging glances. Harry then put his hand on my shoulder and said, 'Na, na, laddie. No like that. Mair like this', and he sang it authentically and what's more, in tune.

'Singin's no your gift', he said kindly.

'Pity Maggie isn't here, though', he continued gloomily, 'She can do a really belligerent 'Eppie Morrie.''

'Maggie, sing Eppie Morrie? With that accent?'

'She may have been to a boarding school, but she never lost her roots.' said Harry with some asperity. 'All the modern gentry aren't wersh as dishwater. They're beginning to come back home, culturally speaking, that is. They're taking their time but they're getting there. Maggie writes songs herself. There's a bit of Jean Elliot and Carolina Oliphant in her. A bit of Eppie Morrie, too', he said, looking rueful.

I could well see the resemblance with the last. A cross between Eppie Morrie and Ursula Cairnwhapple, however attractive the packaging, was a femme formidable indeed.

Michael stood up, shook his head sadly at Harry and said 'If it hadn't been for yon carry on of yours we'd have had the lassies with us still and had a much better evening. '

I agreed, mentioning that the Storm Goddess had a thrilling voice and I'd love to have heard her singing 'Fagail do'n Aite' again.

'Storm Goddess ?' queried Harry.

'Yes, the girl who left with Maggie.' I then realised we hadn't even exchanged names. We'd been discussing much more important things.

Mike at this point rummaged in his pack and brought out some dried bananas. I'll make some bananes brulées for desert he declared, grabbing the brandy bottle and a bag of sugar and moving off to the stove. Meanwhile, I chatted to the now completely revived Harry who was explaining to me in fascinating detail about conversations with W.S. Bruce and some of the difficulties he had in organising the Scotia Expedition. He then told some stories about Raeburn and Naismith, which included some reported speech. I presumed he had culled these from early Journals. Although I am a student of these volumes, I couldn't place the articles. I must have missed them somehow. Over his shoulder, I could see the dark profile of Michael back-lit by the flaring brandy as he brulé-ed his bananas. The brandy must have been well up the proof scale to make flames that size.

The bananas, when they came, were excellent. They were so good I ended by taking up my plate in both hands and licking it clean. I caught Michael looking at me quizzically but I felt too well-brandied to be embarrassed. As the conviviality progressed, he gradually wove the following story into the conversation.

'I would like you to listen to this proposition. Since you are a doctor I can be quite direct and technical about it. Our pharmaceutical division has developed a system that can reverse the process of aging. You don't believe me of course, but let me explain. It's all quite logical. As you know, the body is held together by connective tissue called collagen. Most body components turn over their component molecules; collagen doesn't. Over the years, the amount of it slowly increases and, worse still, changes chemically to become rigid and brittle; we accumulate the stuff round our blood vessels. The nutrition of peripheral tissue becomes diminished; an inner hand slowly strangles us. This gradual deterioration is known as aging. My company has perfected a system that promotes the turnover of collagen. It removes the old stuff, replaces it with new springy, pliable, youthful material. The strangulation is undone and the nutrition of peripheral tissue increases. In short, you become young again, but you retain whatever knowledge, experience and wisdom you have already acquired.

I questioned him about the details of the enzymology and molecular dynamics underlying this hypothesis, and it all seemed to hang together. I really enjoy these surrealistic conversations. I had just had one with the halliracket Storm Goddess when I agreed to join her on Point Five. I also remembered another one in a ritzy ski resort in the Alps when I found myself in a dinner party with some young millionaires. I got so carried away I thought I was one myself and seriously discussed joining a consortium to buy an enormous ocean racing yacht, chipping in my quarter million for the purchase and fifty grand annually for basic running expenses. On another occasion years ago I got a lift from a man who said he was a spiritualist who could foretell exactly the future. Consequently, he could drive without the usual precautions, overtaking on blind corners and so on. He proved his point. Nothing remotely near an accident happened during a hair-raising fifty-mile drive. The present situation was to my mind based more firmly on reality than any of these. The discovery of a cure for aging is much more likely than my becoming a millionaire or someone being able to predict the future exactly enough to risk his and everybody else's life on it many times in the course of a single drive or, alas, my being able to have a convincing go at Point Five Gully and shine in the eyes of the dangerously attractive Storm goddess, a Belle Dame sans Merci if ever there was one, who shed unsatisfactory boyfriends like autumn leaves.

So I led him on; at the very least this was going to make a good story to tell later on round some fireside or maybe even (as it has turned out) as an article for the Journal. Mike was a good storyteller. He made the very valid point that the brain is capable of acquiring knowledge and skills for maybe a couple of hundred years or more, if it could be kept in a physiologically young body. He pointed out that for many intelligent people, it was the rate at which the brain can assimilate and process experience that limits us intellectually. For most of us, it takes sixty years to complete our primary education. By then you've got over most of your hang-ups and are beginning to be really educable. He went on about the new horizons of understanding that could be crossed, the joy of unhurried contemplation of interesting problems and the time to do things properly.

It is good policy in bizarre conversations like this to introduce a practical point to see how they wriggle out of it so I said, 'Mike, this technology is all pretty state of the art stuff, yet you two seem to have been around a long time. You speak of David Hume, Adam Smith and Henry Dundas as if you knew them personally. If you did, how come you knew all this modern molecular biology before it was invented.'

'We've known how to do it for long enough, but now we know why it happens. In the old days we had found out empirically that a certain herbal regime is effective. Now we have isolated the active principles and can do it much better. It would be a disaster if it was generally available, as you can imagine. As it is, we could corrupt anyone we choose, but we do not choose so to do. (He quoted here the first half of Shakespeare's Sonnet xciv - the one that begins:

> They that have the power to hurt and will do none,
> That do not do the thing they most do show,
> Who, moving others, are themselves as stone,
> Unmoved, cold and to temptation free;
> They rightly do inherit Heaven's graces,
> And husband nature's riches from expense;
> They are the lords and owners of their faces,
> Others but stewards of their excellence.

We really try to live up to that noble utterance of the Bard. So we only consider as candidates people who have the intellectual creativity and emotional self-control to cope with it. Most importantly, they must not be cursed with anything so boring and unoriginal as conventional ambition, the ultimate banality when there are so many more interesting paths to pursue; still less do we want anyone with a coarsely competitive spirit or the desire to excel in public; all these defects carry with them the overwhelming need for status, honour, fame, recognition and all that sort of juvenilia. In our field, inconspicuousness is mandatory, as you can imagine. An off-beat, low-profile, late developer like you might be a suitable candidate.'

'Me off beat ? Me a late developer? How come?'

'It's the way you behave. You're not averse to listening and learning and you reach your conclusions obliquely in a way that appeals to me. You also seem to be a case of only mild ambition, almost certainly curable. Besides, when I saw you licking your plate, I knew that in spite of your white hair you hadn't quite yet made it as an adult - you may have some potential left - and that is essential.'

'Well, I'm going to do the dishes.' He said this as if to underline the matter-of-factness of the whole proposition. 'You can check with Harry here. He'll tell you about the disadvantages. He'll tell you why he tried to kill me today and ended up having a bubble in the bunk.'

'Well Harry you didn't look all that happy a while ago. What's it all about? What's the catch?'

'The catch is that Michael is the only one who knows how to do it: he runs the show; he makes the rules. Otherwise it's just as he said; you become physiologically young again. You feel good - physical and intellectual activities become an effortless joy again. What's on offer, mind you, is life not happiness; as everybody knows the two are different. You're not immune to the thousand natural shocks that flesh is heir to and all that. That burden has still to be borne. Also, be quite clear about this, it's longevity we're talking about not immortality. We're dealing with the real physical world, not with metaphysics - that word makes me feel like reaching for my revolver, like Goring when he heard the word 'culture'. Forget Mephistopheles. We wouldn't touch a character like Faust again with the longest pitchfork in the Howe of Alford.

Briefly he explained about the obvious difficulties in outliving your friends and next of kin, the need to disappear and get a new identity every decade or so. They hadn't been back to Scotland since Patrick Geddes's time. They had been in Australia in recent years, hence the Oz-type vowels. It was safe to return to Scotland now that everyone they had known before was 'safely dead' - a phrase that brought out a wry and weary smile. He was currently in love with Maggie, but she was growing broody and wanted children and moreover was becoming a little suspicious that she was getting crowsfeet and he wasn't. She was starting the normal transformation from nymph into matriarch. Maggie was a good sort. He wanted Michael to invite her into the longevity club but the Rule was 'no broody females' - for very obvious reasons. Today

Harry said he'd been badly depressed and had thought of getting Mike to start leading the second rope on Orion and then threatening to pull him off if he didn't let Maggie join. 'You get these black, black, depressions', he said 'But you get over them too, and I now realise that Mike is right. Maggie would complicate things hopelessly; she'd try to found a dynasty - imagine the complications - over the years she'd try to turn the whole thing into a family business with herself as ruling matriarch. I should have thought of Faust before I got involved.

As for you, Mike has made you an offer, that's all. You'll have to do the following up and have a lot, and I mean a lot, of discussion before you are accepted. Meanwhile these drams of brandy seem to have perked you up wonderfully.'

He said this last sentence raising his glass so the light could shine through it.

Michael meanwhile had dried and stacked the dishes and had been outside to look at the weather. It was much better and there was a bit of a moon. He and Harry would go down now to abort any rescue preparations that Maggie had started up.

'Keeping this show on the road is not free from problems', he said cheerfully and then with a kind smile, 'Fortunately we don't need as much sleep as you oldies.'

They dressed up and as he left, Michael gave me a card on which he'd written a telephone number. 'Give me a ring if you want to discuss things further.' We shook hands. Good firm handshakes from both of them. I realised that I actually liked these two odd-balls. I watched from the door as they bounded off into the moonlight as lithe and light as deer. At the bottom of the first slope, they stopped for a moment and turned to give me a final friendly wave.

I returned to the hut. The door clicked shut behind me. I felt I was on the wrong side of it. I sat at the table in the lamplight all alone, solitary and by myself. (The repetition is necessary to convey the echoing emptiness pervading both me and the silent tomb-like hut.) Mike had left a last brimming glass of brandy; he'd taken away the matt-black bottle, alas. The bouquet made me think of a flowery meadow burgeoning with life on a summer morning with maybe a background hint of earth after rain.

The phone numbers of the Storm Goddess and the man who said he wasn't Mephistopheles lay in front of me. I hoped I'd have the sense never to ring either. It would be dangerous to leave the sinking ship of your own generation. Nevertheless, I put the two numbers in my pocketbook, in the slot, as it happened, that also held my Senior Citizen's Railcard where they made a succinct little trio.

Not so long ago, life had been so simple, merely a matter of wandering on downhill until meeting with some more or less disagreeable terminal event to be borne with whatever dignity one was permitted - now the High Country and the Great Climbs were again on offer.

None of this anguish would have happened, of course, if I had just obeyed the rules and kept the bloody door shut.

I.H.M. Smart

Trio

The Shades of Night

The shades of night were falling fast. Big snowflakes drifted down from a gloomy sky, swirling in the occasional puff of wind. Snow-laden woods in the silent dusk of winter are dark and deep and awesome. The two of us were skiing along the floor of a remote valley on our way to climb Mount Assiniboine, the 'Matterhorn of the Rockies'. We were making a raid rather than laying siege, and so were lightly laden. Success depended on moving fast and making no mistakes. In the gathering darkness, we looked around for a suitable tree to bivouac under. This is the appropriate thing to do when benighted in the northwoods. The valley floors in this part of the world are not scoured by fierce winds. Trees grow straight and under vertical snowfall branches are bent rather than broken. The lowest fronds of spruce trees arch to the ground and leave a snow free space between them and the trunk to form a natural igloo where you can create a happy home. You can make a tiny fire from the dead wood of the old inner branches, and relax comfortably after supper in sheltered candlelight, philosophising about the meaning of life while the wild world outside gets on with whatever it is up to when we are not looking at it. It is also a lot more comfortable than camping in a small tent in heavy snowfall.

As we cast about looking at the various residential properties on offer, we came across ski tracks, the first evidence of our own kind we had seen since we left the road a couple of days ago. They were going at right angles to our route. They looked fresh and the tadpole shape of the ski pole marks gave us the direction; instead of remaining steadfastly on our course, we found ourselves following this trace of a fellow human. The tracks continued through the pillared halls of a tenebrous wood to an open meadow. From the far side, a ray of gold shone through the snow-spangled darkness. The kindly light led us to a picturesque log cabin with deep snow on the roof. We unclipped our skis, knocked, pushed the door open and suddenly left the cold dark monochrome world at our backs and entered an alternative universe of warmth and colour. Firelight flickered across the rough-hewn logs of the cabin walls. In the mellow glow of a hurricane lantern, we could see a rifle and snowshoes hung from wooden pegs on each side of the fire. We could feel we were standing on a deep pile carpet of yellow wood chips, richly patterned with bits of dark brown tree bark. The aroma of pine resin, coffee and toasted bread filled the warm air.

A voice from the fireside broke the spell. 'Come on in, you guys. The coffee's ready. Pull up a bench and thaw yourselves out. It sure is one cold night out there. You're mighty lucky to hit this place. There's a grand-pappie of a snowstorm goin' to hit us.' The accommodation properly reserved for us somewhere out there in the swirling darkness could not compete with the opulence offered by the advanced technology that lay before us. We accepted the invitation and spent a very pleasant couple of days in comfort with an interesting companion. As it happened, we would never have got even to the base of Mount Assiniboine. It snowed too much. It was difficult enough just getting back to the road. Nevertheless, we were not to have known that when we deviated from our route. In so doing, we had taken the easy option and lost merit. Enterprises of great pith and moment in this respect their currents turn awry and lose the name of action, as my old friend Hamlet once pointed out.

Stairway to Heaven

We were returning from the ascent of a minor but shapely rock peak of little mountaineering significance. Nevertheless, it had sufficient merit for the powerful Shiva, creator, preserver and destroyer to have shrines on its flank. It had also attracted some exiled Tibetan monks who had built a monastery into its side; the sounds of their horns and chants could be heard rising from time to time from far below. Our camp was perched on a shoulder of the mountain, which we shared with some shepherds and their flocks, a holy man and a few big trees. It was very picturesque.

Each afternoon, towering anvil-headed clouds, harbingers of the approaching monsoon, assembled over the distant plains of India and in the evenings, spectacular lightning played across the darkening southern sky. On our last afternoon, the cloud front moved in unexpectedly and overwhelmed our little Shangri-la. By some trick of light, the hue of the surrounding vegetation was reflected into the air. An unnerving dense green colour filled the quietness between our camp and the cloud base a few hundred feet above. Then, quite suddenly, a dark wind enveloped our ridge, bringing bountiful rain. Bright forked lightning and thunder of intimidating loudness sent a panic through the flocks on the ridge. We abandoned our tents. Everybody, man, woman, sheep and goat headed for the only solid shelter available, a nearby dry-stone fank with a minimal metre-high roof. As I ran, I saw above us two balls of lightning joined by a wiggly band of light, just like you see in horror films.

Inside the crowded shelter, a noisy stream of prayers rose to the heavens. I crouched in the dung in a praying position pressed against a goat, a sheep, a shepherd and a girl from Tasmania while something mighty struck outside. I remember thinking through my fear that, all things considered, this would not be a bad way to go. It would be quite romantic to be struck by lightning in such a picturesque site in the company of fellow mortals all of us fearful of impending dissolution while a stream of interwoven prayers, human, ovine, and caprine, provided a broad ecumenical stairway to heaven.

However it was not to be. After the storm had passed, we found that a tree a few yards away had indeed been rent asunder and some goats sheltering beneath had been killed. Maybe we had been given a warning; perhaps a merciful element somewhere in creation was allowing us all a little more time to obtain a little more merit. According to Buddhist doctrine, merit is acquired by following a life of purity and renunciation and is essential for securing a worthwhile future existence. The recommended route runs uphill, is difficult to find let alone follow, but leads eventually to a restful state of non-being somewhere on the far side of oblivion. On the way, however, there are tracks that lead astray to seductively cheerful log cabins where unsteadfast souls are recycled back to the main road again.

The Aphrodite Moment

Don't get excited by the title. What I am writing about is rather technical and boring and has nothing to do with merit or transcendental log cabins. It is about how we perceive the world, specifically about those moments of heightened awareness we all experience from time to time. Often they happen when we are coming off a mountain in the aftermath of an adrenalin buzz, but equally often they may arrive in a period of tranquillity, the result of mood coinciding with the resonance of a particular place at a particular time in a particular light. On these occasions, you and the ambient world achieve for a moment a numinous, eirenic harmony.

The ancients, being ignorant of modern neurophysiology, used to attribute these supranormal states of mind to possession by forces which were at heart also human, even if a bit more than human. Horace really seemed to think that after a beaker or two of Falernian wine he was in the presence of gentle, jovial Bacchus (Quo me, Bacche?) and in Sappho's poems, there is no doubt that, during these moments of transcendental beauty, she felt herself to be in the very presence of Aphrodite ('...you came to me then.... your immortal face shining'). To the ancients, Gods and Goddesses were metaphors used to explain and make bearable the things they did not understand. Nowadays, the myths we make up about the world are less humane and comforting than the larger than life, but still recognisably human, Gods and Goddesses. We are supposed to be here all alone fashioned from subdividing particles that pop in and out of existence while inside our heads a cocktail of neurochemicals allows us to perceive a limited model of whatever it is that surrounds us.

We may indeed be a marvellous aggregation of transiently ordered particles pushing against the grain of a powerful but mindless universe bent on maximising its own disorder but operationally, that is for the practical purposes of making the most of our subjective inner lives, we could do worse than respond to the aura of the mysterious Aphrodite. Here is how C.M. Bowra recreates the mystery of her presence:

'Aphrodite was not entirely or primarily the goddess of love. Physical desire and passion strictly belong to Eros; Aphrodite's sphere was wider and slightly different from his. She is more the Goddess of beauty than of the desire for it. She is the Goddess of flowers and of the smiling sea. Her power lies in the enchantment that she throws over visible things. In her own way, Aphrodite stands for absolute value, for the magic light that falls at times on life and makes it seem so desirable that men are almost driven to madness. Just as Artemis stood for the remote ideal of innocence, so Aphrodite stood for the sudden unexpected moments of entrancing beauty which occur in the visible world and seduce those who see them into a state far removed from their ordinary experience.'

My most authentic encounter with her was in fact in her native Greece while descending a steep hillside in the fireflied dusk through a grove of dark olive trees under a crescent moon. She, or her equivalent, is immanent in Scotland, too. Most of us have experienced those rare moments of magic that are in her gift. Alas, I suspect they do not stem from some mystical epiphany but result from wobbles in our neurochemistry with no information content other than what we give to them. Nevertheless, there is always the possibility that the wobbles may indeed be caused by the arrival of a message from outside. It might even be a real telephone call from Aphrodite herself. It certainly feels like it at the time.

Far Out on the Far Cuillin

I emerged from the BMC hut in Glen Brittle one brilliant June morning as the brief shadow of the night was fading over the northern hills. The rising sun was just catching the dew drops weighing down the grass, each drop photomultipying the oblique sunlight into a star, achieving effortlessly and in abundance the effect that artfully-cut diamonds strive for; try as they may such artifacts can never be as good as the real thing. The birds were singing, the force of gravity had been turned down to a peep and the midges were off duty. Aesthetically it was a full house, aces on kings, if not the fabled five aces that are said to occur occasionally in skilled hands or in rare transcendental moments - a morning like this seemed to be one of them. As an extra bonus I was all by myself without a companion to disturb the local geometry of space-time.

I intended to contour along the base of the Cuillin to Garsbheinn, come back along the ridge as far as Coire Grundda and return to the splendours of the BMC hut where some slices of filet mignon, assorted mushrooms (morels, ceps and the ordinary ones), new potatoes and mild onions awaited me - a simple repast after a long day on the hill. Oh yes, there was also a bottle of claret, more expensive than I could prudently afford.

I was off to Garsbheinn because it is the least popular of the Cuillin summits yet has one of the best panoramic views of the wide sea to the south and west, the dragons back of the Cuillins to the north, and beckoning Blaven and the receding horizons of the mainland hills to the east. I was going to spend a long time on the summit just enjoying being alive. I would relax with a loaf of bread, a flask of wine, a book of verse and, if I needed a 'thou' or two beside me dreaming in the wilderness, I could summon someone up from the richly populated mansions of the past to share the enjoyment.

One thing I wanted to do was to look down on Soay and remember the day we had tried to get across there to work for Gavin Maxwell in his shark fishery. The arrangement was for us to light a fire on the Skye shore at 2pm on an agreed day and they would come across to pick us up. In spite of a large smoky fire, nothing happened. As we walked disconsolately back to Glen Brittle Maxwell's shark-catching motor torpedo boat sped into the Sound of Soay from the west with a scraggy, sardonically smiling shark no more than ten foot long lashed to its side - their total catch for a week. Gavin Maxwell had been operating the fishery for a year or two and after a period of success, basking sharks, for some inexplicable, osgood-mackenzie-like reason, had all but vanished. Consequently there was no work to be had on Soay. There was a telegram to that effect waiting for us at the hostel when we returned. So we had to make do instead with midge-bitten toil cutting bracken around the struggling foot-high sitkas that now in their maturity dominate the glen.

And so that morning I started off with a spring in my step, but after half an hour or so slowed to a great-grandfatherly trudge; it was after all sixty years since my first visit. By conserving energy, I arrived at the summit in fairly good nick and spent the afternoon there enjoying my flask of wine and book of verse and letting my mind out of its box to soar around looping the loop and enjoying its freedom. It turned into a hot shimmering afternoon and I did a sort of après midi d'un faune for a couple of hours, followed by a substantial zizz in the shade of a rock.

As I was about to bundle and go, I was disturbed by the arrival of two youngish men. We greeted each other and agreed on the superb weather. They dumped their rucksacks and modest rack of chocks and runners, then started admiring the view pointing out landmarks to each other and arguing over some of them. Then taking out their picnic they reverted to the conversation they must have been having when they arrived. They seemed a pleasant couple, light on their feet and obviously fit. Then one of them gave me a second look.

'Didn't we once meet a couple of years ago in the Nevis Hut?' he enquired. 'You helped us during our retreat from a debacle on the Orion Face.'

This could only be the man who was the prime mover on that memorable occasion. Their party of four had straggled down from the Ben in darkness and blizzard and I had offered them shelter in the hut. You may possibly remember that an interesting little bit of theatre unfolded with a colourful *dramatis personae* that included Maggie, the dark dominatrix and the Storm Goddess whose name I never discovered, the *deux femmes sans merci* who spiced up the evening and, of course, there was the hapless Harry. Mike, the leading man on that occasion still had a slight Australian overlay to his clear Scottish consonants and vowels and the same relaxed genial manner.

'Yes, how could I forget? It was quite a night. That was a remarkable bottle of brandy you had. I remember it well.'

'We expected to hear from you again. Did you lose our telephone number?'

'No, I lost my nerve. All that nonsense you talked might have been true. I don't take risks any more. I try to be happy as I am.' I said, sententiously.

You may remember they had come out with some plausible science fiction about their ability to sustain life beyond its natural span. It had been highly entertaining. They had been great company for an evening and, toned down a bit to make it believable; it had made a good story.

'I am disappointed in you,' he said, cracking open a can of beer and handing it to me.

'Well, let me introduce you to my friend Dirk here. He is a sailing man. Mostly square riggers. He's old fashioned, but much sought after nowadays by training ships.'

I exchanged how-do-you-dos with a pleasant man of middle height, rugged appearance, fair hair, blue eyes, a broad smile and a notably firm handshake. It appeared they were off Dirk's boat anchored in Portree. It wasn't a full square rigger, he said apologetically. Well not really. His present vessel was a brigantine. Squaresails on the foremast only. Easier to handle with a small crew. He and Mike were having a day off. They had just done the main ridge in a leisurely ten hours from Sgurr nan Gillian by way of the pinnacle ridge and were going back along the ridge to descend to Glen Brittle via Coire Lagan. They were to be picked up at Glen Brittle House that evening by one of the crew.

'Join us for a bite to eat', he invited indicating a spread of crusty bread, sausage and relish he had laid out on a stone. I accepted, more to be sociable than anything else. I tried to make some mileage with Dirk, reminiscing about the Centennial Yacht Meet and the joys of sailing in state-of-the-art ships of yesteryear. We rambled on but it was an unequal conversation. Rounding the point of Sleat or even Barra Head was a pussy-cat compared to the Cape of Good Hope.

'I'd like to see your yacht', I said to change the subject from my embarrassingly inadequate sailing experience.

'She is not a yacht - she's a brigantine! a real ship', he exclaimed banging me on the head with the remains of the baguette in mock huff. 'Usually I use a belaying pin to correct remarks like that. Be grateful that there isn't one handy.'

And so at their invitation I travelled back along the ridge with them in a late afternoon of purring warmth. We conversed easily together, mostly about history and literature. They were both scholarly souls very well read with a breath-taking historical perspective. I kept up with them conversationally fairly well, but physically I started to lag increasingly far behind on the uphills. The verve of the morning had gone. I reverted to my own leisurely, energy-saving plod. They waited for me at the bottom of the final ascent to Sgurr Dhu.

'Here we must part. It was nice to meet you all again', I said offering a parting handshake. They declined the gambit. Mike made the suggestion that since it was such a fine evening we all saunter slowly to the Tearlach-Dhu gap. I could then join them in a rappel down the short side and then go back down to Coire Ghrundda from the bottom of the gap. It sounded sensible and I was enjoying their company, so I accepted and we plodded communally onward.

I managed the rappel into the gap with a fair show of residual competence. We sat companionably at the bottom, sharing some chocolate. Dirk said it would be really easier for me if I kept on the ridge and went back to Glen Brittle down the stone shoot and home by Coire Lagan in their company.

'We can all go together. No need to hurry. The sun is still high and the colours will get better as the shadows lengthen.'

The offer was confirmed by Mike, 'We'll give you a top rope. It would be a pity to miss the view from Sgurr Alasdair on an evening like this. It will be worth the effort.'

I've seen the day I could have led the steep side but now I knew I didn't have the strength or control to get up under any circumstances. It would be too humiliating to be hauled up like a sack of potatoes. So, I declined. 'No thanks, I'll just rest here a bit and then wander back in my own good time. One of the joys of maturity is that you know how to take your time.', I added, not too convincingly .

Mike looked at me appraisingly and then produced a flask and some small nesting metal cups not much bigger than thimbles from his rucksack.

'Okay then let's have a final dram afore we go.'

'Is it that stuff again? I don't mind if I do. A little snort would do me good.'

'It's not exactly the same stuff, but it's pretty good.'

Whatever it was, was strong - bitter with a pleasant herbal taste, a bit like Gamle Dansk, the Danish pick-me-up. We continued to chat companionably. At one stage they were arguing together about something to do with the next stage of their voyage and I poured myself another dram without being asked. I don't think they noticed. A few minutes later I heard my own voice saying,

'I've got a good idea. I'll just lead this pitch, then we can all go down to the hut and you can have dinner with me before you drive back to your yacht, I mean brigantine. I have some good wine and a bottle of Old Brora.' They exchanged a worried glance.

'Steady on old fellow,' said Mike. But I was already tying on the rope.

Then they gave each other a meaning look. Hendrik nodded. 'Let him try', he muttered under his breath. 'Let's see what he can do. We can catch him when he falls'. I think they both moved to cushion my fall from the first move.

The fact was that I climbed the nasty smooth side with confidence and some aplomb. The rock was much smoother than of yore and unsightly grey, green, greasy limpopo chalk marks were everywhere. Nevertheless, I went up like a competent twenty-year-old. I could feel parts of my nervous system, dormant for fifty years, emerging from retirement. My fingers read the rock like brail and my eyes transmitted data about the geometry and texture of the coming holds. My nervous system integrated all this information, optimised the configuration of my body in relation to the pull of gravity and the expected frictional properties of each hold and organised the sequence of action of the appropriate muscle groups, checking that they could exert the required power, correctly as it turned out. I seemed to be just coming along for the ride. It was a bit like driving a perfectly tuned aeroplane, operating under an efficient autopilot. I got to the top before I was ready, belayed expertly and brought the others up.

'That's a bloody good dram you have in that flask,' I remarked as we untied.

'We'll have to watch you', Mike replied. 'I thought I saw you have a second shot of that stuff. You shouldn't have done that. Never mind. We'll make sure you get home alright.'

'What do you mean 'get home all right'? I've never felt better.'

'I am sure you haven't. Not for years anyway. I mean what you have just done has a cost. The stuff you just knocked back opened up blood vessels in brain and muscle and is even now emptying your liver of glycogen and is starting to catabolise your fat reserves. When we get back to the hut, you're going to have to keep off alcohol and take aboard as much glucose and skimmed milk as you can to protect your liver and let it resynthesise its energy stores.'

'I thought it was supposed to be a 'magic' elixir', I said provocatively.

'You obviously don't know what magic is', he replied. 'We can't break the Laws of Thermodynamics. You always get less useful energy out of a system than you put in. Free energy is a misnomer. In the end you have to repay the bill with interest even if you happen to be a magician.'

'Tell me more', I asked fascinated by this tutorial on the metaphysics of physics, but any further exposition was interrupted by Dirk. 'Enough of this babble', he said. He had finished coiling the rope and was preparing to go. 'There is some magic to be made on top of Sgurr Alasdair on an evening like this. Let's go where the magic will actually happen.'

We wandered on and spent a full hour on the summit while the sun got lower, the colours richer and the shadows longer. It was one of those Aphrodite moments when the mind and the world get fankled up together. This is an interesting subjective state to be in.

Nevertheless, I have little doubt the great wide world out there was completely indifferent to the fact that our nervous systems were transmuting all the mindless radiation it was emitting into a thing of beauty and a joy forever. Although we take it for granted, this ability is profoundly magical. The thermodynamic imperative is transcended by what it gives rise to. I remarked as much to the other two. They asked if I was sure I had got it the right way round.

Then we picked our way lightly down the great stone chute into Coire Lagan, loped with long strides over the great elephantine boiler plates of the corrie floor and on through the rough textures and soft colours of the lower glen, luminous in the afterglow of a magic mid-summer gloaming.

When we got back to the hut they accepted my invitation to dinner. 'Show me your stuff and I'll do the cooking', said Mike. He saw the mushrooms that I had left re-hydrating in a bowl. 'I'll make soup. Dried ones like these have better flavour as soup.'

He sat me down, took out some gadgets from his rucksack and clipped something on to my wrist, which displayed my blood pressure and the rate and character of my pulse. Then he had a look in my eyes with a little ophthalmoscope. 'I never travel without one of these, he explained, 'the retina is the only place you can actually see blood vessels. Yours are all right. Your circulation seems up to it. I am just being careful. Just checking your tyre pressures, as it were.'

'Now go and pour Dirk a dram', he directed as he unpacked more things from his rucksack. 'You'll find him interesting. I'll bring you a liver-saving drink in a few minutes.'

Dirk was an impressive character. He seemed to have sailed everywhere, but he was appropriately foggy about dates. Most of his stories seemed a bit old fashioned, telling them, nevertheless, with grace and interpretive skill. He listened appreciatively enough to my stories of going through the Corrievreckan and the Grey Dog but it couldn't match his story of being dragged by the Benguela current through the teeth of a full gale blowing in the opposite direction in a full-rigged ship without an auxiliary engine.

Mike came through with a drink in a pint mug.

'You must get through another one of these tonight.' he announced.

It wasn't bad stuff – smooth, warm, milky, redolent of honey with a prolonged, rich, nutty après gout. A little later he came back with a couple of bowls of mushroom soup and garlic bread, which he and Dirk supped with great enjoyment. Mushrooms, he explained to me between spoonfuls, had toxins that my liver couldn't handle in its present state. I went off and boiled the new potatoes, grilled the filet mignons and returned with the bottle of claret. This they partook of with relish, commiserating with me but assuring me, while I sipped my liver-protecting posset, that it was for my own good.

The hut was full of climbers noisily reliving the near-death experiences they had confronted during the day. To escape from the clang of decibels we moved outside to a green bit above the road, they with their coffee and drams, me with my second posset. It was a lovely soft summer night with enough of a breeze to keep the midges away.

'Tell me', I said 'what was that stuff you gave me up on the ridge? Was there amphetamine in it? Are you a couple of junkies just keeping going on performance-enhancing drugs? '

'Of course not', Mike replied matter-of-factly, 'we are not escapists, at least not in that sense. We are just knowledgeable about replacement therapy. We are no more junkies than a diabetic is for taking insulin. We have just learned how to use replacement therapy for a greater range of conditions than diabetes. You tune the engine of a car or the sails of a boat for optimum performance, don't you? You do that as a matter of course. Why not tune your mind and maintain your body in optimum condition just like you would a car or boat? We are just knowledgeable about the way our body systems work and can tune them to maximum efficiency.'

'Well why do you risk all this by dangerous activities like climbing and sailing?'

'We climb and sail because both require route finding and calculating risk under stress and have no rules except those imposed by the laws of nature - wind and tide and gravity - against which there is no appeal. Apart from the enjoyable adrenalin-buzz, it is the perfect practical metaphor for us. It helps to steady our nerve for route finding at the wild frontier of the fifth age. We are no longer exploring the edge of our climbing ability. We have done all that. We climb well within our ability. We have new unknowns to explore.'

He and Dirk expanded on this theme for a couple of hours in the deepening summer dusk during which they introduced the term 'Fifth Age of Learning.' According to them the five ages of learning are: first infancy, second conventional schooling, third training in a trade or profession and fourth surviving the vicissitudes and continuous assessments we are subjected to in the University of Adult Life with its incomprehensible examination system that seems unfair and sometimes brutal. To enter the fifth age you have to be fortunate enough to survive the first four stages with enough intellectual commitment to continue your education.

The session ended just before mid-night when we saw the headlights of a car coming down the glen.

'That must be Gourlay', said Mike rising and dusting himself down.

As we walked back to the road he looked at the impeccable sky.

'The weather is stable. There isn't going to be much wind,' he said sniffing the air. 'No good for sailing. Why don't we just stay and do a climb tomorrow? Our friend here and Gourlay would make good climbing partners.'

The car arrived and I was introduced to Gourlay, a big genial rough-hewn man who turned out to be the ship's engineer. Gourlay exuded competence and had a handshake like a friendly velvet vice. The weather report he brought was good for the next twelve hours; then a low pressure weather front from the Atlantic was due to arrive. It was decided to grab the good weather while it was on offer and make an early start.

We managed to squeeze in to the hut to get away from the dew that was settling over us. After a few hours sleep, as dawn's left hand was in the sky and the first birds were tweeting tentatively we left quickly without breakfast, except I had to drink something rather neutral tasting. The dew-laden grass was seeded with pearls gleaming silver-grey in the directionless light – there were no shadows yet. A few strands of mist decorated the black skyline of the Cuillin. The attention to detail that morning was immaculate. We moved fast through the fields of pearls as they transmuted into diamonds under the first sunlight. The rolling flanks of grass and heather gained texture from the first long shadows cast by the oblique shafts of rising sunshine. I was moving easily and seemed to have lost weight.

At the entrance to Coire Lagan we paused to appreciate the ambience and have breakfast. We looked out over the sea to Rum of the fretted skyline, to Canna of the golden sunlit cliffs, and over the Minch to the Long Island, to green Barra of the waves and fair Uist of the songs, all bright in the sunlight and set in a sea patterned in blues, greys and silver. For breakfast I had another pint of the rich emollient mixture Mike had been feeding me with the night before. He also tested my tire pressures and had a cursory look at my retinal vessels, pronouncing my systems to be operationally satisfactory. I remarked on how well I was feeling and asked why I was so spry and light on my feet after all yesterday's activities and so little sleep. He explained that I had used up my brown fat and had now switched over to converting the fat in my spare tire into energy. My fuel tank was emptying, that was why I felt as if I had lost weight. But there was nothing to worry about unless I started running on empty and he wouldn't allow that to happen.

We split into two teams. Gourlay and I were to do Cioch West and Integrity. Dirk and Mike would do the Direct and the Crack of Double Doom. We would meet at the top. At the bottom of the Cioch West, Gourlay insisted I lead the first pitch. The last time I tried a few years ago, I couldn't get off the ground. This time I had the power and control to climb with easy competence. I had the feeling that mind and body, liberated from the shackles of age, were really enjoying themselves. Physical competence in my 'teens had been great but its return sixty years later was even better. Physical well-being was now a mere vehicle for something much more exhilarating. I was more comprehensively aware of the surrounding world than I'd ever been before; a strange sense of intellectual adventure had arrived. You know these pictures made of incomprehensible wiggly coloured lines that were fashionable a few years ago, the ones if you look into them a certain way, a three-dimensional scene, otherwise completely invisible, appears? It was a bit like that. I was sure the unusual insight I was experiencing stemmed from enhanced processing of signals from the external environment and not from the circuits in my brain losing their grip and having the equivalent of a wild in-house party in which guests from the outside world were being tossed in the air from blankets or made to swing from the chandeliers.

We reached the Cioch and sat there, suspended over Coire Laggan, enjoying the sensation of hanging in space above a rugged landscape of gabbro and green pastures. Gourlay was a good companion. He seemed to have a comprehensive practical understanding of how things worked from the mechanics of the Stirling engine to the properties of molecular nano-machinery. He wasn't a boring pedant, merely the entertaining provider of asked-for information.

'So what is all this about the Fifth Age of Learning', I asked, 'I got a bit confused last night when Mike spoke about it as the 'Wild Frontier'.

He was willing enough to explain.

'First you have to understand some basic features about how the brain works', he began. 'Let's simplify things by saying the brain is a machine for processing signals received from the environment, a sort of biological computer concerned with maximising the probability of its own survival in variable surroundings.'

Ordinary computers, he pointed out, are hard-wired, use electronic current, generate too much heat and have to be programmed. A computer with the processing capacity of the human brain made from electronic components would be comparatively big and would generate enough heat to boil a few kettles. The living brain uses the 'cooler' (in the old and modern senses of this word), much more subtle system of ionic current and comes with a program already installed and hard-wired donated by your ancestors. We are dragged through the first part of our lives as our inherited program makes us conform to its priorities; namely to survive and raise another generation.

'As you have no doubt noticed,' he continued, 'we don't always approve of what our inherited program is doing with us. That is because we have so much surplus circuitry in the overgrown human brain that we are capable of exerting quality control on our behaviour – which of course is over-ridden if it becomes too sophisticated and gets in the way of survival. Our soft wiring is configured by our culture and education and over the years tends to become hard-wired. Dogma is a particularly deep and irreversible conversion from soft to hard-wiring. As you know, once you get down to someone's hard wired dogma, quality control is lost and appalling behaviour can result.'

Reclining in the sunshine on the top of the Cioch like an amiable Bacchus (it was easy to transform the sweat band round his brow into an ivy wreath) he explained further: 'once our inherited program has been run through, we as individuals are redundant. Our body has done its biological job and there is no reason for us to hang around cluttering up the system and getting in the way of the next generation. However, when we are freed from the tyranny of the biological program that no longer requires us, we are left for a short period with a mighty intellectual engine with spare processing capacity for which there is no biological need. This is the time of the Fifth Age. The tragedy is that just as we become free to use these latter-day processing skills our support systems start to fail. The metabolic servicing of all our organs, including the brain, which is a metabolically expensive organ to run, declines progressively. Like Moses, we see the Promised Land of the Fifth Age of Learning but we do not have the metabolic wherewithal to enter.

He went on like this for quite a bit. I was fascinated. But I won't bore you any more. I know this is a mountaineering story, and it is not concerned with far-out philosophising. I am only trying to describe a day out on the Cuillin as it actually happened.

Back at the climbing we addressed 'Integrity', a well-named climb of uncompromising verticality, which previously would have tested me to my limit but now was so well within my physical and mental competence that I sang as I climbed. It was so exhilarating to be operating well within the limits of my ability instead of continually husbanding my aging resources to make them last. We met the others at the top where they had been waiting for us, and continued towards Sgurr Alasdair. I really enjoyed the bad step on Sgurr Sgumain; an out-of-balance move I found amusing. The last time I had been there was in winter a few years ago on a windy day with snow drifting around our knees. We didn't have the strength to get up. This time I scarcely paused.

And so we continued on to Sgurr Alasdair and Sgurr Tearlach. On a spur looking out over the Coruisg side, we stopped for a prolonged lunch. Mike explained in his usual matter-of-fact way that life originated as one of the many back-eddies in the downward energy flow of the universe on its way to absolute zero. A back eddy is by definition a local contravention of the Second Law of Thermodynamics in which energy is used to create rather than degrade order.

'Life is a self-propagating back eddy, a special type of wave phenomenon', he declared, airily pointing to the lichens on the rocks and a passing raven that croaked wisely in confirmation (This was probably a coincidence). The particular retrograde surge, which produced life, configured a chemistry that was capable of utilising energy to propagate itself and to create other retrograde waves of increasing orders of complexity. Imagine a swirl in a mighty river with a standing wave going against the current. Life is the crest of a retrograde energy wave with an edge ruffled into a Mandelbrot set. It is distinguished by each fractal of the wave front, before it dies, harnessing more energy from the ambient universe to generate and diversify yet other retrograde wave of increasing complexity – evolution is, I think the appropriate term. We, he indicated Dirk and Gourlay, are just able to keep our own particular little wave going for longer and we know how to make this psychologically bearable by building on our hard-wired desire to explore the Unknown. We are the opposite of Buddhists who strive to put the mind into the neural equivalent of zero degrees Kelvin where everything is still and, as far as we know, nothing much happens except happiness. We feel we have more interesting things to do than await our terminal recycling with minds in tranquil neutral.

Breaking the Second Law of Thermodynamics is, of course, the Original Sin, a capital offence carrying a mandatory death penalty. We have just negotiated a longer stay of execution than most.' Seeing my dismay, he said, 'for goodness sake, cheer up. Don't you understand that the ability to have a conversation like this is a miracle, a view into an unknown world? Entering the Fifth Age is like making an irreversible move over an overhang into unknown problems possibly beyond our capacity to solve. We are trying to find a route on a new mountain where all the usual rules are invalid, where everything is unpredictable. You must remember what that was like - the exhilaration of pushing yourself into the unknown, the creative excitement of making the great irreversible move. The wild frontier of the fifth age is where the action is. Just think of it: no guide books, no artificial aids, no leaders, no foreknowledge of what is beyond the metaphorical overhang. That is a wild frontier if ever there was one.'

We passed the next hour or two in silence and comfortable companionship, each of us utilising energy from the surrounding universe to surf along on the fractal edge of our own little wave. We reassembled ourselves a couple of hours later at what seemed to be the appropriate time and continued along the ridge via King's Chimney and the Inaccessible Pinnacle and then down the long shoulder of Sgurr na Bannachdich to the glen. The weather by then had begun to change, the air turning sultry and close. Tall anvil-headed cumulus clouds approached from the Southwest. The sun developed a halo; colour and relief slowly drained from the landscape. Normally this would have made me depressed, but this time I interpreted it as a different sort of splendour.

At the hut I pressed them to stay for another meal, but they just asked for a pot of coffee and then they'd be off.

'We have a lot to do' Dirk explained 'I have to get the ship ready for a new voyage. We are hoping to navigate through a barrier of treacherous metaphors to explore the uncharted seas beyond.' I am not sure what he meant by this. He did smile as he said it. Maybe he was pulling my leg.

Before he left, Mike tested my tyres again and left me some stuff I was to take in decreasing doses over the next few days added to a posset of skimmed milk and honey with a grating of nutmeg. He warned me to follow closely the instructions he was leaving, and in a few days I would be back to my old self again.

'Sorry about the pun, but here is my card with my email address. Contact me in a few weeks if you like and we can have more discussions about this and that.' Once again he waived his hand about airily.

As we sat having our coffee, the weather broke and the rain started. Nevertheless, they insisted on leaving. I saw them to the car. Curtains of warm, grey rain swept past in the special Skye manner, and thunder rumbled around here and there in the gloom. We rapidly shook hands. Both Gourlay and Dirk said they hoped to see me again soon. After they got in, there was an impressive display of lightning, followed closely by a *basso profundo* roll of thunder. Mike must have seen the expression on my face. He rolled down the window and said, 'don't look at me like that. This extravagance has nothing to do with me. It's too theatrical. I'm embarrassed.'

They drove off in a cloud of spray turned silver by a wan shaft of sunshine that momentarily appeared. I ran back into the hut into the smell of wet clothing, tinned soup and someone's burning toast. Mike's card was damp and the print discretely small. I was about to start looking for my glasses when I found I could read it easily without them. My eyesight seemed to have improved.

I.H.M. Smart

Suleiman's Pilaff

We arrived at the hut in the freezing cold of a gloomy dusk. During the night, a wind shook the building and a couple of feet of snow fell. By sunrise the storm had passed, leaving behind a white, white world under a clear blue sky. All things were now bright and beautiful but, of course, much more dangerous. Avalanches of fine powder swept down the gullies billowing into the corries. Only fools would rush out to climb on a day like this. Since this was, in fact, the case, we optimised our chances by choosing the safest route. We could see the wind blowing streamers of diamond dust from the crests of the ridges. These would at least be clear of suffocating snow. We took the easiest ridge on offer, and late in the afternoon arrived on the plateau.

We walked to the summit with our heads in sunshine and our feet hardly visible in knee-high spindrift. At the summit, the wind dropped and life became easier. We dallied as long as we could to enjoy the spectacular winter sunset of blue and gold behind the several horizons of snowy mountain-tops and deep glens filling up with darkness.

Then we paid the price. In the gathering dusk we descended into Corrie Leis where the powder had accumulated in deep drifts. Two miles of unconsolidated fluff lay between us and the hut. If we had had the strength of former years we would have ploughed our way back to the hut without stopping. It would not have been macho to do otherwise. Now, as card-carrying Senior Citizens, we had to take our time whether we wanted to or not. In the prevailing conditions, this was no hardship. There was no wind. We were warmly clad and had husbanded our strength. The photomultiplying effect of the snow on the starlight allowed us to progress without using our head torches. Every few hundred yards we had a rest and relaxed comfortably in the soft drifts, enjoying the austere beauty of the ghostly walls of the glen and the roof of bright stars. In our earlier days when our priority would have been to move as quickly as possible, we would have missed out on these periods of contemplation under the wonder of a starry heaven.

On occasions like this, my friend Carlos Macintyre tends to have bouts of introspection. One of them overcame him as we lay on our backs in a comfortable snowdrift looking at the immense universe above us: a black sky full of fixed stars that twinkled, wandering planets that gave a steady light, and every now and then a shooting star that, for the brief period that it advertised its presence, did both.

Carlos had only recently discovered science, and was full of wonder at the new world that had opened up to him. He opined, 'All that starlight is out of date. All the information we are receiving from that weighty matter out there is light years out of date. We are living in the past.'

Most of us know this, but to Carlos, product of several conventional religions based on revealed truth, it was a novel thought.

'Yes, oh sage,' I replied to keep him going.

A profound silence followed.

'The light we are receiving now was released long ago', he continued, 'it is arriving with obsolete information about events that happened in the past. Some of it must have started out before there was life on earth.

"And we who now behold these present days

Have eyes to wonder, but lack tongues to praise."

There is nothing we can do about it', he continued, 'except enjoy the fact that we are stumbling around in an antique shop full of past history.'

When Carlos starts off on one of these soliloquies he makes the clichés sound as original as they must have been when newly minted. I knew from experience that we were now going to get a quotation from the Rubaiyat of Omar Khayyam, the philosopher whose writings he had encountered during his years in Persia. He had learned enough of the Farsi language during his time in Iran to have read and understood the idiom of the original and, better still, actually to have heard it recited by a native speaker; so he knew both the poem and its spoken music. He was of the opinion that Fitzgerald's English translation was separately inspired, and that the poem had actually gained in translation if such a thing is possible. The main loss was not in meaning but in the beauty of the script in which it is written; Latin letters were somehow too stark and angular compared to the grace of the flowing cursive Farsi script. He found Omar's civilised fatalism very congenial and he frequently returned to it in spite of his familiarity with so many prestigious philosophical systems and divinely inspired religions

So out it came, a stanza based on the thoughts of a long-dead Persian astronomer, philosopher, mathematician and poet translated into a different language and recited by an old man lying on his back in a snow drift in a remote highland glen gazing up at Orion and the Pleiades.

'And that inverted bowl we call the sky

Whereunder crawling cooped we live and die

Lift not your hands to it for help,

For it rolls impotently on as you and I.'

He obviously felt much better after that and struggled out of the comfortable armchair he had created in the soft snow. Regaining his feet he remarked that that was one of the most comfortable bits of armchair philosophy he had enjoyed in a long time.

And so we journeyed slowly on, leaving a gently winding trench in the snow behind us. Every hundred yards or so our tracks were punctuated by the imprints of two chaises longues where we had reclined comfortably in the soft powder and contemplated the inverted bowl whereunder crawling cooped, we live and die. At every stop, Carlos had come out with another philosophic gem from his old pal Omar, either in the Persian original or Fitzzgerald's translation. I learned that a thousand years ago, this man was not only a poet, but an astronomer of practical ability and mathematical competence. He had calculated the length of the solar year correct to six decimal places, and had demonstrated convincingly that it was the earth that rotated and not the stars. Naturally, he got into trouble with theologians who knew from their books that this was not the case. He had the good sense to keep a low profile. Less controversially, he wrote a treatise on algebra and conceived a general theory of cubic equations. This was safe territory, as it did not threaten the theologians.

After a happy couple of hours, we arrived at the hut about an hour past moonrise. We left a silver world of hard monochrome beauty to enter the bubble of gold on the other side of the hut door. In the warmth of the refuge, we relaxed in our shirtsleeves before a cheerful fire, enjoying a dram of summer sun distilled years ago on the fair Isle of Islay.

Carlos that night, in honour of Omar, made something he called Suleiman's Pilaf, a rice-based dish of many ingredients. The hut filled with the rich aromas of spices from distant subtropical lands, redolent of warmth and lush vegetation while the cold moonlit world outside the hut, in all probability, went on being austerely beautiful even if no one was looking at it. We went out from time to time to check that this was so.

And of course, to the memory of Old Khayyam, polymath and poet, we dedicated a glass of wine, red wine, 'that subtle alchemist that in a trice life's leaden metal into gold transmutes'. Carlos, mindful of the last quatrain, turned down an empty glass as a gesture of fellowship with the absent Omar:

The Big Eye of Summer

"And when thyself with shining foot shall pass

Among the guests tar-scattered on the grass'

And in thy joyous errand reach the spot

Where I made one – turn down an empty glass!"

It all goes to show that in order to have someone proposing your health and enjoying your company a thousand years after your death, you have to write some poetry that resonates in the civilized mind.

I.H.M. Smart

Rounding Cape Horn

I know from conversations that many people use their mountaineering experiences to relieve the excruciating boredom of long committee meetings, particularly those in which they are powerless participants. Cases of brain damage from unprotected exposure to such meetings are common. In this context, the recycling of mountaineering experiences is a useful technique with many successes to its credit. I know someone who claims to be the first person to have mentally climbed all the Munros during a single committee meeting (Munrosis psychorepetans or, I suppose, in some cases, Munrosis waltermittiensis). According to him, he survived unharmed while everyone else suffered severe psychological collapse. These notes describe a fairly pedestrian, run of the mill application of the technique. I remember it because off its ending, which showed me I was not alone. I am sure others have more exciting accounts that could be added to the literature on this commonly used but little written-about form of committee survivormanship.

'I was almost at the top of 'Integrity', a climb just within my ability. I seemed to be climbing solo and yet enjoying it immensely, moving skilfully on the sun-warmed rock, relishing the exposure. I stopped for a breather before finishing the last few moves, sensing the vast emptiness of Coire Lagan behind. I looked between my feet down the cleavage of the east face to see the Cioch with some aspirant climbing on to it. I topped out from the crack with a few more confident moves, walked over to the skyline and beheld Rum and Canna, and let my eye roam over the silvery sea cats-pawed with little breaths of wind to the low profile of the long island. Just then, a voice sounded somewhere to my left. It was saying, 'And what conclusion has your sub-committee come to on this matter, Dr Smart?' I had been waiting for it and knew what to do. I mentally abseiled down from Sron na Ciche . . . .

. . . . *into a committee room in the University in the middle of a meeting planning yet another curriculum reform. As I was re-entering my body I heard my preprogrammed voice saying*

'Our sub-committee agrees with the conclusions of the main committee on this matter and has nothing to add.' I sensed all round me the general approval of the good sense of our sub-committee. Originally, we had been enthusiastic and creative, but this only caused trouble. We were now more mature, and had given up wasting the time of our betters by having a mind of our own. The next item I would be required to agree with was much further down the agenda, so I was free for at least another half hour. To endure the intervening tedium while remaining fully conscious of the present would be dangerous. Preservation of sanity required another journey into the astral plane. So, setting part of my mind listening on the emergency channel I teleported the rest of it back to the Cuillins . . . .

. . . . This time I found myself walking up to the Coire Tairnealar on a hot summer's day. I stopped for a dive into each be-water-falled rock pool as it passed by, enjoying the tingle of cool, clear water against skin and seeing the sun-dappled surface from underneath as I rose up from the pebbled bottom where the shadows played in jumbled colours, then the pleasure of drying off luxuriously on a warm rock slab while watching the breeze ruffling the feathers of the little poplar trees. Eventually, I reached the inner Coire and started up the vast intimidating boiler plates of Mallory's climb. This time I wasn't in such good form as on Sron na Ciche; the old familiar fear radiated from the pit of the stomach. I definitely needed a companion. Tom Weir appeared from somewhere. We had an exhilarating time, particularly when a warm wind got up and tried to pluck us off the slabs. We then went up Bidein Druim nan Ramh, my favourite peak, and had lunch on its platform summit. It was a clear day, and the view was great. 'A real magic moment', I heard Tom saying as clearly as if he had really been there. . . . .

. . . . .By way of contrast I then changed channels to the top of Sgurr na Lapaich on a winter's day of some sunlight and a lot of moving shadow. The glen bottoms were filled with glooms of navy blue and black; lonely patches of sunshine wandered around the upper snows sometimes keeping up with the gaps in the clouds and sometimes getting lost and dying. It was a day of high drama - I was so grateful to be there. Five other people were also present: two Snaddens, a couple of Slessers and our national hero, William Wallace - all good company on the hill. When I arrived, they were about to ski back down again towards Glen Strathfarrar. A brilliant rainbow now appeared spanning the glen in front of us. The others took off. They spread over the slopes of the curving corrie, turning gracefully like autumn leaves floating down in the wind until coming together again as black dots a few hundred feet below, under the enchanted arch of many colours. I enjoyed the loneliness for a moment, savouring the ambience. Before following on, I sharpened up the focus of the landscape to reveal more detail, adjusted the contrast between light and shade to add to the drama, and modulated the colours of the rainbow to the maximum glory consistent with retaining the aesthetic balance of the whole. On occasions like this, you might as well take advantage of all the facilities available. I could hardly believe my good fortune to be skiing down after the others amid so much space and colour. It was good Spring snow, the turning was easy, I could hear the skis biting in at each turn. The rainbow and the autumn leaf effect of the skiers must have cross-referenced in my mind for suddenly I found myself . . . .

. . . . miles to the Westward on the shoulder of Beinn Dearg Mor, looking north across Strath na Seallag on a luminously gloomy day with little wind. It was indeed autumn, because the birch trees were yellow in the bottom of the glen. A half rainbow with its open side directed to the west arched over the head of the Loch, brilliant against the blue-black raincloud with trailing silver showers veiling the brooding bulk of An Teallach. Just then, a skein of about a dozen geese (barnacles I think) flew honking down the glen. They entered from the darkness on the right into the brightness within the arc of the rainbow and as they caught the sunlight, the voice again obtruded . . . .

. . . . *and I was back in the Committee room. My voice was saying, 'Yes my committee would gladly consider the changes that had just been proposed and I would bring back their agreement at the next meeting.' I would of course have to find out from someone what the required changes were. My answer phone had failed to record the details. I spent the next ten minutes hanging around in the meeting. Those who had power were manoeuvring around trying to use it, most of them (to be just) with the best intentions. Once I was sure there was no way I could usefully contribute I left and found* . . . .

. . . . myself at Loch Scavaig enjoying an evening beer in the cockpit of the yacht 'Goodbye Girl' which was riding at anchor there on a calm summer's evening. My friend Phil was on the foredeck playing 'Farewell to the Creeks' on his pipes, and the vale profound was overflowing with the sound. We were pleasantly tired after traversing Sgurr Dhu na Da Bheinn and, as we sipped our beer, felt some detached sorrow for the campers on the nearby shore being driven crazy by the midges. . . . .

. . . . The scene then changed of its own accord to another time and place. I found myself on Ladhar Bheinn on a sunset evening. It must have been a clip from the time in the late forties when I dossed there on a fine night of high summer with Hamish Nicol. He was a student friend who, after graduation, vanished somewhere down south and nevermore was heard of again in the land of the living, a pity because I seem to remember he was an amusing character. . . . .

. . . . I then fast forwarded memory forty years on to another time on Ladhar Bheinn on an equally fine evening. We had ascended directly from Loch Hourn and could see our yacht anchored below our feet in the shadows of the coming night. . . . .

. . . . Then I hopped a few miles south into the rough bounds of Knoydart and wandered about on Sron na Criche for a while, watching the glens fill with midnight blue before descending . . . .

. . . . to the meeting again in response to bad vibes arriving on the emergency channel. I seem to have missed the best part. There was a stushie of some kind going on. The plot, as far as I could gather, was that some of the people who had power had ganged up against one of their own number and had stabbed him fair and square in the back. Blood was everywhere. The stabbed one was not rendered silent until he had delivered a plangent terminal aria and some accusatory recititivo. Ham acting is an under-rated branch of the thespian art which, nevertheless, has its learned aficionados who remember great performances; when it is good it can be very, very good. The silence was pregnant with enthusiastic one-handed, zen-type hand clapping. It had really been quite a creditable performance. Things were going to be quiet for a bit as the body was dragged off and each side regrouped, so I hopped into the teleporter and beamed up again to the astral plane . . . .

. . . . This time I landed up on the top of Blaven and took control of events. I started with a clear fresh dawn with one star still awake and made the sun come up over the mainland until the world was filled with light. As the morning wore on, the shadows shortened until the glare of noon flattened the landscape, the profiles of the world becoming blurred in heat-haze. As the torpid afternoon progressed, shadows gradually returned and the trembling land regained relief. The mellow evening progressed. A full moon rose exactly opposite a setting full sun, which is, of course, how it should be in real life at high latitudes at the summer solstice. The panorama of sea and mountain changed to silver and shadow; the stars came up and a mild summer's night gradually entered into another dawn. . . . .

. . . . a quick nip back to the committee - all seemed well - so I returned to the astral plane . . . .

. . . . I speeded up the moon so it kept up with the earth and was always in the full position. This must have done something terrible to the tides but I couldn't work out what even on paper. Easter and other lunar dependant events would have had problems too. Then, transporting the scene to the equator. I brought the sun straight up from the horizon, overhead at noon and straight down again so that night fell with a bang somewhere behind Benbecula. It made a noise a bit like the one o'clock gun in Edinburgh. The southern constellations then blazed in a black velvet sky. Skye itself had already shrivelled under the noonday heat into something resembling the Sinai peninsula. I don't know what the good people of Skye were thinking while this was going on, but no doubt it has all been recorded in the West Highland Free Press. Certainly it must have thrown astrologers into confusion. Being fairly confused myself by now . . . . . .

. . . . . I returned briefly to the meeting, where the top predators were repressing an attempt to come back from the dead by the disaffected victim, who seemed unable to accept the brilliant success of the original ambush. He thought he had been misunderstood. They were trying to get through to him that he had been understood (that was the major part of his problem) and that he should shut up and settle the matter later in private with his fellow carnivores rather than embarrass his peers by carrying on in such an unsophisticated manner in front of the herbivores forming the rest of the committee. We herbivores sat there with eyes averted placidly munching away at the low-calorie intellectual diet that was our lot. For a little respite from life at the bottom of the pyramid I . . . .

. . . . teleported to Greenland, to a fine day on a granite ridge on a peak at the head of the Roslin Glacier in the awe-inspiring Stauning Alps. It was one of those overwhelming Greenland days of windless silence. Frost and granite crystals were a-twinkle in the morning sun, and the clear air brought the structural features of distant peaks into sharp focus. I was just beginning to enjoy the fabulous panorama. In fact, Malcolm and I had started to inspect a knot of spectacular rock spires to the north. We were discussing possible routes when I had to leave Malcolm there alone as I sensed the meeting was about to end. (He must have got back alright because I saw him again recently.) . . . .

. . . . *The Chairman was saying, 'Before we adjourn could I ask Dr Eccles if he has done anything about the accommodation required for the new course we have been discussing ?' There was dead silence. The Dr Eccles referred to, a herbivorous nonentity like myself, was sitting next to me and his eyes were fixed on the horizon. He vouchsafed no answer. The chairman repeated the question. It was obvious to all that Dr Eccles was not with us, so I gave him a gentle prod. He jumped a foot and started to talk incoherently; he was obviously under considerable stress. I knew he was a fellow space traveller and recognised that he was having a malfunction of his teleporter. I threw him a lifeline , 'Say , "The matter is receiving urgent consideration"', I hissed at him. 'The matter is receiving urgent consideration', he dutifully intoned. 'Do you think it will be satisfactory?' Prolonged silence. Charles was still somewhere else. I think his teleporter had got fankled up in the coordinates of space-time. (Easily done, I have often had that trouble myself). I could hear him broadcasting an SOS on the psychological equivalent of the international distress frequency, namely 121.5 kilopsychles. 'Say "Yes"', I broadcast. ' Yes, Mr Chairman' announced Charles, 'It should be all right.' The emergency was over. He had returned and was coherent again.*

After the Meeting he said, 'Thanks for your help. You got me out of a tight corner. I really was in great danger. I had been sailing alone around the world. I was off Cape Horn; I could see it through the rain less than a mile away. The boat was being driven before a wind of gale-force, maybe more, gusting, I'd say, to Force 12 at times; even the storm jib had been carried away and I was running under bare poles trying to keep her from broaching. I had one hand on the helm and was struggling to get some warps out of the rope locker to trail behind to slow her up. That was when you poked me in the ribs; I thought the tiller had broken off. No wonder I jumped; I thought I'd had it.'

I.H.M. Smart

Weathering the Storm

What's in a Name

On this stormy day in the Black Cuillin, the wind reverberated in the great dark corries and beat its fists against the steep walls of gabbro. The head of Loch Coruisg is a forbidding place in such weather. The tent leaked. We were bored. We had to do something. We set out for one of the buttresses on Bidein Druim nan Ramh which loured above. We did in fact do a wind-plucked climb there somewhere, a few not very good pitches. I don't think I could ever find them again. But 'Bidein Druim nan Ramh' - now there is a name to make you pause a while in wonder. It must surely offer some interesting route finding.

The first pitch of the name is 'Bidein'. This pitch is easy to surmount but presents one problem. In Gaelic 'bidein' means a peak or point and is singular. According to my Gaelic dictionary the plural is bidean. The summit in fact has three parts close together but with a substantial drop between them. So, it should be Bidean Druim nan Ramh. But then, from a distance and from most angles the three tops look like one, so Bidein is alright after all, unless you are a pedant, and there are plenty of them around. Route finding for the first time through this trifurcated mass of steep rock is quite difficult. The main top is a flat platform big enough for several people to recline on; it is one of the best eyries for viewing the interior of the range. I remember having a long lunch hour there on a hot summer's day and thinking . . . . I can't remember what about but the thoughts can only have been pleasant. However, we digress.

The next pitch is Druim, which in Gaelic is a masculine noun signifying 'back' or 'spine' as in:

'Ach tha slat airson druim an ti a tha as eugmhais tuigse'

'A rod is for the back of him that is void of understanding'

(Proverbs Chapter 10, verse 13).

Now this will cause problems with modern educationists. But I can think of cases and circumstances where people void of understanding would have been the better for a rod across their backs. The authors of the Book of Proverbs were hard men who laid down stringent rules of behaviour. They were more concerned with human responsibilities than human rights. They would not have made good speech-writers for any politician who wished to be elected.

A druim can also be viewed from underneath and be used to signify 'roof'' as in:

'Gu druim Sheallamha shin mi mo lamh,
Tha'n fhardach gun druim ach adhar.'

which translates literally as:

'To the roof of Sealma I stretched my hand;
' The abode is without a roof but sky.'

which is from the 44th poem in the Reverend John Smith's collection of Sean Dàna, or Ancient Lays which, according to Professor Derick Thomson, show a great familiarity with Ossianic 'matter', but whose style belies the claim that these are genuine traditional poems.

Druim, according to the Highland Society Dictionary, is probably also cognate with 'drum' in Chaldean, which signifies 'high'.

That pitch we have just done I would grade as an onomastic 'mild severe'.

The third pitch also has a severe move at the beginning, and then eases off a bit.

'nan Ramh' expresses the genitive plural of 'Ramh' which means 'oar' as in:

> *'De dharagaibh Bhasain rinn iad do ramhan' –*
>
> *'Of the oaks of Bashan have they made thine oars'*
>
> (Ezekiel, Chapter 27, verse, 6.).

In Chapter 27 Ezekiel gives a rambling account of constructing an extraordinary opulent merchant vessel. Oaken oars from Bashan were only a minor item. The sails were fine linen with broidered work from Egypt died with blue and purple from the isles of Elishah, and so on. The vessel came to a dreadful end. 'thou shalt be broken by the seas, in the depths of the waters thy merchandise and all thy company in the midst of thee shall fall (verse, 34.). It was an allegory of the city of Tyre, which achieved a market economy as ruthless and indulgent as our own. The Lord took a dim view of it all. We have it on the authority of Ezekiel that the Lord pointed out to Tyre that it would all end in tears: These were His very words (verse, 31). 'they shall weep for thee with bitterness of heart and bitter wailing'

Ramh is cognate with the Latin 'remus' as in:

> 'Quinquereme of Nineveh from distant Ophir.
> Rowing home to haven in sunny Palestine'

In the Cuillinic use of the term, the 'oars' are the buttresses, which descend in pairs on each side of the druim, which is a broad ridge running south-eastwards from the summit, to which it gives its name. After threading our way through these difficult pitches, we descended along the ridge delicately, pussyfooting gingerly like cats on a cold, stone roof as we followed the mighty druim not to distant Ophir, nor to Nineveh, nor sunny Palestine, but to the dark, windswept waters of black Loch Coruisg in the shadow of the black Cuillin.

Weathering the Storm

Loch Scavaig is a place where Rugged Grandeur is spelled out in Capital Letters. At its head is a little harbour contained within two great paws of gabbro thrust out from the base of the Cuillin. It is an impressive, steep-sided place; it looks sheltered, but in a storm it is like anchoring in a washing machine. We entered the harbour on a fine evening in mid-September. Fine weather at any time of year is a bad sign, but particularly bad at the equinox. We dined that night on moules marinières, fresh from the local rocks. The background music was provided by a rising breeze playing on the harp strings of the rigging. During the night, the storm got going in earnest. The wind twirled the rain-lashed boat round and round its anchor rope like the galley, galley ship in the song. At one stage, a particularly violent squall blew her over on her side, but the boat was well-designed and righted herself. The rest of the crew had such confidence they hardly noticed. Those on the lee side were rolled in their bunks; those on the windward fell out and climbed back in again muttering complaints.

In the morning, we bore the slings and arrows of outrageous weather as best we could. I was impressed by the state of the anchor cable, a pleated rope affair, stretched to such tightness that it twanged at middle C. Some tents that had been pitched on the shore the evening before were now no longer there. A poignant story must have unfolded there during the dark hours. The equinox obviously had the weather by the throat and wasn't going to let go no matter how much it struggled. So we went ashore or, rather, we allowed ourselves to be blown ashore in the dinghy. John and I went to explore the watery glooms and manifold dooms of the unfrequented southeast side of the Cuillins between the main ridge and the black broth of water boiling in Loch Coruisg. This is a rough terrain of hanging corries cradling dark lochans. The corries are separated by stepped buttresses and steep boilerplates of abrasive gabbro. It is jumbled country, which is why it offers so few sustained climbing routes. We spent the day exploring its interesting crags and terraces and secret places. Ezekiel would probably have found it commendably apocalyptic. We gradually adjusted to this environment of rain, buffeting wind and waterfalls blown uphill and accepted it as normal, even revelled in it. This was stern and wild country, a land of the mountain and the flood, strong meat only to be relished by the strong and the sane. Pastoral colours, calm seas and balmy winds are for emotional vegetarians and intellectual pansies - for the 'pallid pimps of the deadline and the enervates of the pen', as Robert Service described them so well.

An Old Dispensation

A long time ago, when the world was a lot less affluent than it is now, we could never have aspired to a yacht of our own, even on charter. And so we made journeys in the Western Isles in a heavy wooden dinghy driven by a 'British Seagull' outboard. One day, the engine failed and we had to row a few miles to the shore. After the first irritation had passed, we adjusted to the slow tempo of the swinging oars and went back to an older passage of time. The raucous outboard became a still life on the transom, a magic symbol of movement without effort. The rhythm of the waves and the creak of oars now measured the passage of the hours; we even sang to the slow rhythm of the strokes. It was a fine summer's day. The sea twinkled in the sunlight, and a light breeze wafted us towards an island a few miles away. In the late afternoon we came to a little bay of jade sea ruffling gently along a white sandy beach. We pulled up the boat and made camp on a patch of greensward patterned with daisies and silverweed. A little brown burn emerged from an acre of meadowsweet, scenting the air with the incense of summer. The place was in a 'mood' of some sort. I had the impression that it had been through this many times before. We were re-enacting a scene that has been repeated often enough through the ages. We were in direct apostolic succession to our predecessors in the Stone Age - a small band of men rowing in to an island to camp by the shore. We, in our turn, lit a fire and cooked our meal and relaxed in the amber light of the evening. A passing shower had freshened the air about an hour before, and raised the smell of earth and flowers. It was completely still. The cries of distant sea birds came clearly across a flat sea.

I went for a walk over the island towards the village marked on our map. I found a path and followed it through the stillness. Coming round a corner near the village, I suddenly came on a statue of a young Madonna and Child. It stood in a recess painted white with the Madonna's robe in blue. I know I went pale, and the hair on the back of my neck stood up. It wasn't just because I am a cradle protestant. I think it was partly the surprise and partly that it short-circuited Christianity. It was the powerful re-appearance of the primal Mother Goddess, the gentler Deity who pre-dated the hard patriarchal God conjured up by pastoralists in the intimidating deserts of the Middle East, the God Abraham saw when he looked in his mirror.

A small bunch of flowers and a few coins were there as offerings. Also a slip of paper kept down by a pebble. On it was written:

> *'O holy Mary, Mother mild*
> *Thou Mother of the Jesus Child*
> *For me a wretched sinner plead*
> *Both now and in death's hour of need'*

This was a disturbing experience for a hard-bitten, rational agnostic brought up as a protestant, under the baleful shadow of the psychopathic Calvin. Nevertheless, I left some buttercups of my own. There was a remote possibility that it might be remembered.

By the time I got back to the camp the light had faded. I could see the campfire from afar, a candle in the dark. When I got there the others had fixed the outboard and its raucous voice announced the return of the god of engines. It destroyed the cathedral skies of a magic summer night. These noisy, patriarchal Gods are difficult to handle and can be unreliable unless continually serviced.

I.H.M. Smart

One Autumn Day

Quite unexpectedly, I ran into my old friend Quintus Horatius Flaccus. It was one of these sunny mornings you get at the back-end, when the air is clear, and sharp and the floors of the glens are dusted with the gold leaf on autumnal birch trees, and everything else is silver with frost. I had just crossed the River Etive by the stepping stones and was passing in front of Jacksonville on my way to the Buachaille when he emerged from that fabled howff. He left with a cheery, 'Valete, sodales'[1] to those inside. He was followed by equally civil wishes from the inmates. I could make out:

''I in pace, O Horatio'[2]

'Bene ambula et redambula'[3]

'Deos obsecro, ut te nobis conservent et valere nunc et semper patiuntur.'[4]

'Πολύς ταραγμος εν τη τοις θειοις ενι

Κ'αν τοις βροτειοις.'[5]

Then, from someone improvising Julius Caesar's celebrated introductory line,

---

[1] ' Farewell comrades'

[2] 'Go in Peace'

[3] 'Fare well and haste ye back'

[4] 'I implore the Gods to preserve you for us and to keep you in health now and always.'

[5] ' There is as much confusion in the world of Gods as there is in ours.' This quotation from Euripides was not a bad effort at nine o'clock in the morning from a man with a hang-over.

'Heh, Horace - 'In Scotia hiemes longae sunt!''[1]

The voices carried quite clearly in the still air. It was all a great credit to the old system of schooling in Scotland.

'I didn't know you were a member of the Creag Dhu', I said as we saluted each other.

'I've just been made an Honorary Member for my poem on Soracte and some of my more earthy songs which were judged true to reality.'

He spoke English with a pleasant Scots accent. He did indeed have a slight Glasgow intonation, which was not surprising considering the company he had been keeping.

'They are a good lot', he said, nodding towards Jacksonville, 'Remind me of the Thracians in my time. We had a party last night. I introduced them to the delights of undiluted Caecuban wine, and we sang songs together in the pentatonic scale. Got a bit racy by the end, but we Romans can handle that. The Caecuban wine seems to have got the better of them; they're a bit hung over this morning.'

Quintus Horatius Flaccus, let me remind you, is/was a sturdy man of middle height with a young face and prematurely silvering hair. He was dressed in a sort of hippy kilt, acceptable enough by today's standards.

---

[1] 'In Scotland the winters are long.' The first line of 'Caesar in Britain and Belgium' begins: 'In Gallia hiemes longae sunt'. This used to be the standard book that every school child had to translate in days of yore when Latin was considered a normal part of the curriculum for a civilised European. Many students never seemed to get much beyond this initial sentence. The speaker was well aware of this. The line was, of course, delivered on this occasion in appropriately flat-toned, dead-pan Glaswegian.

'So how are things up there in the Elysian Fields?' I enquired companionably. I always feel relaxed in his company.

'I am not going to waste a day like this going into the metaphysics of Paradise with someone who isn't dead yet, and therefore has not the conceptual vocabulary to talk about it. Let's just enjoy the here and now. I can tell you, however, that although Elysium is a very fine place, it's not as good as Scotland on a day like this.'

I have always suspected this. It was nice to have my intuition confirmed by someone who really knew for sure.

We climbed to the foot of the Curved Ridge talking about the qualities of different landscapes. I was fascinated by his descriptions of Athens and some amusing stories about Catullus.

At the bottom of Rannoch Wall, he said he would really like to do Agag's Groove and the Crowberry Ridge.

'They all say they are classics.'

'They?' I queried.

'Yes, Bill, Hamish, Alec, Tom, George all the members of your Club I meet up there in Elysium.'

I was understandably silent for a while, sorting this one out. I could see him watching me from the corner of his eye. We reached the foot of Agag's.

'I'll lead,' he said gently, 'If I fall off it won't matter since I'm dead already'.

This seemed logical in a surreal sort of way.

He made a good job of it, moving lightly from hold to hold, belaying skilfully. Whoever had taught him the basics had done it well. I did suspect him of cheating once or twice, or at least relying on special attributes, for he appeared to levitate up the crux.

'I shouldn't like to have done this when I was alive', he said, 'It would have been more terrifying than at Phillipi.[1] It's surprising how bold and reckless the living can be.'

We crossed over and came down the Curved Ridge. Then we did the Crowberry Ridge in similar style, stopping frequently to admire the view. On the crux, he even paused for a few minutes, holding on with one finger and the toe of his sandal while he turned to explain about the siege techniques of his day. They often used pitons and chocks as aids to get up citadel walls, he informed me. When I expressed surprise, he said pitons were not new even in his day. Alexander the Great had used them. He had heard of spikes being used in Homeric times, probably made of bronze then. Wooden wedges were used, too. A wooden wedge was a trivial thing to make compared to a wooden horse. He recommended to me a smith named Hephaestos, the head of an old-established firm that had a name for making good state-of-the-art pitons.

On the summit, we tarried, admiring the view over the vastness of Rannoch Moor.

'They were right', he said, 'Your range of blues are better than anything we ever had in Italy or Greece; even the Elysian Fields couldn't do better than this.'

We walked back over the moor, and reached the King's House as dusk was falling. Maybe half a dozen people were sitting around in the lounge. The barman was someone I had never seen before - a genial soul with a beard who wore a colourful robe of superior

---

[1] Horace, you remember, was on the losing side at the battle of Philipi. Although a senior officer, he prudently fled when things got too dangerous, and threw away his shield. Donachaidh Ban MacIntyre also threw away his sword when retreating early from the field of Falkirk. Had they not done so and been killed, the world would be a poorer place.

make with a geometric design in gold round the hem. He looked like a well-to-do hippie left over from the swinging sixties. Surprisingly, he seemed to know Horace; they greeted each other warmly and chatted away in a strange tongue I eventually recognised as Classical Greek. Some really charming loose-girdled barmaids polished glasses in the background. Things had certainly changed here since my last visit. I assumed the old Kingie had been taken over by some Hellenic entrepreneur, probably the inevitable Rio Stakis.

Horace seemed to confirm my guess when he introduced me to what I thought he said was his 'Old friend Rio'.

'Pleased to meet you, Rio', I said

'No, no, my name is Dio - not Rio. Dio - short for Dionysus.'

I did a double-take. They both laughed.

Dio spoke English with a pleasant Hebridean accent. When I remarked on it, he said it was because he came from the Greek equivalent of the Hebrides.

'I come from the fair isle of Chios. It is a sort of Aegean version of Islay, except we produce good wine there instead of good whisky. Try some of this. It is the Chian equivalent of Lagavuillin.'

The girls brought us each a silver tassie half-filled with the sea-dark wine. Horace paid with a gold coin he produced from a leather purse. Without pausing in his conversation Dio picked it up, flicked it in the air, caught it, then tossed it towards the till some feet away. The drawer opened to receive it and then closed. Quite a trick. Horace gave him a look. 'Don't overdo it', he muttered.

Horace started topping up the glasses with water.

I tried to stop him. 'Hey, what are you doing?'

'Oh sorry I forgot. Here you drink wine undiluted. I don't advise it. That's why the Dhu were so hung over this morning. Still this is the famed Chian wine. We'll have the next glass undiluted.'

Horace and Dio chatted away amiably about arcane matters I couldn't quite follow. Then I got them on to talking about the mysteries of such well-known mountains as Olympus, Helicon and Parnassus. They told me a lot, but first made it quite clear that it was privileged information and was only to be passed on to people responsible enough to receive it. I tried to make some mileage by proposing that the clashing rocks encountered by both Odysseus and the Argonauts were icebergs.[1] I mentioned that I had some experience of sailing among such things myself. They could easily be interpreted as icy mountains not fixed to the seabed. Phoenician sailors who had been beyond the Pillars of Hercules, I continued, must have picked up the story from the locals and taken it back to the Mediterranean where they became floating rocks, as no one knew about floating ice. There was a silence. It was broken by Dio shaking his head sadly and saying, 'Odysseus was an awful liar and Jason was not much better.' By implication I was included among that august company. I felt flattered, even if classified negatively as a teller of tall tales. This was the first time I had ever been

[1] It is not impossible that Odysseus reached the Hebrides and even further north into iceberg country during his ten years of haphazard navigation, and even if he didn't, he wasn't above taking a good story as his own and embroidering it to make it even better. A deplorable habit that persists to this very day. The classical accounts of the narrow, turbulent, rock-infested straights of Charybdis, for example, correspond exactly to the description in the Clyde Cruising Club Pilot of the tide race through the Bealach a'choin glaish – the narrows of the grey dog between Lunga and Scarba. Scylla who lived in a cave above the tide race was, of course, a dog-headed monster or at least wore 'a girdle of dogs heads about her loins'...

bracketed with larger than life heroes unless, of course, you include my associations with members of our Club, notably with such people as Slesser, Peden and Hay.

I started to order another round but Hora (I was now using the familiar diminutive form of address)[1] said, 'Tonight is on me. I owe you such a debt of gratitude.'

'You owe me a debt of gratitude. Come on. How? Why? It's the other way round surely.'

'I'll maybe explain later', he said, then turned to the others in the lounge and invited everyone to come over and join him in a glass of Chian wine.

I may say that the conversation in the rest of the room had stopped long ago; the others were watching us from their tables with wide eyes and dropped jaws as they registered wonder, even frank dismay. This was understandable. The crowd I was with were arrestingly picturesque.

And so we all ended up leaning on the bar - us patrons on one side and Dio and his strangely sophisticated barmaids on the other. The wine loosened tongues and the party got a glow on. The barmaids radiated charm. Our personalities and conversational ability

---

[1] There is no reference in classical literature to Hora being used as a diminutive for Horatius. I think I heard Dio using it and followed suit. It is declined like 'nauta', a sailor - one of the few masculine nouns of the first declension. The feminine noun 'hora' means an 'hour'. I tried to make a pun of this by coming out with the well-known motto still found on present-day sundials 'Horas non numero nisi serenas' - 'I do not count the hours/Horaces unless they are serene.' He looked pained and said, 'You're two thousand years too late with that one. Besides, if I were you, I wouldn't experiment with that word with these girls around; you could use it wrongly and offend them; that could be dangerous.'

expanded and the ambient world seemed brighter. I became involved in a conversation with one of the barmaids. It became fairly deep. She possessed disquieting intellectual and artistic insights. She was quite a lass.

Horace rather fancied one the girls on our mortal side of the bar. She acted a bit snooty but otherwise was a fair stunner. I was sure I had seen a picture of her on the front cover of one of the climbing glossies, looking lithe and sinuous in a grass green lycra leotard with swirls of yellow that accentuated her curves. Horace was fascinated. He started to chat her up. After a time, she seemed to become more compliant and I recognised his Ode III, xxvi coming out.[1] Fortunately he declaimed it all in Latin. I was very glad of the absence of Classics from the modern school curriculum, otherwise her boy friend, a hulking brute from somewhere up in the Grade VIIIs, might have taken offence. Even so, he started to close his fist as if he sensed something - particularly at the last couple of lines when Horace put his hands together in the praying position and looked towards the heavens. He really was enjoying himself - Horace that is - not the boyfriend.

All this was interrupted by the phone ringing. Dio answered.

'Yes, I'll tell him.' He turned to Horace,

---

[1] In this delightful ode Horace addresses the Goddess Venus asking her not to involve him and his old bones in yet another affair of the heart - except maybe . . . well, perhaps . . . maybe, just this one more last time. The poem ends something like this:

'Here is my last request,
Goddess ruler of the blest
whose sublime whip bends
proud girls' knees -
one last little flick for
snooty Chloe, please.'

'That's MacAenas on the phone. He'll pick you up outside right away.'

Horace's face fell. He turned to the crowd saying

'I must go now. Valete sodales', then to me, 'Come, see me off.'

We left to the farewells and expressions of regret from the others. At the door, I turned to wave goodbye to the mysterious barmaid.

'See you later', she said. She was a disturbing girl, probably had other sides to her character, probably good with the scissors.

'Much later, I hope,' I heard myself saying. She gave an entrancing smile as if to say, 'Don't worry, it may not be all that bad.'

Outside, some kind of vehicle was waiting. Harness clinked in the darkness. It was difficult to make out anything in the shadows.

Horace turned and said, 'Once again, can I say how grateful I am to you.'

'Oh come off it. How do you get that idea?'

'If it were not for you, I really would be dead. You and people like you are my monument more enduring than bronze.[1] If people like you didn't exist, neither would I. I would have to spend all my time in Elysium - which is okay but, all things considered, it is not as richly rewarding as being alive and in Scotland. You can't understand yet how good it is to have a day off with congenial living company. The poor souls in Elysium who aren't remembered

---

[1] He was referring here to his Ode III, xxx. The one that begins, 'I have made a monument more enduring than bronze . . .' It continues . . . 'because of my poems, . . . non omnis moriar. . . not all [of me] may die . . . .'

by you mortals, never get a day off. That's why I'm grateful to you, my friend.' He laid his hand on my shoulder and said.

'Before I go I would like to give you this blessing. "May Providence bestow on you good health, a sound mind, relish for life and an old age that still maintains a stylish grip on the lyric metres."[1] Or in your case, since you have no sense of rhythm and don't really understand what a lyric metre is, let's say, "A stylish grip on the handholds of life."'

He embraced me, mounted up beside the driver, and the vehicle, whatever it was, passed towards the bridge. A fairly large coin was tossed to a shadowy figure lurking in a gloomy booth.[2] The conveyance crossed the river. As it faded into the darkness, the sound of hooves and wheels merged with the noise of the river. I can assure you it was no spooky phantom carriage that bore him away, for it left distinct wheel marks in the gravel.

I hope I see him again. I would like to ask him more about the climbing gear Hephaestos used to make; it would be interesting to know if we have re-invented the wheel.

---

[1] He was paraphrasing here from his Ode I, xxxi:

[2] The Styx has evidently been bridged. The ferry has been discontinued and Charon degraded from skilled boatman to menial booth attendant. The tolls have, of course, been increased; the size of the tossed coin was much bigger than the original obolus of classical times. Evidently Pluto, originally a grim, unpitying deity, a severe punisher of wrong-doers (whose psychological function in the Classical World was to serve as a metaphor for incorruptible standards) has responded to the mood of our time, and in order to receive attention (the food of the Gods), has become market-orientated and acquisitive in order to mirror the vulgarity of his worshippers, but see Note 5 above.

Expedition to the Dark Island

My friend John Hay organised at very short notice a two-man boat journey into the inner recesses of Scoresby Sound (East Greenland about latitude 70 N) in the autumn of 1997 when the Arctic tundras were a-glow with browns, reds and yellows. Our destination was the Dark Island, which lies towards the western end of this mighty fjord system. We picked this distant isle as our destination partly because of its scenic position in the middle of a confluence of terminal fjords, but mostly because of the romantic connotations of its name. Neither of us had been there. It just looked good topographically. We knew not whether it was darkly sinister or darkly romantic. We had no specific plans, except to get there and reach its five hundred metre summit. The whole trip was romantic and none the worse for that. We seized an opportunity to make a bold journey, and the Goddess of Fortune favoured us. The Dark Island lay about 300 kms (a ba' hair off 200 miles) from the airstrip at Constable Point where we landed. The round trip with diversions for ice and accessing a fuel dump was roughly the same distance as circumnavigating Harris and Lewis from Oban - with Oban as the last inhabited place. No mean journey, even in the less windy seas of Scoresby Sound. I had been half way there in the seventies as a boy with Douglas Scott, Charles Eccles and his son Chris. We didn't get further than the Bear Islands that time, because during the air drop the parachute to which our outboard engine was attached didn't open properly. After that experience our antiquated, now slightly bent 'British Seagull' could only push us along at one knot. Like that, it took a long time to pass an iceberg. This time we had a good inflatable with a forty horsepower motor. We were lightly laden, and could get the boat up on the plane and travel at twenty knots. We were living in a more prosperous time. We even wore survival suits, which were impervious to the cold. A subjective account of the trip now follows. It is not to be read as a tale of derring-do but as a lovesong to life and the bittersweet danger of being alive.

Greenland, the grey

'Here is your anchor', said Sigi, handing John Hay and myself one of those folding galvanised iron contraptions. He shook my hand, looked me in the eye and said, 'Be careful'. This ceremony happened on the 25 Aug 1997 on the bleak airstrip at Constable Point. Greenland was at its most uninviting. It was overcast and grey and a bitter wind blew from the north. Two Swedes who had had the boat before us looked dour and chastened, 'It was a tough trip', they said as they climbed thankfully aboard the returning aircraft. We learned that the 1997 summer had been bad in East Greenland, with overcast skies and a lot of rain. The sullen ice had lain against the shore around the Scoresby Sound settlement all summer and had restricted movement even for small boats. The visitor accommodation at the airstrip was full, and the chief of the station said, 'You would be better to camp so that you can make sure that all your equipment is in working order.' He gave a knowing look and waved a hand towards a dismal windswept expanse of tundra. This is what I like about Greenland, you are expected to handle problems yourself. After a bleak supper, we went to look at the boat we had hired. A four metre zodiac lay on a deserted sandy beach about a mile away beside a grey sea with grey horses galloping southwards on the cold grey wind. Sand had blown inside the hull, gritting all the equipment. The propeller had a blade missing. We fitted a new one but clumsily lost the only split pin. Finding a replacement was an exercise in problem solving, but that is a story in itself. We walked back to our tent against a bone-chilling wind. I was depressed at the prospect of two dreich weeks stuck among dismal grey ice floes; John Hay never gets depressed.

Arctic Riviera

The next day Greenland smiled; the sun shone from a cloudless sky and the sea was calm. Then came the most difficult part of the expedition - getting the unloaded, but still heavy, boat down the soft sand into the water. After that, the rest was down-hill. We left at two in the afternoon and planed over the mirror-smooth, reflection-filled sea, slalomed through twenty miles of ice floes and, as soon as we could, made straight for the Bear islands, a direct forty-mile crossing of the inner Sound through a city of shining icebergs. A hundred miles from our starting point at the time of the midnight shadows, we entered the narrow cleft between the steep sides of the two most southerly of the Bear Islands. We suddenly lost the photomultiplying effect of the reflections from the open sea and entered the shadows. In this awesome spot we ran out of petrol. In the gloom and silence that suddenly surrounded us, we refilled our tanks from the reserve drums we carried in the hold.

A gift from the past

I had been to the north end of the archipelago a quarter of a century before, and was suffering from confused memories. The boat, however, seemed to know where to go and guided us to a dimly remembered beach ten miles away at the northern tip of the right hand island. We disembarked in the increasing light of the new day. I was fairly sure this was the place where we had left a food dump twenty-odd years ago when I was a boy. I walked to where it might still be and there it was, intact and undisturbed. This was just as well. John Hay had done an impeccable job in organising the expedition, except for the food. Out in the field, John does not eat very much unless he can actually shoot it. This time, he had forgotten to multiply the slender basic rations by two. The antecedent Swedes had left some dried meat in the boat, but even with that we would have been on scant rations. There didn't seem to be much to shoot either. The vintage bully beef, sardines, biscuits and chocolate from the old dump saved us from hardship. There was of course plenty of whisky; in this department John is more than competent.

The Bear Islands

The islands lie in the angle between the ramparts of Milne and Ren Land. There are about a dozen, each one different: some are rolling boiler plates of bed rock cradling picturesque lochans, others are sharp fins of vertical strata with serrated edges, some are round, others are long and thin, some are mere skerries; one runs a curious wiggly course for ten miles or so, a branching thread bearing different types of mountain. The rock varies from good to dreadful. Dougie Scott and I had climbed the highest fin (2100 feet, with some diff and v. diff. pitches) twenty years ago on a memorable day of silence and colour. The islands are separated by narrow channels opening into bays and secret places; architecturally interesting icebergs drift around the waterways grounding from time to time and then journeying on. Our arrival coincided with the first flush of autumn colour, when the leaves of the six-inch-high birch and willow were beginning to glow in the sunlight.

La dolce vita

We cruised the archipelago for some days on an aesthetic high, exploring each island and climbing to the top of the less precipitous summits. We had time to choose pleasing campsites with memorable views and to revel in extended lunch hours on honey-coloured promontories or ambience-prone isles. I remember with gratitude an afternoon of contemplation spent on an intricate islet of jumbled ice-worn rock patterned with multicoloured lichens and rich autumnal leaves. A further item of aesthetic excellence at this time was the waning yellow moon; as each bright day ended it would lean for a while against the dark blue northern mountains before sinking behind them, leaving us in the brief transparent darkness that at this time of year precedes a new sunrise.

Corridor of power

We eventually continued our journey westwards into the steep-sided Island Fjord leading to the distant Dark Island. This mighty cleft is 40 miles long and 4 miles across. The sides are formed by buttresses rising straight from the sea to icecaps 6000 ft high. The fjord is a major wind funnel channelling strong catabatic winds from the inland ice and dissipating their energy from its mouth. Biggish glaciers breaking through the ramparts on each side contribute their own catabatic cross-winds which generate periodic stretches of extra turbulence. At its west end, the fjord is split by a large eponymous central island with three thousand foot cliffs. Here, we reasoned, there must surely be converging orographic winds from each side making a spectacular turbulence where they met. It could be a nasty place.

The buttresses that face the fjord, by the way, are formed of igneous rock - excellent stuff - polished by ice and done in light shades of ochre and honey. There are also pinnacles and blades of rock separated from the main escarpment. There is some excellent climbing here, but few landing places and fewer harbours.

Alea jacta est

We approached on a smooth sea, but were turned back by the white horses galloping from the fjord mouth. We dithered for a day in a calm corner of a nearby island, watching for the moment the horses would return to stable, wondering how the dice (or the icebergs) would roll. The weather turned a bit gloomy. Then John got hold of the tiller and committed us to a counter-gallop against the enemy cavalry. He is not known as the 'Kami Kaze Kid of Loch Mullardoch' for nothing. We crept across the fjord, nipping from the lee of one iceberg to another. When he was sure it was too late to turn back, he slowed the engine and said, 'It should be a joint decision whether to go on or not.' We went on, even though the objective signs were that things would surely get worse.

Land of the great silence

Anyway, the theoretically violent catabatic cross winds did not amount to much. After entering the north branch of the fjord the wind gradually died and we emerged into an inland sea of flat calm, silence and golden evening light. Willow down floated on the smooth black water filled with the reflections of mountains and sky. The cliffs gave way to milder hills cradling broad valleys of richly autumnal muskox pastures. We entered Rype Fjord and camped on a platform carpeted with the russet and gold of dwarf birch and willow with a panoramic view towards a wide glacier descending from the inland ice. The next day, we climbed the mountain overlooking the entrance to Rype Fjord, taking our separate ways through the bronze and yellow of the autumn landscape, meeting muskoxen and, on one occasion, each other. We separated rapidly. The finer aesthetics of a place can only be fully appreciated when alone. That evening John returned with a white hare he had shot. I have a picture of him skinning it. A lawyer splitting a hare is in his element.

The dark island

On the morrow, we made for the Dark Island through two sets of icebergs: the real ones and their exact reflections in the still waters of the sea. The island was roughly round in shape and a couple of miles in diameter - small enough to be intimate and large enough to be mysterious and have many secret corners. We climbed its highest peak, about 1600 feet, through mats of chocolate green cassiope, yellow willow, darkly crimson blaeberry and dwarf birch. The colours of the latter ranged through yellow gold, orange, bronze and various shades of deepening red, a tour de force in this part of the electromagnetic spectrum. Let me try to describe the view from the rocky summit. To the east lay the ice-capped cliffs and glaciers of Milne Land, to the north the big island that had bisected our line of approach, to the south and west open water, and beyond that, the spacious russet valleys and broad glaciers descending from the inland ice itself. All of this rugged grandeur was reflected meticulously in the mirror of the sea. There were of course icebergs, the sea was filled with them. Then there was the silence.

The heart of lightness

The following day we spent exploring the island's sunny southern coastline, wandering slowly from one richly embroidered bay to the next, and finally crossing through the interior. Here on the summit of a pass, we encountered a lochan surrounded by autumnal cloth of gold. The reflections in its polished surface were sharp and exact. It was difficult to determine where the shoreline was, where the boundary between reality and reflection lay. The reflections of the mountains of Milne Land were in fact crisper, richer in colour and much more convincing than the reality they portrayed. I have photographs to back up this statement. I am sure there is some deep metaphysical point to be made here if I could only think of it.

Stretching a point

One morning, we loaded the boat and were ready to depart. At this point, we both wandered away in different directions vanishing into the ambient colour and silence. Subjectively at least, it is possible to stop time and expand the transient present into a long moment of detent when the mind can be undividedly part of everything. We knew that when this moment of departure ended we would be cast out of the garden; we would lose grace and return to the world of good and evil, that is, to the world of thermodynamics and the dreaded increase in entropy. In the end, we pushed off with decision and seamanly competence. We might be romantics but we were also cautious, practical men; otherwise we would not have got to where we were. It is not easy being a romantic; in my experience it has always involved a lot of hard work. Nevertheless, to prolong the moment of grace we stretched space-time a bit more by circumnavigating the island amid the clarity of its confusing reflections.

Leaving the island

In the end, in spite of our ability for time-stretching, we had to turn westwards through the icebergs of Snow Sound and back through the now glassy calms of the once turbulent Island Fjord. On the way, John found a tiny harbour on the north side from where a system of terraces, each richly loaded with autumn colour, led up the steep rock of a beetling buttress. From the top of this narrow zigzag on the frowning cliff, we scanned the vastness of the landscape and felt fearful and bold, intimidated and elated, in fact, the full chromatic scale of opposites in this part of the emotional spectrum; then we had a lunch of vintage sardines, obsolete brands of chocolate and biscuits a quarter of a century old, still scented with cinnamon.

Hubris and humility

By now we were getting used to being intimidated, and could apply more and more brain to the aesthetics of our situation while retaining enough parallel processing to anticipate any dangerous configurations that might start to form around us. It was, it must be said, imprudent for only two men and one boat to be wandering around in such unforgiving territory beyond the edge of world. Minor acts of carelessness, failures to foresee, failures to react quickly enough, particularly when you are tired, can result in a variety of terminal scenarios or, worse still, one in which you might have to face the humiliation of being rescued. Our main vulnerability was lack of physical strength. We had not the brute force and stamina to unload the boat each evening and pull it up on the shore a safe distance from the sea. If it had been washed up on the rocks by a wave dissipating the energy from a capsizing iceberg or a big berg undergoing catastrophic sundering, we would have had trouble man-handling it back in. The problems of a forced landing on a stormy lee shore or changing a failed motor in a rough sea did not bear thinking about. None of this happened, but you can't be lucky for ever. If you use up too many of your good statistics, only the dud ones are left and that makes you superstitiously prudent.

Evensong in the islands

We escaped from the confines of Island Fjord and reached one of our old camps on the Bear Islands. From here, we beheld two colourful sunsets: the real one and its immaculate reflection in the mirror of the sea, the one separated from the other by a jagged band of black land. We wandered around reverentially in the stained glass light of the roofless cathedral that surrounded us, aware that this was one of these moments of numinous tranquillity far removed from ordinary experience. There are doubtless boringly prosaic neurophysiological reasons for these states of mind but for all that, they are best regarded as rare gifts from whomever She is who actually runs the universe.

An islet in the storm

The next day, complex cloud layers covered the sky and striped the cliff faces. We crossed the ten miles of icebergs and open water to the South Cape on an immaculately calm overcast evening specialising in shades of translucent greys and blues from silver to black. We found a little island with traces of palaeoeskimo stoneworks to camp on. Here we were storm bound for a day or two by a fierce cold wind. During this period the sunlight returned, but it was as hard and cold as the wind.

Brief encounter

Then, proceeding eastwards in a change to sombre weather, we met a German sailing ship, looking for somewhere to get frozen in for the winter; the crew were surprised to see a small boat emerge in a gloomy evening from beyond the greyness marking the edge of the world. The yacht was a rebuilt Esbjerg cutter. They knew about the similar Ada Franzen (one of the boats on our Centennial Yacht Meet). The Dagmar Aaen and its picturesquely romantic young skipper had spent the last seven winters in the Arctic. They had been through the NW passage to the Bering Sea and the NE passage as far as Cape Chelyuskin - seven winters locked in ice. They were specialists in this particular genre. We were invited aboard for coffee and a chat about things Arctic in the yellow lamplight of the warm saloon.

Into the gloom and the gloaming

We proceeded eastwards into a grim evening and a rising headwind. In the end, we got stuck in the pack ice in the first real darkness - the equinox was only a couple of weeks away. We had difficulty getting back to land because of the extreme shallowness of the sea along the flat, featureless Jameson Land coast. The boat kept grounding in a foot of water while still hundreds of yards from shore. The pack ice and grounded bergs at least protected us from the onshore wind. Otherwise, we would have had to travel among the waves in deeper water four to five miles off this dangerous lee shore. Things might be better when the tide rose. We eventually found a landing and camped a couple of hundred yards inland on the first firm tundra beyond the shifting sands, sleeping intermittently, checking the boat every hour to make sure it did not get blown ashore or hit by a piece of moving ice.

A grey dawn breaking

Later, as we set off in the small hours of the morning, an immense land- and seascape, intimidating and austere, emerged from the darkness. On the rising tide, we escaped from the trap by dint of luck and resourcefulness and loosening floes by bashing the edges with the heavy anchor. (The Goddess may be implacable but she sometimes rewards you if you act intelligently and do not despair). Our escape, however, was mostly due to a change in the wind direction; it started to blow from the west. The forty miles of pack ice between us and journey's end began to loosen and move out to sea. We reached the settlement of Scoresby Sound after a final long day of surfing on the backs of the waves, following the loosening ice floes as we all galloped eastwards together in intermittent sunshine.

Alas everything comes to an end

That evening, after sixteen days of higher education in the wilderness, we were in a warm house dining off arctic char, smoked seal, mattuk, and fresh bread while watching the sun set in splendour from our dining room window. We also noted that the ice had returned, closing the route we had come. We had been lucky to arrive at the beginning of the only long good weather window of the entire summer. The journey had required no more of us than basic competence. We could easily have been more severely tested. When I showed my snapshots and told our story to my old friend of fifty years, Professor Slesser, doyen of Arctic travel, he observed with experienced accuracy, 'Never try to do that journey again.'

I.H.M. Smart

Ride of the Valkyries

One New Year's day, I found myself scudding south down the Sound of Mull in wild Wagnerian weather under gloomy clouds with a shaft of sunshine illuminating our white sail against the wine-dark sea. In real life there is no background music, except on rare occasions. This was one of the exceptions; the ride of the Valkyries was being played by a full orchestra discretely hidden somewhere off stage. I know in this location it should have been heroic Fingalian music, but the fact is it was Wagner. We zig-zagged south in the gathering storm without being chosen, and at dusk escaped from the white-horsed sea into Salen Bay for the night. We had a nebulous plan for climbing Dun Da Gaoithe, the 'Hill of the Two Winds' on the morrow. It was a spectacularly Wagnerian night: sheet lightning backlit the snow-capped mountains, and phosphorescence glowed along the heaving anchor chain. Down in the Valhalla of the cabin, the whisky glowed in the light of our swinging kerosene lantern, and we fell asleep rocked in the cradle of a shallow sea to the sough of the sea-dark wind in the rigging.

The next day, we left this exposed anchorage and sailed twenty miles south through squalls, battering rainstorms and riding Valkyries. In the gathering dusk we entered the Poll Dobhrein, a bomb-proof anchorage, overcrowded in summer, but now lonely and forlorn with the winter sea growling outside its gates. In due course we made our way through the trackless bogs to the pub. We were offered a lift to the local dance by two kindly Englishmen. It was a West Highland Dance in the old style. There were still enough locals around for it to be authentic. The dancing was vigorous. Nae cotillons brent new frae France but hornpipes, jigs, strathspeys and reels put life and mettle in our heels. We reeled, we set, we crossed, we cleekit till ilka carlin swat and reekit. Then changing gear someone would sing. I am sure I heard Fagail

Liosmor, Mo chailein donn, Cruachan Bheinn, Bratain bhana, Fagail do'n Aite and of course, Calein mo run-sa. It was so refreshing to escape from the heavy theatrics of broody Wagner. I danced with a girl who said she remembered me well, that my name was Spike Maxwell and when was I coming to see her again. I remember doing a schottische with a wee smasher who wore a luminous blue bangle on her ankle. All in all, aged, unshaven and wellie-booted though we were, we seemed to be doing well. We had, I suppose, a sense of mystery. We were off a yacht in a stormy January night. 'A likely story', said the luminous blue bangle. Anyway, the time passed and the dance ended at God-knows-what hour. I confided to the blue bangle that we were indeed the Flying Dutchman and his crew, and that this was the one night in seven years we were allowed ashore, hoping that some damsel would take pity on us and save us from our doom of sailing the seven seas forever. I got the impression that blue bangle and her friends would willingly oblige.

We got a lift back to the bridge with the two obliging, but culturally disorientated, Englishmen, crossed the hill path in the wind-tossed darkness back into Wagner country again. The Firth of Lorne shimmered in the light of the full moon, with silver horses galloping across undulating fields of heaving pewter. Clouds scudded across the sky and when they covered the moon the scene became dark and ominous, and the tone of the hidden orchestra as it played the Dutchman motif became more menacing. The next day we rose late and decided to postpone the ascent of Dun Da Gaoithe till another time. It was, in any case, a piece of hubris to approach a hill with a name like that in midwinter in a yacht.

Looking back on all this, I now realise that everyone has got the Flying Dutchman story the wrong way round. The Dutchman epitomises the gallus, carefree bachelor sailing the seven seas of adventure. The symbolic night ashore is the perennial risk of meeting a heroine and his doom is landing up with a wife, a family, a pram, dog, a mortgage and a suburban bungalow with a lawn needing to be cut, while his heroine turns into a matriarch. From time to time, the erstwhile hero sees the ship of adventure sail for some far horizon without him and is duly perturbed. As the years go by, his inner eye grows dim and eventually he sees such things no more. Such an ending, although biologically satisfactory, is without romantic interest. And so, for the purposes of making decent drama, it is necessary to introduce a role reversal by inferring (oh, irony of ironies) that freedom is the doom from which we must be rescued by some heroine with a luminous blue bangle round her ankle.

I.H.M. Smart

The Mantrap Conference

Three men on one rope slows the party down. However, if the climb is not hard enough to frighten you out of your wits, you can have interesting conversations, particularly when two are together on the same stance, waiting for the leader to make some progress.

And so it happened that I was left with the middleman, securely belayed in the sunshine on the capacious first platform while the leader footered around on the next pitch. The middleman was new to us; we had picked him up in the hut the night before. He seemed a scholarly soul, well-read, with a lot of arcane, slightly zany lore at his fingertips. For instance, not many people know that harp strings chopped small, when sprinkled on hot meat, wriggle like maggots. This knowledge was used in the more robust times of the late middle ages to hasten the departure of unwelcome guests. (I am going to try it out myself sometime when I get my hands on some harp strings.) During the course of the evening, he mentioned casually that he was completing a book on Eschatology. The announcement caused a pause in the conversation. No one knew what Eschatology was. I assumed it was some branch of statistics.

‘Is that related to stochastic analysis or regression theory?’ I asked tentatively.

‘Oh no,’ he replied, ‘Eschatology is the study of the 'final things' - death, judgment, heaven and hell.’

An appalled silence followed. Some of us looked at our boots, others at the ceiling.

‘Cheer up’, he continued seeing our discomfiture,’ It's not as bad as all that. Fascinating study, really. It's not just about sitting on clouds playing harps or shovelling coal into furnaces. The subject is much more subtle and intellectually satisfying than that.’

We shifted uneasily in our seats. Someone said, 'It's cold for the time of year. Anyone like a cup of coffee?' In the event, it turned into quite a fascinating evening as he took us on a quick tour of the various types of heaven and hell and judgement systems that were on offer. However, this is all by way of background, and has no direct bearing on the story I'm trying to tell you. Suffice it to say that we ended up asking him to join us on a climb the next day. The forecast was good, so we went to bed early and slept well in spite of all the hellfire and damnation that had been flying around after supper.

We got off by first light and reached the foot of Raeburn's Arete while rosie-fingered dawn's left hand was just appearing in the north-eastern sky. We climbed in silence, appreciating the haunting ambience as the new day stretched out its arms in benediction over us. Our new and untried friend turned out to be competent and nimble. He carried a well-used rack of gear commensurate with greater climbs than mere v. diffs. So we all climbed relaxed and were able to respond completely to the glory of the surrounding morning. At the first platform below the Northeast Buttress (where this story properly starts), we stopped for breakfast. While we were tearing into our rolls and cold sausage, our new friend remarked apropos of nothing,

'It all makes sense once you know about Part 1.'

'Come again? Part 1 of what?'

'Hamlet, of course'

'I didn't know there was a Part 1.'

'I know you don't. I've never bothered to tell anyone about Part 1 until now.' He made this portentous announcement while airily waving a sausage around to indicate the splendour of the rising sun. Then he continued, 'That's why Shakespeare's Hamlet is such an enigma. Until now, we didn't know how he got to be the way he was. Unless you know about the beginning of the story, you miss the meat; you don't get the full irony that Hamlet was Claudius's son and that Ophelia was his half sister.'

'And where did you pick up all this tittle-tattle? '

'Do you really want to know? '

Before I could reply he was off on his 'subject'.

'Well, I was working away in a gloomy recess of the Vatican library. I have to do this, as I am tracing how the concepts of reward and punishment changed in the Northern World during the transition from Paganism to Christianity.'

He said this casually as if referring to the change from DC to AC electricity which, in a way, I suppose it is.

'Anyway,' he continued, 'I found, among a lot of uncatalogued stuff, a collection of Icelandic manuscripts - really beautifully vellum codices; the calligraphy was excellent, very easy to read. Probably they were part of the tribute Iceland sent to the Holy See along with more saleable things like seal skins, whale oil, walrus ivory, unicorn horns and what not. They were mostly the well known sagas; But one was entitled 'Gudrun's Saga'. It was the lost 'Ur-Hamlet' that everyone has been looking for.'
'What on earth is an Ur-Hamlet'.

'The original story Shakespeare based his play on, of course.'

'Enough of this chatter, declared our leader. It's far too fine a morning for all this heavy literary speculation. I haven't thought about Hamlet since I was at school, and then I found it boring. Stay in the sunless vaults of the Vatican if you want. I'm off to enjoy myself in the present sunshine. You two just keep your minds on the rope.'

I believe in taking ropework seriously, so I did in fact pay attention to the rope rather than the conversation. Nevertheless, in the background I heard him explaining that the lost saga he had discovered tells the whole story from Gudrun's, that is from Hamlet's mother's, point of view. Hamlet appears late and at first has only a supporting role.

Then it was his turn to go. As he left he remarked, 'You are a doctor, aren't you? You must know that before you can assess what ails a patient you need to know his case history. If you were Hamlet's shrink you would need his whole clinical history in a folder in front of you before you could give an opinion, wouldn't you? '

He vanished heavenwards, singing happily to himself, something in Old Icelandic by the sound of it. As I payed out the rope, I remembered we had been taught as medical students the aphorism: 'no case history - no case'. Hippocrates said as much while teaching under his olive tree on the isle of Cos. I had never been very convinced by Shakespeare's plot; the final scene is a mess. Stripped of the memorable language, you are left with Adam Macnaughton's summary.

Then a few tugs and a shout from above told me I must follow. Climbing on good rock in the early sun of this burgeoning summer morning was a joyous experience. The force of gravity seemed to be having a day off and movement was easy, or maybe it was just the verve and suppleness you get when plugged in to the great cosmic battery, which on mornings like this seems to deliver élan vital or whatever it is at particularly high voltage.

The climbing was so enjoyable I arrived at the stance before I was ready. The scholar and our soi-disant non-literary leader were deep in conversation and hardly noticed my arrival. The scholar had obviously explained to him what Shakespeare's play was all about and how the plot didn't add up. Our leader, however, a practical unsentimental man, was now doing the talking; he was explaining to the scholar that most of Shakespeare's tragedies could have been prevented if a good social worker had been available to sort things out before they got out of hand. His wife, he was pointing out, was in Social Work, and some of her cases would make your teeth curl. This Hamlet business was a minor domestic problem, a run of the mill episode that social workers were dealing with all the time. 'For example, ...' He started to relate some horror story of contemporary life when I interrupted.

'Pay attention to the bloody rope.', I admonished getting my own back as I led through without stopping. In spite of the surrounding sunlight and shadow patterning the north face, and the emerging panorama of sun-dappled hills, not to mention the essential commitment to the climb, I was intrigued by the thought that Hamlet was, like the rest of us, a minor character in a bigger plot which we don't really understand. Our scholarly friend was right. We come into Shakespeare's play at the endgame of a longer story. We don't know the case histories of any of the main characters.

I arrived at the top of the next pitch and brought the scholar up, my mind full of questions. As his head appeared below me I said, 'Okay, so tell me more.'

He stopped where he was with his arms laid across the edge of the stance, his chin resting on his hands.

'Well, as I was saying to your friend just now, Gudrun's Saga tells of what happened before Hamlet was born. It is the old story of an attempt to end a feud between two landed families by a dynastic marriage. Gudrun is a young, intelligent, bluestocking; she has a forceful personality and gets things done. She is persuaded to marry Gudric, the chieftain of the powerful opposing family, and so end generations of strife. Gudric is okay, but a bit of a huntin', shootin' and fishin' bore. Moreover, he spends a lot of the time on trading voyages. He also finds Gertude's company a bit overpowering and brings the occasional slave girl home from abroad for a bit of relaxation. Nevertheless, he is a formidable patriarchal figure with a commanding presence: he and his doings, and Gudrun's ability to keep the show on the road, dominate the first part of the saga.

The talking head resting on the ledge below me continued,

'Well, the emotionally neglected Gudrun plays her part as best she can in keeping the two dynasties away from conflict, but by and by, during one of Gudric's absences, she falls in love with Gudric's brother Kolbein (Shakespeare's Claudius) who has the next farm. Kolbein is a peaceful, cultured, scholarly man with a sense of humour and much better company than boring old Gudric. Anyway, as you might expect, 'Hamlet' is the result of their liaison, although Gudric doesn't know this.'

He heaved himself up onto the stance, settled himself comfortably and continued,

'Kolbein/Claudius, although a nice guy, also finds solace from time to time with Unn, the frustrated wife of a 'gay' neighbour named Pol (Shakespeare's Polonius), who needs a woman to run the farm and nothing else. By her, Claudius has a son Lars and a daughter Olof who are of course the originals of Laertes and Ophelia. These were robust times, remember: no television, only houghmagandie to while away the long winter evenings. The point is, of course, that Hamlet, Laertes and Ophelia are all siblings with Kolbein/Claudius as their biological father. This lack of parental knowledge is one of the ghosts that haunts the story. It is, after all, a wise man who knows his own father.'

An impatient voice came from below. Obviously our leader, now relegated to last on the rope, was feeling out of it and wanted to join the seminar. He came up faster than I could take in the rope and arrived with a few coils in his hand.

'So what happened next', he demanded while half way onto the stance. We brought him up to date. He was hooked. Our scholar was now lecturing an attentive audience. He scratched the two family trees on a convenient rock with a pebble and summarised further:

'There is still strife between the Gudrun and Gudric families. Personal and clan rivalries do not go away with a marriage. Quarrels over inheritance and land rights grumbled on, with Gudric and Gudrun as central characters. After a quarter of a century, a crux in the story is reached with the murder of Eirik, a family retainer of Gudric, and foster father of Hamlet. Eirik was found cutting wood in disputed land and was killed by Fothra, a leading member of the opposing family. In revenge, Hamlet, as he is obliged to do, waylays and kills Fothra. For this, Hamlet is banished by the Law Court at the Althing for three years exile. In Shakespeare, this episode is converted into Hamlet going to Wittenberg to study. He is pursued abroad by two members of Fothra's family, Runulf and Gizur. When they catch up with him, Hamlet, no slouch with the sword, is obliged to kill them both. (Rosenkranz and Guildenstern are dead).

Eventually our leader, resuming his rightful position at the head of the rope, set off, saying, 'I must think about this; it sounds just like one of the dysfunctional families my wife has to deal with.'

And so, as we climbed, the story unfolded further, the delays at the stances became longer and the story more intriguing. By the time we reached the Mantrap we had learned that while Hamlet is away in exile, the mighty Gudric (now an old man) starts to deteriorate mentally. Today he would be regarded as a victim of Alzheimer's disease. He stravaigs the countryside somewhat demented, muttering paranoid accusations. He becomes his own wraith. One of the dramatic cruxes of the saga is the mental decline, Lear-like humiliation, and ghost-like wanderings of this once powerful character. ('Call no man happy until he is dead', as my old friend Solon so wisely remarked to the fabulously rich Croesus).

Gudric dies, probably from natural causes: at any rate, he goes out one stormy winter's night, and is found dead the next morning in the farm midden, the final undeserved humiliation of a good man. There is of course, the inevitable rumour that his departure was hastened by Claudius, who if he did not actually push him out in the storm, at any rate did not go out looking for him. Gudrun and Claudius get married soon after. Gudrun is now Shakespeare's Queen Gertrude. They had to move fast to protect the family inheritance from predators. Hamlet is wandering abroad, an outlaw under banishment, and the other lot had got a good lawyer and were trying to declare him ineligible as heir. In any case, as the saga makes clear, Gudrun/Gertrude and Claudius get on well. They are now in their fifties, and want to enjoy the last of their lives together in a 'mature relationship', as we would say nowadays, and of course they want to preserve the inheritance for their son Hamlet.'

About this stage, we got a fankle in the rope as well as in our understanding. After sorting out both, our scholar continued his summary.

'Hamlet now becomes the character around whom the system collapses. He returns from exile to be told of his 'father's' demise and terminal wanderings, also to rumours that it was Claudius who pushed him through the one-way valve of death - that bourne from which no traveller returns. The gay Pol, the nominal father of Laertes and Ophelia, has fallen into debt. He too is going a bit gaga and garrulous and tries to blackmail Hamlet about his paternity. Hamlet, horrified, kills Pol for slandering his mother. As custom demands, Lars/Laertes duels with Hamlet to avenge the death of Pol, his 'father'. Hamlet kills Lars, and so unknowingly commits fratricide. Hamlet, now he has got his hand in, seeks revenge against Claudius for killing Gudric. He leads a raid on Claudius's farm, and kills him. Hamlet, instead of avenging his father's supposed murder, has unknowingly committed patricide - a bit of Greek Tragedy here. Alas, poor Oedipus. Gudrun's tragedy is that she knows that her son has killed his father. She gains true heroine status by her efforts to keep the situation stable. It is after all 'Gudrun's' Saga, and Gudrun was, after all, a descendant of the formidably effective Aud the Deep-minded.

We had been going very slowly. It must have been midday when we reached the Mantrap. We lay there in the warm summer sunshine having a leisurely lunch of feta cheese, bread and olives. Our leader had even brought three of these small cans of wine - I have already mentioned he was a practical man. We must have looked like Gods on Olympus toying with the fate of mortals. But enough of such hubris; it is bad style to mix one's mythologies. The climb, as you will have gathered by now, had lost its momentum. The Mantrap is, nevertheless, a spectacular location, and there are more ways of travelling than moving bodily from place to place. An hour or so later, our leader, waking from a comfortable doze, remarked,

'All this is plausible, but why didn't Shakespeare do the whole thing?'

'It was too big a story, too rich in subplots to put into a single play. Shakespeare used the Hamlet sequence to present the inner conflict of a man of action maturing into an ineffective intellectual. The interior monologues recreate the thought sequences of a decent man trying to make the right decisions on the basis of a lot of dodgy data. Thomas Kydd, a few years before in his play, had also altered the original plot a little. His play balanced the double doom of Claudius's fratricide and Hamlet's patricide. The important point is that the audience knew the background; Shakespeare didn't have to etch in the details.'

'You are sure of this?'

'Yes, there was a lot of general knowledge of European literature among educated people at that time. Kydd's play would have been widely known. Saxo Grammaticus' account had most of the story, but in a very brutal version, with Danes replacing Icelanders, lacking the high literary quality of the Icelandic original. Saxo probably got hold of it from uncouth seamen in some drinking den in Hedby. Saxo's version was a debased tabloid press version for splitting the ears of the groundlings. The original Icelandic Gudrun's Saga may even have been in circulation and known to the educated as late as the fifteen hundreds. The Vatican copy can't have been the only one around. BelleForest knew of the affair between Claudius and Gertrude at any rate, and he didn't get that from Saxo. Different playwrights just selected different aspects. The Germans, for example, like Kydd, were more interested in Claudius's alleged fratricide of Gudric, and made that the central plot; Hamlet was a mere instrument of retribution in their version.'

The scholar started wandering off into arcane territory while flicking pieces of breadcrumb off his knee over the Orion Face.

'Okay, okay, go on with the main story.' We hauled him back from the dusty corridors linking the twelfth and sixteenth centuries.

'Ah yes, where were we? Well, the characters in Shakespeare's play, particularly Hamlet, were acting out their roles on the basis of incomplete information, but the audience knew the whole plot. Imagine the extra frissons of watching Hamlet unknowingly slaying his half brother and then his biological father and dithering over whether to . . . or whether not to . . . with Ophelia, perhaps half aware from rumours around the court that she was his half sister. However, the great Shakespeare had taken out the Hamlet revenge motif from its context and, brilliantly though he presented the sub-plot, was left with all the loose ends. Like MacDuff, it had been ripped untimely from its mother's womb. The Bard didn't have to worry about what went on before, but in order to end the story dramatically and within the time limit, he had to telescope the final ten years into ten minutes and kill off all the characters - hence the dreadful last act that even good actors have difficulty in presenting plausibly. Have you ever tried to force someone to drink poison in public? '

An hour or so later we managed to get going again.

'You will lead the crux', we informed the scholar. He did so with ease, pausing in the middle of the difficult move to mention that the gravedigger scene had extra poignancy for the Elizabethan audience, who would have known the skull was that of Erik, whose death Hamlet had avenged (Alas, poor Yorrick . . . .).

'What about the ghost?'

Oh, that was easy. Gudric had been carrying on like that for a year or so before he died. According to the saga, the locals knew he wandered around talking to himself and would appear from time to time at social functions and make speeches, much as he did in the play. They also believed that after he died, his troubled ghost still walked the night, paranoid and accusing.'

'And Horatio?'

'A snake in the grass. A faux ami. In the saga he is an Iago type character. All along, he was Fothra's man. He and Fothra's son did for Hamlet in the end and Fothra's son, alias Fortinbras, bagged the whole inheritance.'

'And Ophelia?.'

'Oh, she married Thorstein Black the Wise (who discovered the principle of the intercalary week) and lived happily until they were both accidentally drowned crossing Breidafjord.'

'And Gudrun?'

'She was a formidable woman. She went to Norway where she married again - to Ulf the Unwashed. Don't look so dismayed. His name is a bit of Norse humour. He was noted for his cleanliness. Shortly after, Ulf got killed while out raiding with Sigurd Longhair who, incidentally, was bald. Gudrun returned to Iceland after that, weary but unbroken. She entered the convent at Helgafell and took over as abbess after the death of Gudrun Osvif's daughter.

Quite a girl, Gudrun. In real life she was a practical woman who ran a disciplined ship. If Shakespeare's Hamlet had mooned around looking soulful and having soliloquies in the real Gertrude's household, he would have been underfoot all the time having to lift up his feet every time she passed with the hoover. Dramatically, it wouldn't have worked. Just try having soliloquies in your own house when the roof is leaking, or a drain needs sorted, and see what happens to you. In the play, a no-nonsense Gertrude would have ruined Hamlet's act. So, she and the others had to be tuned into the background to keep attention directed on Hamlet as an icon for civilised indecision and a master of the interior monologue. The practical demands of a two hour play also required a quick end, so Shakespeare had to finish them all off in the last ten minutes. If he had let any of them survive as in the original saga, it would have unbalanced the drama. It isn't easy to reorganise someone else's story seamlessly, even if you are Shakespeare.'

The scholar completed the crux and vanished out of earshot.

'Plausible bugger', I opined to our quondam leader.

'Yes, he's more sensible than I thought. He would get on well with my wife. She has to deal with equally bizarre dramas from the great soap opera of life. Only hers are happening today - now - as we speak, some indecisive ineffectual is probably trying to screw up courage to do in his uncle who is probably his father. You don't have to grovel in the bowels of the Vatican to learn about domestic strife.'

Then his eyes surveyed the distant horizon. He was lost in thought. At length he came out with an opinion,

' I think Gudrun's Saga is genuine. It is the mirror image of Njal's Saga.'

'Njal's Saga? Don't tell me a practical man like you has joined the amateur literati?'

'Look, I may be a man of action, but I'm not bloody illiterate. The Sagas happen to be my "subject". I didn't let on in case I put him off his stride.

'You see,' he continued, 'In Gudrun's Saga everyone, especially Hamlet, is acting on the basis of incomplete information. None of the characters know what is really going on. None of them understands the plot.'

'And in Njal's Saga?'

'Njal's saga is the story of a man who has all the facts. He does understand the plot and can foresee the results of each course of action. He tries to avert disasters, but there are too many variables in the social equations he tries to balance. Each wise solution is unbalanced by people who cannot control their dislike, envy or desire for revenge, even if they are damaged in the process. Pitfall and gin beset the road of the well-intentioned. Self-centred blindness and sheer ill-gaitedness are ever present.'

He continued drawing on an unexpected fund of learning,

'Njal tries to manage every situation to minimise conflict. Even then, the whole thing collapses and ends in a final grand punch-up. The greatness of the saga is Njal's civilised attempts at maintaining stability, and the final reconciliation between Kari and Flosi, the leaders of the two factions, two decent men who have had the obligation of exacting vengeance thrust upon them. The final scene is brilliant. After years of bloodshed between the two sides, Kari is shipwrecked in an autumn storm. He and his crew get ashore, and after nightfall reach a farm in a snowstorm. The door opens, and it is Flosi standing there. He treats them hospitably and with honour. They both see the futility of it all, and realise they have been manipulated by events, mainly by the stupidity of their relatives.'

He sighed and then added, 'I prefer stories that end happily. Real life is too full of grief. But you never know, the good variables must come into sync from time to time and produce a fairy tale. Very important to be ready for it if ever happens,' he concluded.

We got to the top, strolled about the summit plateau, identifying all the hills and reminiscing about past adventures, then descended the Tower Ridge.

We arrived back at the hut in the golden light of the late afternoon. Our scholar left us immediately, as he had to get back to Edinburgh on some pressing eschatological errand.

Before he left we asked, 'When are you going to publish all this interesting stuff?'

'Never.'

'Never?'

'Never! While we were talking it through up there in the Mantrap, I realised that Gudrun's saga does not give the case history of Shakespeare's Hamlet. The Hamlet of the play is not an Icelandic farmer, nor an Oedipus nor an Orestes. Shakespeare rearranged elements of the original story to give a brilliant study of an indecisive intellectual confronted with a moral problem requiring action. Today he would be a well intentioned liberal worried about the legality of using force against an unprincipled aggressor.'

'But if you published you could become famous, properly handled, even rich!'

'I'm both already', he replied, 'My income is sufficient - that makes me rich. And I am famous - all my friends know who I am. I couldn't handle any more fame than that. No, no, no,' he said this three times with increasing emphasis. 'If Gudrun's Saga ever got out, it would generate a huge lit. crit. industry and, even worse, a series of PhDs. The poor bloody Hamlet of the play should be left to get on with his problem as best he can, as Will Shakespeare intended.'

We shook hands, hoped we'd meet again and, to increase this possibility, we exchanged the names of the pubs we generally frequented. He set off down the glen, en route, no doubt, to rummage around in the dusty oubliettes of the Vatican.

The hut was empty and dank (it was in the days before the windmill), so we sat outside having a little dram and musing in the evening sun. I was ever so slightly niggled at my leader's unexpectedly virtuoso intellectual performance in explaining about Njal's Saga. I sat there thinking, and eventually came up with the following.

'You know this is not the first time this sort of thing has happened.'

'Eh? What sort of thing?'

'That discussion we had at the Mantrap. There we were in a little notch in a vast ridge of steep, intimidating rock, surrounded by authentic rugged grandeur, and we were discussing arcane details about Icelandic sagas and Elizabethan theatre.'

'You mean such things happen often?'

'No, but it has at least once. The whole episode reminds me of a painting by the Chinese master Gu Yun.'

I paused to let this sink in.

'I saw it in an exhibition of paintings from the Shanghai Museum. In the Chamber's Street Museum, as a matter of fact. It was a scroll about five feet long that seemed to cascade down the wall. It depicted a mountainside, rugged and untamed, full of steep jumbled rock with trees and tanglewood clambering up from the depths of a deep glen. The title was 'Literary gathering by a stream'. The 'literary gathering' was an easily-overlooked detail towards the bottom left where there was a small finely-drawn pavilion before which a few sages were sitting. On the authority of the artist, amid all this grandeur they were discussing literature.'

I was getting into my stride, so I continued,

'I imagine the deep metaphor the painting was expressing was the fragility of civilised human intellectual activity in the face of the unintellectual thrust of creation. It represented the eternal triangle - the tension between the phenomenal universe, represented by the surrounding geology subservient to the Laws of Thermodynamics, life itself exuberantly and defiantly surging upstream against these Immutable Laws, albeit temporarily, and the epiphenomenon of tiny human beings exercising the gift of detached thought in the immense uncaring universe that surrounds them.'

My friend gave me an oblique look, patted me on the shoulder and filled my glass to the brim with golden Lagavuillin.

'There, there,' he said 'Drink that and then you'll feel better. I'm not going to let you go climbing with an eschatologist again. It's not good for you.'

Midnight on the Capel Mounth

Midsummer at midnight in our northern latitudes is a magic hour if you are lucky enough to hit both in a spell of tranquil weather. It occasionally happens - to me at least three times: one on top of Ben Alder and another on Carn an Righ. On each occasion the sky was clear and the flat tops of these remote mountains were so windless that the primus stove purred away without shelter and the pleasing aroma of toasted oatcakes and whisky drifted in the mellow air. As everyone knows, the olfactory nerve that samples airborne molecules is not really a nerve; it is an extension of the forebrain; it carries sensations straight to the base of the higher centres without much filtering. I think this is why many religions swing incense around during their services. It helps to switch the congregation on and alerts their brains to the arrival of some supra-rational information. Frankincense and myrrh are all very well for up-market religiosity, but are a bit over-sophisticated, even fantoush, compared to the good honest indigenous aroma of whisky and toasted oatcakes. They tune you in to a more fundamental harmonic, one broadcast by the land itself, unprocessed through the belief systems of someone else's brain. The third time, the one I would like to tell you about now, occurred near the summit of the Capel Mounth.

I was walking over to Deeside from Braedownie alone and had settled down somewhere near the summit to relax awhile and enjoy the serene ambience of space and soft colours that hang in the half-light between dusk and dawn on the night of the summer solstice. I had just got nicely tuned in when a man approached. He must have been following ten minutes behind me, yet I hadn't noticed him when I looked back. He had, I suppose, as much right to be there as I had, perhaps even more; he looked somehow as if he belonged.

Nevertheless I was enjoying the solitude and felt a little miffed at the intrusion.

'A fine night', he remarked.

'It is that.'

'Mind if I join you?'

'It's a free country', I said without enthusiasm.

He sat down facing me looking south, silhouetted against the brightest part of the sky. He lent, or rather reclined, against a boulder with his arms behind his head. His face, therefore, was in shadow framed by two triangles of bright light between his bent arms and head. I made him out to be strong featured and athletic. He seemed to be relaxed about his intrusion and in a leisurely mood. The last thing I wanted at that moment was a chatty companion getting between me and the approaching magic of the mid-night hour. I radiated displeasure. He didn't seem to notice.

After a period of silence he said,

'You are looking in the wrang airt, my trustie fiere'. He nodded towards the south,

'Tak a long look ahint you.'

I didn't like his patronizing tone and anyway I don't like doing what I am told, so I did not move.

'Sunsets are for beginners, intellectual halflings. You aye see mair if you look the other way.'

That remark appealed to me more; it had hit one of my weak spots, looking the other way, that is, so reluctantly I turned.

'Look carefully', he said.

Gradually I realized the subtlety of the scene. Looking sunwards to the bright north the hills were in shadow. To the south, however, the ridges were luminous in the soft afterglow and were separated by the dark intervening glens. The colours were soft and subtle and merged gradually towards the distant horizon. I was surprised at how much quality was there. Somewhere beyond I could sense the presence of Strathmore and the Howe of the Mearns and felt a foreboding.

I forgot to be unimpressed and said, 'Aye, there is quality there in the afterglow, I have to admit. You miss it if you look sunwards into the glare.'

Then, after a pause I felt the sense of foreboding again.

'But when I looked south I seemed to see over the hills. I saw big new towns and motorways covering Strathmore and the Howe of the Mearns,

'That is the future', he said simply.

I was beginning to be intrigued by this man, even beginning to co-operate.

'You are not a latter-day Brahan Seer?,

Na, na, I hae mair respect for my skin than Coinneach Odhar had for his.

Anyway you don't need to be a seer to predict the obvious. The population of your world is increasing. Surplus people have to go somewhere. That's bairns' stuff; anyone could foresee that. I could lead you into far greater mysteries if you have a mind.'

'No doubt you could but I don't like being led.'

'I am sorry, that was ill-stated. What I mean is, if you like we could enhance each other's understanding. You are receptive to new ideas and in exchange you could no doubt enlighten me on many things.'

He had spoken in a good Scots accent with pure vowels and clear consonants with, as you have doubtless noted, an occasional old-farrand turn of phrase. However, for me this man had too good a conceit of himself - too 'pro-active' to use a modern term. I retreated into my shell.

I could feel he had his antennae out. He was registering whatever it is that sensitive people are able to register about other people even when they are in their shells.

He waited a decent interval and began again.

'As it happens, laddie, I am a literary agent. Would you be interested in writing a best seller? I ken weel the gate o sic things. You could scatter your thochts like oats and barley from the seed-basket of your mind and reap a golden harvest.'

This evoked a memory of childhood. I remember seeing farmers walking up and down fields scattering seed from a cloth basin hung from their necks, a handful to right and left. This man was adept at evoking older, deeper memories. I could make him out more clearly now, He was dressed in countryman tweeds of a distinctive pattern, blues, greens and browns like a summer hillside. I noticed his waistcoat was uncompromisingly black.

Then he blew it. 'I could make sure anything you write will sell well. I could make you weel-kent and rich.'

I now knew who I was dealing with. I too can be proactive when roused. I went for his jugular.

'You are Mephistopheles aren't you?'

Blandly he replied. 'No, as it happens, I am His Satanic Majesty Himself.'

'The de'il you are!', I exclaimed without thinking.

'At your service', he answered. 'People don't usually recognize me quite so quickly. It's usually a wee bit too late for them when they do.'

'Look, Your Majesty,' I said, with my birse getting up, 'Haven't you anything better to do than wander around highland hillsides trying to corrupt peaceful non-entities. I would have thought you were engaged in greater enterprises considering the present state of the world. Why don't you just b***** off.'

'Aye, you're a thrawn de'il yourself, if I may return the compliment. No one is a non-entity to me. I depend on entities; I am one myself. I'll maybe explain that later', he added. 'But to answer your question, I am redundant. I have been overtaken by events.'

Things must indeed be hard if the Prince of Darkness is surplus to requirements. I almost said "Poor devil", but stopped myself in time.

He must have sensed the thought for he said

'Don't feel sorry for me. It's gey and restful to have my quality time to myself. I have spent millennia on a full time basis pushing poor souls down the path of intellectual degradation. It is enjoyable at first, like trundling loose boulders down a cliff, but in the end it's tedious.'

Changing tack, he next said. 'Look, is it not a pity to waste a fine night like this in idle blethers. Let's go down to the Dhu Loch and do a climb together. I have a rope in my sack.'

Well, what the hell, I thought, without realizing the appropriateness of the expression. Why not go for it? I have spent a large part of my life in the company of eccentrics. I could surely handle this one.

'Okay, my friend', I replied, 'as it happens I have a lang spoon with me, so it should be safe enough.'

This amused him greatly and we set off together heading across the upper bowl of the Allt Dhu towards the west side of Central Gully.

As we walked I asked him to explain why one so mighty was not surfing the growing waves of evil presently afflicting the world. He explained his problem thus:

'One of my titles is "Lord of the Air". Not so long ago I could travel freely through the ether but now I am crowded out.

You mean there are too many aeroplanes buzzing around?'

'Aeroplanes are least of my worries.'

Too many of your fellow demons, then ?

'No.'

'So what's crowding you out?'

'You humans.'

'Us? - I thought it was the other way round - that *you* bothered us?'

'Not now. Your invasion of the ether has ruined our privacy. If you could only sense the continual buzz of signals infesting an ether that was once so pristine and empty. The blether from mobile phones is unbearable, broadcasting fills the demon world with moronic noise and television signals are never-ending bad dreams. For us demons it's like flying through treacle - worse than that - like flying through a cesspit. That's why I'm down here on the Capel Mounth – just for some peace and quiet and, as it happens,' he bowed courteously, 'some agreeable company.'

'Have all you demons been driven out of the ether, then.'

'Of course',

'So what are all displaced demons doing?'

'Needs must when the humans drive, if you'll pardon me using such an expression. If you can't beat them, you maun join them.'

'What does that mean?'

'Instead of using humans as intermediaries we are now moving in as direct participants. We have pushed people out of their bodies. My kindred now roam the broad lands of global trade where there are no boundaries between crime and legitimate business. It's much more enjoyable actually being corrupt yourself than degrading others. Besides, being lords of the ether we have free access to people's identity.'

'If business is booming why haven't you joined them?'

'Because I am a Calvinist demon.'

'Eh?'

'Why does that surprise you? I am your personal manifestation of the Prince of Darkness as you call me. Calvin was one of my most successful cases. I really screwed him up and you inherited his screwed up thoughts.'

I put this interesting information on the back burner for later consideration.

'But all this must be working in your favour', I argued. 'It is opening up new avenues for evil – that must please you.'

'Aye the wark gangs bonnily on as I once said when I was with the Calvinist divines at the massacre after Philiphaugh. But things are now going so fast I can't keep up. You buggers have now discovered electronic money. In the old days gold was heavy and palpable. It was obvious and took time to move around and usually needed some kind of violence to get hold of it in any quantity. I now realize I had an easy time then. Electronic money is unstable. It can't be kept; it has to be exchanged into something else as quickly as possible. Hence, the exponential rate of growth of the world economy and the increasing rate of consumption - if you'll pardon me lapsing into modern parlance. My former clients are off tapselteerie doun the brae on a bogie roll to the everlasting bonfire before I can even give them a push start. Electronic money has even made war obsolete.' he added as an afterthought.

'Surely not, there are still plenty of wars around.'

'Aye, I still have a bit of fun there, but war is no longer efficient. It is much more cost effective to buy a country and occupy it peacefully by immigration. Better value for money that way, cuts out the middleman and no need to buy military hardware.

'Religions must surely still give you some opposition.' I queried.

'No, they never have. In the end I have always used them. I put my people in and turn them to violence or to accept violence from wherever it comes as the punishment inflicted by divine wrath. Surely that must be obvious?'

'So there is no opposition?'

'I never said that, but as is normal it is having a hard time.'

'So where is the opposition?'

'Look,' he said, 'I'm fed up talking shop. Have you no sense of aesthetics? This is as fine a midsummer's night as I can remember. The air is still; the acoustics are perfect. Let's rest for a while and amplify the ambience with a little music. As it happens I have my fiddle in my sack here.'

We stopped close to the Allt Dhu. He swung down his knapsack, took out a case and withdrew a venerable, well-cared-for instrument and spent a moment tuning it. I sat down while he played a set of tunes. Some I recognized; others were unfamiliar – wild and strangely beautiful, all played in the eastern style. Gow and Skinner and a hundred others would have recognized the roots from which their inspiration sprung.

After this unexpected recital, we sat for a moment in silence while the emotional harmonics died away into a restful tranquility.

After some minutes he seemed to recover his old self

'Now where were we? Ah yes, I mind fine, you were asking about the opposition to my triumphal march.'

'Yes I would like to know.'

'It lies in the superabundant information processing networks of the human brain.'

I must have looked baffled because he sighed again, as if unnecessarily pointing out the obvious. 'Let's get this over with so we can enjoy the rest of our time together. Your brain has two conflicting processing systems. A large part is devoted to ensuring your long and short-term survival, at almost any cost and in any situation; your 'hard-wired core processing systems' take their task seriously. Therein lies predestination. You are predestined to make the best attempt you can to survive. Theologians get hot and bothered about this. Under my direct personal supervision they evolved the doctrine of Predestination. They adapted it to ensure their own survival as the Elect and the predestined damnation of their competitors. Establishing psychological dominance is common practice, a standard biological survival strategy. It is so easy for me to corrupt religious literalists. There's no real challenge.' He sighed with boredom, shrugged his shoulders and smiled sadly.

'And the other processing system?'

'You humans are also endowed with far too much surplus brain power. The evolution of the human cerebral cortex was a big mistake. It has landed you with a prodigious ability to process information and modify the behaviour of your core program for good or ill; therein lies 'Freewill' or less grandiosely the woblinesss of your emotions. The conflict between what you call good and evil is deciding how these groups will control each other.'

He paused'

'Go on, I know all about wobbly emotions.'

'Your superabundant circuitry is capable of sophisticated analysis of signals arriving from the world around you. Therein lies the opposition. You humans have an immense capacity for understanding how the world actually works. Freewill has the ability to arrive at intelligent solutions. It requires controlling your emotions. Training your superabundant circuitry is like domesticating a confused wild animal. Some brains never escape from the core survival program, others maximize civilized behaviour by controlling their core program and maintaining what you would call standards. There are a lot of thrawn people around who won't do what I tell them. They use their circuitry to arrive at practical solutions I don't approve of.

'Would more brain help us?'

'More brain? You must be mad! It would only introduce more variables into the system. It would make you more neurotic and emotionally unstable. You can't handle the superabundant circuitry you already have. Just learn how to do that. You can't excuse yourselves by pleading inadequate brain power.'

'So whose going to win? '

'Win? What a curious notion. No one will win. Things will go on as usual only more quickly and at a larger scale.

Now that's enough practical theology, let's get on with enjoying the here and now.'

In the here and now we were crossing the shallow bowl of the upper Allt Dhu when we heard the sound of bagpipes. In the improving light we could make out a small tent about half a mile away on the slopes of Broad Cairn and a man was standing beside it playing a salute to the dawn. I recognized that most soaring of all pibrochs, 'The Old Men of the Shells." The notes spread over the plateau lands and soared over the Dhu Loch adding an aural dimension to space-time. The tenor and bass drones seemed unusually sonorous in the still air forming a three-threaded background tapestry to the singing of the chanter. (Incidentally if you ever want entry into appreciating piobaireachd, 'The Old Men of the Shells." is the one to begin with. I have only heard of one other instance of playing piobaireachd on mountain tops at midnight and that was by a lecturer in the old Queen's College, Dundee, way back in the sixties before that institution became a supercharged electric chair of scientific progress. According to legend he played the 'Cailach of Beinn a' Bhric' one Halloween on the summit of Beinn a' Bhric itself; there were, alas, no supernatural manifestations, the Cailach did not answer the call, at least on that occasion. But I digress.)

We stood for a moment while land, light and music interwove in a sett of harmonious sensory impressions. Mindful of the introductory paragraph I produced my flask of malt; His Majesty, not to be outdone, produced some oatcakes from his sack. They were freshly toasted and still hot. I didn't ask how He had managed this but with His background it was probably a trivial feat.

We savoured the subtle aromas and in so doing alerted our superabundant processing power to the arrival of sensory data requiring supra-rational interpretation – in this case music deeply rooted in the land and its history. All the ambient resonances were in phase. Deep in our surplus brainpower an awareness of ancient days generated itself. I suppose it was what is sometimes referred to as 'folk memory'.

We wandered off to central gulley and in the improving light picked our way to the foot of the cliff. On the way I said to him, 'You are a piper yourself according to legend. You did well in Kirk Alloway by all accounts. Your performance in the winnock bunker in the east is still remembered, still commented on world wide each 25th of January.'

'Aye, thon was a great party. We used to have them like that in thae days. There was none of that mindless stotting around full of lager and alcopop. I don't know who is responsible for such degradation. I may be evil, but at least I have style. There must be something even worse than me around – some banal force that has no sense of style. It shows that even we demons can't enforce standards in our flock these days. However, I suppose it maximizes profit and so it meets our basic criterion and must be alright.'

He was silent for a few minutes, obviously thinking of the "good old days".

He eventually said reflectively, 'Yon cuttie-sark was a roch wee lassie. A halliracket quine if ever I met one - a wee bissom, the first of the mini-skirts – but she had style.'

While on the subject, I was interested in his opinion of the great Ball of Kirriemuir. 'Were you involved with that?', I asked.

'No, that was sheer native exuberance. I was there of course - but only as a guest. Now *it* had style and the ballad about it has great literary merit, both technically and conceptionally. The verse about "fifty acres finest flax fairly ****** flat" is an alliterative and imaginative masterpiece.'

We had now arrived at the foot of a likely looking crack. 'This will do', he said taking a rope of scarlet silky material from his sack.

'I'll lead of course.'

'Of course,' I agreed. 'This is all your idea.'

I wouldna be muckle sure of that, laddie.', he replied.

We climbed the cracks, corners and overhang with easy competence.

At the terrace we sat down for a rest. I asked him, 'What did you mean by inferring this might be my idea?

'I am a construct of your own mind. I reside in your superabundant circuitry. Nothing that has happened this evening was not already in the model of the world created in your own neural networks - in your mind if you wish to call it that. If you happened to fall just now and ceased to exist, this particular version of me would cease to exist too. That's why I am seeing to it that we dinna gang tapselteerie doon the brae together'

'So what are you doing wandering about in my mind. I can't remember inviting you in.'

'You acquired me. Like most people of your generation you had a religious upbringing. I am your implanted quality control system, part of your hard-wiring. I try to make you claim you have done all the Munros when you haven't – just to find out what stuff you are made of - that kind of thing. For example, will you claim to have climbed Black Mamba?' (That, as it happened, was the climb we were on!)

'Well many years ago I was dragged up this far, behind Allan Pettit with Malcolm in the middle of the rope; then it started to rain and we had to traverse off - so it wouldn't be a complete lie, this far anyway.

'Well the next bit will be. We are off to finish the upper crag.'

We couldn't find the route in the dimness and finished up somehow at the top of the rocks on the edge of the broad plateau just as the sun was rising. The piper on Broad Cairn was mow playing the "Desperate Battle of the Birds" – another good piobrach for the apprentice aficionado.

'That last bit we climbed might be a new route.' he said, 'I think we were off the line of Blue Max. If it is, what would you like to call it? You choose.'

'How about 'The Exciseman'?', I suggested.

This amused him no end – he had a weakness for feeble jokes.

'Very good', he said

'Well I must go now I think I'll have a word with yon fellow piper. He is good. I happen to know him; he's one of us. I'm going to ask him to play Neil Munro's "Lost Pibroch", and if you know anything about that I would advise you to get out of earshot before he starts. Psychologically you are in a bad enough state as it is.'

As he walked away towards Broad Cairn, he turned and said,

'By the way I left my Aston-Martin in the car park at Braedownie.

I don't need it anymore. You can have it with my compliments. The keys are in the ignition.'

So that was that. The supposed figment of my imagination walked off with his back to the dawn.

It was never my intention to return through Braedownie; the offer of the Aston-Martin must have been his last Parthian shaft of temptation. I continued north on my original errand to visit a friend at Logie Coldstone just on the other side of Muir of Dinnet.

A couple of days later, however, I read in the Dundee Courier that a search had been mounted for someone who had left a customised Aston-Martin DB5 in the Braedownie Car Park with the doors unlocked, the key in the ignition and a case of the rare 'Tir nan Og' whisky in the boot. The search for the missing owner went on for days with all the stops pulled out - sniffer dogs, the Pitfoulie Mountain Rescue Team, helicopters an' a'. No one was ever found. There was a bit of a stushie about the ownership of the car, however. The registration document in the glove compartment gave the owner as a certain O. Nick of Flat B, El-Zabbub Apartments, Mahoun Square, Kensington. The occupant of that up-market residence was a successful merchant banker, named Goldie MacMammon who oiled the wheels of international trade by specializing in 'currency transfers'. He was correspondingly powerful and had unassailable political connections. Goldie, in fact drove a Lamborghini Gallardo and didn't think much of Aston Martins – 'far too staid'. He had never heard of an O. Nick. Neighbours thought the previous tenant might have been someone with a name like that, a Russian gentleman, a Mr Oleg Nikov who had something to do with the oil industry; they were too cagey to remember much more. The apartments were rented from Walpurgis Developments, an international conglomerate registered in the Cayman Islands where, of course, the trail went cold. There was a general appeal for information. Unsurprisingly none was forthcoming.

A year later the unclaimed car was auctioned. It had become in the meantime a 'mystery car' and every rich vulgarian in the world was after it. It was bought by a dubious middle-eastern playboy called Sheikh Djinn al Toniq and 'muckle guid it did him', as Robert MacQueen, the famous Lord Braxfield would have said. The Sheikh failed to take a corner on the Corniche somewhere above Monaco and went tapselteerie doun the brae; both he and the car ended in a spectacular fire ball that was seen for miles.

The money from the sale went to the education of handicapped children. By some fortunate mistake, it went to a group with a particularly dangerous handicap - those cursed with a high intelligence. If they are let loose into the world with their superabundant circuitry programmed by the wrong people they will, indeed, exert a degrading influence on the future.

The whisky was also auctioned off, but discretely as single bottles. It was a very old distillation; it attracted the attention of connoisseurs. I felt I had to buy one for old time's sake. I shared it with friends one fine summer evening sitting outside Gelder Shiel looking over the Dhu Loch towards Black Mamba and the mysterious 'Exciseman' finish. It goes without saying we had our dram with freshly toasted oatcakes. The complex blend of delicate bouquets seduced our superabundant circuitry into generating ancient folk memories of wisdom and mother earth. It was well worth the ransom it cost.

Flashbacks

Total recall is a disconcerting experience; at least in the way I experience it. I will be engaged in some task or other when, without warning, for a second or two, I will be back in an event in the past. For a few fleeting moments I experience all the sensations of the five senses that were arriving at some particular moment in the distant past. Most interestingly I experience the moment with the unsophisticated psyche I had at the time, not with the psyche I have now: battered and disillusioned by the attrition of subsequent living. These flashbacks seem to arrive spontaneously without being triggered by Proustian madeleine cakes or any other contextual reference. Ordinary memory by comparison is a woollier picture, an old dog-eared snapshot pulled out consciously from the untidy filing cabinet of the mind and seen by the 'me' I am now, not by the previous unsophisticated 'me' that was there at the time the event happened. The total recall I am referring to is a sort of epilepsy of the memory centres in the temporal lobe, an involuntary re-play of some event in the past. Some of these recalls are pretty dreadful others are happy. Here are three happy ones.

i

I was on top of the Cat Nick on Salisbury Crags. It was a peaceful morning. The whin was yellow and the grass a fresh green. Beside me was Bob Grieve. I could smell the smoke of coal fires and a whiff of Bob's asthma tobacco. There was no sound of traffic. I could hear church bells striking all over the old and new towns. I could see the pall of smoke from the household fires over the tenements of the Dumbie Dykes and the Pleasance. My hands were glowing from clutching holds all morning. I heard Bob speaking. I could make out only one word of the sentence he was uttering. It was: '...morning...'. I had at that instant no memory of anything that had already happened in my later life, just a feeling of being aware of the present and feeling happy before the whole scene vanished.

The greenery and yellow whin indicates that this scene must have taken place in early summer. It must have been just before eleven on a Sunday morning to judge from the quietness and the church bells. The date must have been some year of the late forties.

There is a lot of social history in this transient flashback. Sunday mornings were quiet because there was no traffic. Car ownership was low and I seem to remember you were not allowed to park cars in the street after dark unless you left the lights on. In those days cars were kept in the local garage and taken out at weekends, a bit like yachts in marinas today. The breakfast fires were lit late because a Sunday morning 'lie in' was for most people less of a luxury than a physical necessity after a six day week under what would today be considered brutal and illegal working conditions. Our future President Professor Sir Robert Grieve was at that time a minor functionary in the civil service with his coming greatness unsuspected. He was smoking asthma tobacco in his pipe because it was cheap. By smoking this dreadful stuff he was gradually saving enough to buy records of the Beethoven symphonies. The records would have been 78 rpm, played on a wind up gramophone with a fibre needle. In those days technology was basic and affluence was not widespread. Many Edinburgh professional families were satisfied to take their annual holiday in remote resorts like North Berwick or the adjacent slightly more up-market Gullane (pronounced 'Gillin', if you were the sort of person that went there).

ii

I was standing outside the bothy at Upper Steall. It was dark. It had just been raining. A warm wind was blowing clouds across the stars. I could hear the roar of the great waterfall across the glen. Two people were standing next to me. One was saying, 'We are sib to the wind....'. I could hear his accent and voice as if it was happening in real time, whatever that is. I felt an overwhelming sense of freedom and discovery as if I had escaped from a cage into a magic world where few others had entered.

This event I now remember took place in the mid forties of last century. I was fifteen and going through an animist phase. Every rock and tree had its spirit, every glen and mountain a presence of some kind. In lonely places the sense of the ambient world was at times quite frightening. In those days Upper Steall had a roof and walls that kept out the rain, if not the wind, a battered caravanserai in the wilderness of remote Glen Nevis. Now all that is left of its once-sheltering halls is a crumbling gable end and a pile of rubble. It is passed by scores of walkers each weekend, if not each day.

On the occasion of the flashback I can recall from ordinary memory that I had arrived at this desolate ruin late, late in the gloaming about the hour that Kilmeny came home. I had been camping alone for some days in the Mamores and White Corries. I tried to enter the darkness of the surviving habitable room. Compared to a tent the place seemed a haunted cavern wherein a presence lurked. I was on the point of pitching my cotton tent outside instead of braving the unknown forces within the gloom of the ruined house when another rain squall arrived and provided the courage to enter. I gritted my teeth and stepped into the wood-smoked darkness and lit my candle. Things weren't so bad once I got a fire going, better still after a primitive meal. My memory of these days was of constant hunger kept inadequately at bay with dried egg, baked beans, bad margarine and Beattie's bread. Only the beans survive, the rest are now happily extinct. But there were still shadows moving around and the wind soughed in the roof tree and there were of course 'unidentifiable sounds'. We animists find it bad enough in the daylight but in firelight and shadow the world is full of unchancy things. Then I heard footfalls. Panic and a flood of adrenalin. Fortunately the footsteps came from mortals, two boys from Falkirk. The older was a soldier on leave and the other was about my age and being taken on his first trip to the glens. The fear and emptiness vanished. We talked far into the night of bothies in the snowy north and places ill tae ken. We felt that our presence here showed we had broken out of the conventional world and discovered the real Scotland for ourselves. Having done this we were 'special' in some way and belonged to an elite group; we were 'sib' - to use a forgotten term that describes that feeling of brotherhood between free and equal spirits who had independently broken through without any psychological support.

I find the scene I have been describing unbelievably Arcadian. Was the world ever really like that? Could three reasonable intelligent teenagers raise their arms in the night air, to the throbbing waterfall, to the starlight and scudding clouds and say sincerely and without embarrassment, 'We are sib.... sib to the wind!'?

There must surely be a few odd balls still around, unprofitable people, the despair of admen, who won't buy what they are told, who walk through the prevailing fashions without noticing them in the way ghosts pass through walls as if they weren't there. You occasionally pass a youth, obviously in the possession of his own unmarketable vision, walking Alastor-like uphill into the gloaming while the rest of us are proceeding downhill to the pub as fast as our fading nervous systems will allow. Sometimes I feel as if the figure might be me walking out from the past through a chink in space-time which, of course, just shows that even a hard-bitten realist can write sentimental nonsense.

iii

I was lying on the stern of a boat. I could smell the aroma of old rope and hear the low throb of a big engine. Around me there was space and light and colour. I felt luxuriously fulfilled and happy and a great sense of the future.

Rummaging around in the untidy filing cabinet of ordinary memory I recall that this must have been another clip from the late forties. We were returning from an illicit visit to the forbidden Isle of Rum where we had spent a week climbing on Ruinsival, Trallval, Hallval,

Askival but for some reason not Barkeval. I was with young versions of the Great Slesser and the Great Dutton. (Even at that distant time they were under heavy suspicion of future greatness.). We had stayed in Canna after our return from Rum while the rest of the party returned to Embro. Lorne Campbell had given us permission to sleep in the loft of an outhouse down by a little bay below the old castle where the princess was held prisoner. We had intended to achieve fame by making daily first ascents on the cliffs above the harbour or on the north coast. The weather was against such crass activity. We were in the middle of a long heat wave. (There used to be such things.) The sea was glassy calm and had been so for a long time. The atmosphere was too heavy and soporific to do much except eat Tennysonian Lotus. We passed the time serenely watching yonder amber light that would not leave the myrrh bush on the height and drowsing beneath the craggy ledge from which the poppy hung in sleep. And all the rest of the Lotus land experience. Even the Great Slesser was moving in slow motion. Canna and Sanday at that time had a substantial native population and were not often visited. As rare strangers we were treated with distant politeness. When we first asked at the farm for butter and milk we were provided with it diffidently. The next day we were judged by our polite behaviour to be harmless and were invited in for a strupach and a ceilidh. Milk, butter, eggs and home-baking survived unrationed in these quiet places.

The next boat to come was a dilapidated freighter. In the glory of a summer's evening she wove her way into the harbour and amid a flurry of ringing bells she hit the pier with a crunch that cracked the pier's woodwork. The captain peered over the bridge, looked at the altered geometry of the wood and muttered, 'That bloody pier is always getting in the way'. Macbrayne's had freighters in those days - old tramp-like vessels with a proper straight funnel that emitted abundant smoke. These picturesque vessels took occasional passengers and we were given deck accommodation to Mallaig. Sobriety among captain and crew was not considered essential in these less prissy times. For most of the voyage the crew assembled on the bridge absorbed in some discussion. Meanwhile this latter day Birlinn Clann Ranald steered for Mallaig imparting from time to time an interesting pattern to its wake - an occasional shallow curving zig followed eventually by a more positive zag. In those days the Western Isles still had a whiff of the old frontier between two civilisations.

Anyway, back on the coiled rope hawser on the stern of this romantically ramshackle vessel I was surrounded by an extravagant sunset reflected in a smooth oily sea, full of the reflections of the surrounding mountains. For a brief second or two I had been who I used to be with no memory of the future. But that's normal - not being able to remember the future, I mean. Unless, of course, you have the second sight.

Madeira Wine

Madeira wine improves in flavour when carried around the world in the hold of a ship. So is the memory of a good expedition if allowed to rock around for a few years in the bottom of your mind. The original experiences grow or diminish in relative importance and achieve a balance unsuspected at the time when they were being harvested from the ambient universe. The immediate account of an expedition is the new wine drunk fresh from the bottle, sparkling and immediate. The beaujolais nouveau for the 1985 summer expedition to Petermann Peak in northeast Greenland has already been provided by Malcolm Slesser (SMCJ, 1986, xxxiii, 177, 283-287). As expeditions go, it was a good vintage, and what follows is a flagon drawn from the same cask ten years later. It seems to contain endless glasses unequally filled and obviously poured from the bottle of the mind by a shaking hand. Since few readers reach this remote corner of the Journal, maybe one every twenty years, now that you are here, why not relax by this little campfire in the wilderness of time and savour a glass or two of vintage '85 while I enjoy your company?

Moveo ergo sum

The weather in August 1985 was perfect for travel, the sun shone day after day, and there was no wind. The big fjord leading north, however, was filled with heavy pack ice. After a day or two of pushing floes apart, we made it as far as a little island in the sun that lay a few miles off shore, the top of a drowned escarpment of red columnar basalt an acre or two in area. We landed in a minute bay on a few yards of dark sand. From a nook at the top of its northern cliff, we watched the surrounding ice for signs of movement. The hours passed and merged into days. The sun circled the horizon. The pack drifted to and fro with the tide but didn't loosen. The island, meanwhile, started to make itself felt. It was a colourful, intricate place. Little terraces led off from a central basin of red gravel patched with grey, black and bright orange lichens, white and yellow flowers, light green willow, and dark cassiope. It was like living on the palette of an artist confident with primary colours and bold forms. From the centre of the magic island, the outside world was invisible except for the bright blue sky. The patterned terraces led the few yards to the sea and the sight of the surrounding hills: the jagged Stauning Alps, the distant profile of Ella Island, and the long horizon of Traill Island, fifteen miles to the East. A peace began to descend on the mind. The magic of this island was unused, very different from the more experienced magic of a Hebridean island. Ideas started to stir. A month spent here would be an interesting educational experience. This led to questions. Was all this desire for movement merely an excuse to avoid thinking? Were we missing the point? We had maps of everything ahead of us, aerial photographs too; others had been this way before. Were we passing the time playing a hands-on computer game in real time in a sort of actual reality instead of trying to do something original? This island suggested there were unexplored territories on offer to a mind not preoccupied with movement. Intellectual vistas on the other side of the backdrop of the apparent scenery kept opening up for attention. This would never do; people were fidgeting and pacing about restlessly. We were getting nowhere fast. We must set off and at least try to accomplish something; otherwise we would have no story to tell, no slides to give a show with, no achievement to show our worth, no sense of fulfilment, no story to sell. As we loaded the boat, I had a wild urge to throw out a few foodboxes and say, 'Pick me up on your way back'. If I had, I might have done some original journeys into wild and wonderful new territory. It was very tempting to snatch such an opportunity for original exploration but, alas, I had not the strength of character to bring off so bold an act. I got into the boat reluctantly, the last to do so. I had to: I was supposed to be the leader.

Quinquereme of Nineveh

The south side of Ella Island presents a wall of near vertical rock rising straight from the sea for four thousand feet. A waterfall at its centre bounces once or twice on the way down. The rock looks good, a prize ascent for some lucky climber of the future. We sailed below it in a matronly fashion in an underpowered inflatable boat towing another smaller one behind and making about four knots. We were grossly overloaded with ration boxes crammed with food from half the world: pineapple from Hawaii, spices from the Indies, royal game soup from Fochabers; we had high-tech tents, sleeping bags of the finest feather and clothing of such oversophistication it was almost chic; we had jerry cans of refined fossil fuel and the complex engineering to transform it into movement; we also had a state-of-the art radio with which to talk to the world and a rifle to neutralise the local wildlife should it become too uppity. We chatted urbanely about the hundred and one exotic places we had visited at one time or another. We read sophisticated novels, some of us indulged in the affectation of playing liar dice to while away the time. From time to time we looked at the view through the portholes of our minds. And so we crawled along the foot of this beetling cliff like a caddis fly grub, our soft parts armoured against the world by a carapace of material and psychological comforts or, more vaingloriously, (and why not) we sailed like a quinquereme of Nineveh our five banks of oarsmen rowing rhythmically within our engine like genies in a bottle bearing us along with our cargo of apes and peacocks, cedarwood, sandalwood and sweet white wine.

Respect for Professionals

As you travel the empty coasts of northeast Greenland, you come across good camp sites and find that someone has been there before you. The most humbling of these relics are low walls of stone and turf with a lintelled doorway, the winter houses of an Inuit population that survived here for a few hundred years, dying out last century just as Europeans reached this area. Scoresby described their empty settlements. A small band was seen once in the middle of last century and then no more: maybe they were the last of a population that once numbered a few score, the maximum this bare land could support. These were the professionals, and one ought to tread deferentially in their empty homeland. Their minimal technology was of such a high standard that they were able to survive entirely on the thin resources of this indifferent land. The only import they had was driftwood from the Siberian rivers delivered by the sea currents. All other materials were of local origin: bone, skin, sinew and a stone or two. Even in what might pass as good times, Northeast Greenland is borderline survival country even for an Inuit band. It is a chastening and therefore beneficial exercise for the summer visitor to pause for a moment, and in his mind switch off the daylight and imagine the vulnerability of life here in the winter dark at the absolute zero of human ability to survive. An oil lamp under a low roof with a squalor of meat and blubber represented security for the foreseeable future. In this minimal condition, they created some sort of psychological home to protect their souls from the stark pressures of an uncertain, ungenerous land; they told stories, made jokes, sang songs, made poems, carved toys for their children. Sooner or later a hunter did not come back from the ice, and his dependants died, for in hard times the remaining hunters, if there were any in the area, could not take on the demands of someone else's widows and orphans. It was of no great moment anyway because death was only the process you had to go through before rejoining your ancestors in a generous hunting ground in the sky where their was no cold and hunger; such a place certainly existed, because those who had gone before held parties up there that were so wild they could be seen in this world below as the Northern

Lights. Or, then again, the dead might wander about in the cold moonlight, malicious and restless and envious of the living. More prosaically, premature death by accident or hunger depleted a dangerously small gene pool, so diminishing the ability of those remaining to cope with a borderline existence.

Nansen survived one winter in an underground house with a skin roof, but he shot enough animals in the Autumn to leave a pile of meat and blubber outside the door sufficient to last till Spring. Steffansson speaks of the 'friendly arctic'; he lived off the land for three years, but in a much more prosperous part of the Arctic than this. Both Nansen and Steffansson had guns, steel knives, matches and other locally irreplaceable artefacts. Also they had companions as resourceful as themselves who didn't get killed or incapacitated to leave the survivor frighteningly alone or, worse still, lethally burdened with an invalid. Most importantly, they didn't have families of vulnerable children to maintain; without these, individual survival is of no biological value. Mighty men though they were, they were essentially visitors from another planet living on imported psychological and material reserves. Our expedition, by these standards, was a summer holiday, or at best an educational tour for aging yuppies long past their arctic shelf life.

Play Boys of the Western World

We entered the shadows of Kaiser Franz Joseph's Fjord towards midnight. It is a lonely, forbidding place at this shadowy time, a narrow slit, steep-sided and filled with unstable icebergs calved from the glaciers at its head. The event I remember so clearly is the occasion Slesser and I had our turn in the small boat. Unloaded and powered by the spare outboard, it could get up on the plane and scoot around at ten or twelve knots. We did this occasionally as a relief from the sedate progress of the stately quinquereme. We skimmed away into the shadows and slalomed among the icebergs, which rocked decorously and dangerously in our wake. We paused a couple of miles away, on the smooth black water out of sight and sound of our material support. The bergs caught what little light remained and glowed spookily in the gloom, dimly teetering around their centres of buoyancy as the universe worked out the mathematics of whether they were going to topple into the here and now or remain ghostly metaphors of uncertainty. As we all know, there is a wild delight in voluntarily playing under the paw of the great cat, putting a toe over the line and imagining what it would be like to cross it without the possibility of coming back. We, of course, were playboys, and kept well on the safe side of the line. After frightening ourselves for a little while, we returned to the mother ship and rejoined our lumbering capsule of protective artefacts.

A Sense of Place

We emerged from the narrow part of the fjord into the broad waters at its head just as the light was improving. This is a magic time in the Arctic, and it coincided with reaching the inner sanctum of this mountain fastness. Awe is an unfashionable word, and it has lost most of its emotional charge from overuse. However, the feeling it used to describe is still to be experienced in places like this if you are that way inclined. Here there was space and silence, a wide sea filled with icebergs and reflections of icebergs, and all around were mountains of light and shadow and great valleys leading into a mysterious interior. Emotionally, it was a bit like crawling out of a window in your mind and finding yourself exposed on a high smooth face without a hold in sight while the mind rummaged around for a metaphor to chock into some crack to provide the semblance of security. I think the trouble was that we had passed a psychological barrier, and had entered territory not yet appropriated into our scheme of things. This was not a place you could walk back from, either on foot or in your mind. Maybe I was alone in this feeling, but I think the rest of the party was also a bit subdued.

Holiday Camp

Half a day after our arrival, we had tramped down a platform in the emptiness, and were well secured with psychological belays. Our tents were pitched on a sandy platform a hundred feet above the icebergs. The sun shone; there was no wind; it was very hot; we sunbathed in our underpants. It was a moment of detente before back-packing into the interior. Malcolm, always at home in the Arctic, lay around starkers reading a racy novel. Pat set up the radio aerial, and after unfankling a wandering muskox from its coils chatted urbanely to the Danes in Mestersvig; he also recorded the sweet twitterings of Horneman's redpoll. Phil tootled on his penny whistle, cogitating on his future. Roland remained quiet; he was lean, fit, and self-sufficient; he had no need to do anything else. I continued to investigate who was in charge of this remote area. Thus each of us was making a statement, some more amusingly than others.

The Room at the Top

One day, we did get to the topmost rocks of Petermann Peak by two routes of modest difficulty. It was a magic day of light and cloud shadows. We were on the highest point for 600 miles; it was all there below us: mountains and glaciers, receding eastward into the mysterious inland ice. This was the fourth ascent, but we were so bemused by all the ambience that we quite forgot to scrubble in the cairn for any record left by previous visitors. In order to achieve this remote position, we had exercised a fair amount of organising ability, physical effort, determination in the face of adversity and frank mountaineering competence. These virtues are already the stuff of a thousand climbing narratives, and their further consideration here would be boring. The uniqueness of our situation was that we had a special freedom denied to most other expeditions in the sense that we were self-financed. We had no need to do science, no need of success or disaster to enhance the sale of a book, no obligations to have something interesting happen to entertain future audiences with slide shows. There was untrammelled room at the top of this particular mountain, and the freedom to be conscious in the present without past or future strings.

The Scale of it All

We had travelled the 125 miles from Mestersvig to the head of our Fjord at an average speed of 4 to 5 knots. This is equivalent to putt-putting from Oban to say the head of Loch Torridon by the Sounds of Mull, Sleat and Raasay at a time when Scotland was emerging from the ice age. No human artefact would be lying around in this proto-Scotland except for maybe the ruined camps of some dead nomadic hunters who had arrived before the country was really open for business. The Staunings, like the Cuillins, rise straight from the sea, but are well over twice the height, and cover several times the area. The fjords were anything from two to twenty miles across; some were narrow passages with steep walls, others were bordered by rolling musk ox pastures. From the head of our Arctic Loch Torridon, we relayed food and equipment for 35 miles inland, say from Inveralligan to Beinn Mor Fannich elevated to three times its height. I am not telling you all this to solicit your admiration. This type of journey after all, if you watch your step, is a lot safer than driving from Blairgowrie to Glasgow. I think I'm trying to make myself realise what a high privilege it was to travel in this vast unpopulated wilderness.

The Hunting Band

The experience of being a member of a small free-travelling band of competent equals exploring new territory is satisfyingly atavistic. It is what the much-maligned male version of the human mind is good at. There are, alas, no longer any unknown oceans to navigate or Bering land bridges to be crossed into unpopulated worlds. Failing the real thing, we are driven to do something unusual requiring skill and nerve. It is apparently something to do with mate selection. To do something bold and original with a bit of violence thrown in shows you have plenty of biological reserves at your disposal and so demonstrates that you are the possessor of a genome with spare capacity for the competitive game of life. Some biologically aware female may therefore select you for matrimony, after which your biological competence is utilised for supplying the resources for raising a family of dynamic offspring. Thereafter, the demonstration of exploratory prowess for its own sake becomes socially taboo. The various substitutes on offer, such as driving a commercial opponent out of business or its somewhat more respectable analogue, namely, ram-raiding a shopping mall with a borrowed Range Rover, are both said to be pretty good, but they can't possibly be as satisfying as the real thing. The present journey through the wilderness of East Greenland with self-reliant companions was a homeopathically diluted version of the fulfilment of our basic design, and gave a vestigial feel of what the Real Thing must be like.

Our Particular Band

There were five in our band. None of us were hunters. We were all sophisticates of one kind or another. If we hunted at all, it was after involved metaphors that we associated with successful living. None of us were natural leaders, and none of us liked being led. Malcolm was the most experienced and widely travelled mountaineer of us all. He came nearest to being a natural leader. I suspect that the expedition was his idea. His major contribution was supplying energy and initiative, and if need be the quick thinking, competent action and reliability required in an emergency. The reason I was the leader was the result of losing the chess game in the opening stages of planning the expedition. Leading an expedition with my good friend Malcolm in it was a complicated business. Things had to be stratified into several levels with minimal intermixing. Occasionally leaks occurred. At one time I heard him remark with some irritation, 'There are decisions being taken in this expedition that I don't know about.' I have given up leading expeditions. It was not my metier. Oh yes, another of Malcolm's attributes was that he was a starter of interesting conversations.

Pat was a man of many talents. He hunted bird songs and was an internationally acclaimed recorder of birdsong. He was also technically competent in many other fields from tram-driving to falconry and a possessor of vast stores of arcane lore on a variety of subjects. Musically literate, he was an aficionado of Haydn quartets. On the downside, alas, he had lost the original lenses in both eyes due to cataract; nevertheless he drove sports cars and motorcycles and had retained his pilot's licence and was proficient in aerobatics. As an additional quaint paradox, he was the senior electrician of the Gas Board.

Roland, a Luxemburger, was a widely experienced mountaineer, wiry, superbly fit, and utterly competent. He was a scientist and an intellectual who wore his European learning lightly. A lone hunter, he flew aeroplanes, from microlights to his own up-market monoplane. In the former, specially adapted to carry a variety of sensors, he surveyed territory in third world countries, and in the latter went weekending from his home in North Italy to Crete and Malta.

Phil was a polymath mathematician with a wide range of skills and experience, and possessor of a fund of diverse learning from Beowulf to the literature of classical Greece. At the time, he was starting up his own software business in the States and his mind was preoccupied with working out the next crucial decisions in his life. He was wont to tootle pensively on his pennywhistle, producing semi-competent renderings of folk tunes. One day, Roland picked up the whistle and played exquisitely a fragment of

Mozart with all the twiddly bits. He then put the flute down and made no further comment. Phil seemed to miss the point and continued his tootlings unabashed. Malcolm, Pat and I were pushing sixty; Roland and Phil were in their thirties. Without them, we geriatrics would never have made it; they carried more, relayed more, and climbed a more difficult route on the mountain than the rest of us.

A sixth intended member, a friend of Malcolm's, who couldn't make it at the last moment, was the former Italian ambassador to Argentina during the Falkland's war. His presence would have enhanced the texture of the group by another magnitude. So we had to make do with what we had.

The Chocolate Mountain

On our return journey, we made a side trip along a sound running to the north into a curiously different landscape. Its western shore was dominated by ruined mountains shaped like ziggurats, the highest, the Devil's Castle, about four thousand feet; they presented a striking horizon when silhouetted against the setting sun. The other shore, the one we followed, was steep too, and made up of loose contorted strata of browns, yellows, and whites. Some of the strata were wavy and as thin as a biscuit; others were monstrous layers of flaky pastry. We reached a small bay on the east side of Ymir's Island, which marked a transition to a stepped hillside cradling little lochans in its treads. Above this stepped pedestal there was a mountain of chocolate coloured rock, steep but disintegrating. One of its hanging glaciers had pushed a steep frontal moraine of chocolate rock onto a grassy meadow; you could see the bright greensward disappearing under the rich brown jumbled blocks as if they had toppled on to the fresh green grass the day before. I showed a photograph to a world famous glaciologist who also found its origin mysterious. Whoever constructed this area had unconventional ideas about mountains.

Being here broadened the mind. This area was actually brilliantly original, a virtuoso performance in the art of orogeny, free of repetition and without a single orographic cliché.

The Iceberg in the Distance

We camped that night at the little bay, looking across to the many-banded ziggurat of the Devil's Castle on the opposite shore. The Sound was three miles across here. Maybe a score or two of icebergs were scattered around. If a big berg overturns, the wave it creates can be substantial, and in a narrow fjord its front is throttled by the walls, and a tsunami can flood thirty vertical feet up the shore. We were safe here in calm, wide, open water so we moored the big boat to the shore by its bow, keeping its stern out with an anchor. Nevertheless, from force of habit, we pulled the small boat twelve feet above high water. After supper, as we sat communing with the work of the Great Artist, one of the distant icebergs slowly keeled over and its new summit spire metronomed against the dark opposite shore. Thank goodness it was such a small one and so far away. So we could relax. Then there was a roar. Sound travels more slowly than light, of course. Then there was this wall of water coming at us. Help! Get the boat further up. We had moved it a few feet when the wave hit, carrying the boat still further up the shore. The bigger boat lifted its stern anchor off the sea floor, and gave a mighty twanging tug at its bow rope and then almost crashed against the bottom of the bay as the wave receded. That was the worst over; the subsequent tsunamis scaled themselves down progressively. It was only a small iceberg as icebergs go - about the size, say, of Edinburgh Castle, well at least the size of Stirling Castle, certainly as big as St Gile's Cathedral, and we were three or four miles away at, say, the bottom of Calton Hill or the Abbey Craig. If the berg had been a bit bigger and the tsunami correspondingly higher and more energetic we might have been bereft of everything, having to face the winter without even skin, bone or sinew, well not as bad as that, but we would have been very humbled by our carelessness, particularly if the magic, all-singing-all-dancing radio had been silenced. This was not a place you could walk back from.

Sunset Song

North of Ella Island, five sounds meet, and at the centre of their wide confluence is a flat looking island with a rounded hill on it. The map indicated its height was 530 metres. As we emerged into the confluence from Antarctic Sound on our way home, it looked like a good place to camp with a view point for an after dinner stroll. We approached over a calm sea amid lengthening shadows. The form of the island became more complex; the level base was a barren expanse of dark jumbled rock, the hump a fin of steep unstable slabs. The coast presented a line of low fractured cliffs with a few black sandy beaches. We landed on one and tried to break in to the interior. There was no level ground for a tent, only jumbled rocks. There was also an atmosphere of hostility. The place had an aura. This was one of these islands that didn't like to be visited, at least in its present mood. We coasted the southern shore to the far end where we found that the edge of the fin came down to the sea. We landed again in the shadows of a narrow strip of cold gloomy beach. I sensed that we were not welcome. Fortunately, we had people with us who were able to handle situations like this, and we began to climb the revolting unstable rocks. The beginning was a series of steep loose gullies. Perseverance lead us on to a ridge of stable rock which took us, by pleasant scrambling, to the top. We made it in under an hour; we were fit by now. The summit of this shadowy citadel was paradoxically a bright friendly place, like the top of an iceberg emerging into sunshine from gloomy submarine depths. We were above the horrors in a still evening of soft colours with the sun just about to descend below the northern horizon. It would take too long to describe the total experience: the colours, the silence, the feel of air so clear the furrows made by a family of eider ducks were clearly visible on the smooth sea far below, the mysterious Vega and Sofia Sounds leading easterly to the bear-prowled outer coast, the sunny unexplored northlands and the dark, sunless south whither we were bound.

We reached Ella Island later that night and rounded its eastern cape deep in the midnight gloom, feeling our way along the dim shoreline, bumping into a submerged rock with a resounding jolt but nothing worse. We camped at the head of a bay. A driftwood fire made a little globe of yellow light on the edge of the immense darkness to come. Thank God we didn't have to face a winter here using skin, bone and sinew to win sustenance from a bare land so far beyond everything that the Northern Lights flicker in the *southern* sky.

A few days later we were back in Scotland, one of the better-off residential estates of the world, living among intellectually well-to-do friends who weren't stuck for the odd sirloin steak and bottle of good claret. By and large, balancing this against that and taking one thing with another, it is really not all that bad being a playboy; there are worse belays on the Eigerwand of life.

High Noon

The heavy aroma of honey filled the summer air. The heather track with heaven in its wiles led to the summit cairn and I collapsed thankfully in the small shade cast by the mid-day sun. I had bread and cheese, a bottle of real ale and at that moment a tranquil mind. When this happens you have to seize the moment and enjoy it to the full. I lay quietly by the cairn simply appreciating my surroundings. I had spent all my life 'doing things'. I was now old enough to begin exploring the completely new dimension of just 'being'. An hour must have passed me by in gentle contemplation. Then I noticed a figure coming up the hillside from the east. You can't get away from people these days. A man clad in tweed knee britches and a white, loose-sleeved, open-necked shirt approached. His legs were bare and his feet were in leather brogues. He had a black waistcoat open down the front. As he reached the cairn I noted he had strong features and dark tousled hair. It took me a moment to recognize him as the eccentric wanderer I had met a couple of years ago on the Capel Mount, the man who had introduced himself as His Satanic Majesty.

"So it's you again, my friend.' I said without enthusiasm. I was in two minds about his re-appearance; he had been an interesting companion, but he had obviously tried to land me in mega-trouble with his mischievous Aston Martin ploy.

'Aye indeed, I am pleased to see you looking so well and enjoying the view', he replied.

'I can't say the same about you. Mind, last time we met you tried to trick me into accepting an Aston Martin of dubious provenance.'

He laughed and said, 'Och I kennt fine you wouldna fall for that ane,. I did it mair for your entertainment. You did say you kennt how to use a lang spoon. I just thocht I'd try you out. I saw the car when I was passing through Braedownie, and an Aston Martin DB5 was too good a cliché to miss. It was quite a story, and it turned out well by all accounts.'

Aye you're a richt ane, Your Majesty', I replied in my mother's tongue. I should explain that speaking to this man both he and I switched between Scots and Standard English. He explained to me why later in the day.

'So what brings the Prince of Darkness out into the bright sunshine of the high noon of a summer's day? What devious ploys have I to watch out for on this kingfisher day of innocent blue skies and fleecy clouds?

Och, on a day like this it maun be a truce. We'll just hae a blether and give the problems o the warld a miss.

'How can we with you here. *You* are the big problem screwing up the world. Your very purpose is to lead us astray.'

'Na, na laddie, I'm not a prime mover. I'm just a catalyst. I facilitate actions I don't initiate them.'

He reclined leisurely on the ground between me and the view. I had a good look at his feet; they were not cloven and there was definitely no hint of horns. His ears were perhaps slightly 'pointy'. He also cast a definite shadow. He caught my wandering eye and obviously guessed what was going through my mind. He gave a chuckle.

'No, I am not wearing my regalia. That's only for the gullible minds of halflings. We two are beyond such juvenilia. Remember we're grown ups.'

'Okay. So tell me more about Predestination and Freewill. Last time we met you inferred they were the eternal battle between our two basic programs.'

'Do you really want to talk about that dreich subject on a bonnie day like this?'

'Yes, I don't see you everyday and you are the first person I've ever heard talking sense about the subject even if you are the de'il himself.'

'Aye, man, you're a fair glutton for punishment.', he responded.' But I suppose I should feel flattered that you find my opinions so informative.'

'Well it is your special subject isn't it? Who would know more about damnation than yourself?'

'Aye, true enough. Well let's get on with it.' He lay back with his head pillowed on his knapsack looking at the sky. His eyes were heather coloured, matching the green, brown, purple mixture of his tweed britches.

'The battle between our two programs you say. If you want to put it so starkly we can't proceed very far; it's the wrong metaphor. '

'Well, you said that Predestination was the way the hard-wired core program in our brain drives us to survive and Freewill was the control exerted by our superabundant signal processing power. That's sounds like a battle.'

'Its not a battle, it's more like a rider on a spirited horse, The horse is wilful, has a mind of its own and is intent on survival; that's your core program; these circuits permeate all parts of your brain. They run the internal economy of your body and try to ensure your future. You are in the grip of that predestination whether you like it or not.'

'And the rider?'

'The rider is confused and emotional and only dimly aware that he or she is on a horse and anyway only crudely understands the principles of horse control. Over the years schools of equestrianism have evolved that have tried to control the horse. But the horse is very, very experienced and worldly wise. It was there long ages before we acquired our superabundant signal processing systems. The horse is intelligent and has learned to control both the rider and his teachers.'

'So you are saying that the schools of equestrianism are the various religions and philosophical systems, and the horse is our self interest guiding the rider and his mentors in the way the horse wants to go.'

'Well it's a metaphor and a metaphor is never exact because it is a representation, it is not the same as the thing it is trying to model. Nevertheless, it takes us into murky depths of some of the fundamental verities.'

'"Murky depths", now that really sounds like the territory of the Prince of Darkness. This should be interesting. You must be good when you are on your "subject"; it's too hot here in the midday sun. Let's go for a canter in the land of shades.'

'Man, ye're a hopeless romantic; you're expecting fire and brimstone and de'ils wi' horns and forky tailies. It's not going to be like that. Your core program doesn't understand romance; it is ruthlessly practical '

'You mean red in tooth and claw?.'

He looked at me despairingly,

'That's a romantic cliché'.

'But surely violence is involved somewhere?'

'You have been reading too many cheap novels, my friend.'

He paused and gave me a searching look.

' I am not sure you're up to this.', he continued. 'It isn't going to be what you expect; you may be fell disappointed at what I'm going to tell you. You may even have to *think*.'

'As a last resort, I'm wiling to try even that.'

'Hold tight then we're going for a brisk gallop through some very flat country; its not going to be what you expect'

'Leese me on, dainty Davy,'

He smiled at the reference

'Your core program', he began, 'keeps you going from minute to minute, day to day and down the long sequence of generations – yesterday, today and tomorrow. Basically it is concerned with preventing you from falling apart.'

'Eh?

'You have heard of the Laws of Thermodynamics, I hope?'

'Ye-e-e-e-s,' I replied slowly, wondering what he was getting at. 'What's that got to do with your core program, with survival using tooth and claw?'

'Everything.'

'Oh come on, the Laws of Thermodynamics are abstruse physical laws. They are arcane concepts that can only be understood by the hyper-intelligent. I've forgotten what they are, if I ever knew, and I'm surviving okay. What have they got to do with real life?'

'Everything, my friend. Forget Predestination and Damnation – immature concepts both particularly if you spell them with a capital letter - we are about to explore the dark territory giving rise to real life.'

He paused, or I should say 'reined in' to sustain the metaphor. Then, as it were, he shook the reins and started off again.

'Life broke the Second Law of Thermodynamics - that was the Fall from Grace that theologians go on about. Breaking the Second Law is *the* fundamental Fact of Life; unless you break it you can't live. By breaking this fundamental Law life committed *the* Original Sin and the penalty for that, of course, is Death.'

'Please, my devious friend, we were getting on so well and now you throw me this wobbly. What, may I ask, is the connection between our core program and the Second Law? I don't find it obvious. Remind me about the Second Law.'

"It's simple; it merely points out that to create an ordered system you need to put in energy and to maintain that order you need a continuous input of energy or it will fall apart. A simple example is your living room. If you don't put effort into tidying it up all the time it gets progressively disordered. The Universe is a giant room becoming progressively disordered. One day it will run down into a uniform state of minimal order carrying us with it.'

'That's a gross oversimplification surely. You shouldn't listen to what scientists tell you. They are an airy-fairy lot. That's just one of their speculations; it could be wrong.'

'It's not only scientists who have this opinion; Theologians agree, too.'

'Och away, they don't know anything about thermodynamics.'

'No, but they read the Bible.'

'The Bible approves of thermodynamics?'

'Yes, most definitely; remember the verse from Isaiah:

"*Every valley shall be exalted and every mountain and hill laid low,*

The crooked straight and the rough places plane."

That's a fairly succinct statement of the Second Law of Thermodynamics. The Bible is talking about everything running down to a uniform zero degrees Kelvin where order is minimal and uniform. You couldn't get a more authoritative or unequivocal seal of approval than that. The Second Law is a statement that is biblically orthodox. It couldn't be revealed to Isaiah in terms of thermodynamics. He wouldn't have had the conceptual vocabulary to know what God was going on about. God, it seems to me, was trying to get through to the good prophet that the Laws of Thermodynamics were His Laws and we had better get on with learning to live within them.'

I was trying to voice an objection, but he anticipated me.

'You are going to say, " The devil can cite scripture for his own purpose."

'Well, yes, something like that. It sounds like a quotation. Where does it come from?'

'You learned it at school when you did the Merchant of Venice' it's a "get out clause" that some theologians find useful when they encounter alternative interpretations.'

At this point, I remembered the night class I had attended on Shakespeare's sonnets.

I had been particularly impressed by one of them and had tried to learn it by heart. A few lines of it came to me at that moment. and I quoted :

. *"Oh, how can summer's honey breath hold out*

Against the wreckful siege of battering days

When rocks impregnable are not so stout

Nor gates of steel so strong but time decays."

Is that not a memorable statement of the Second Law, as you call it?'

'Weel done my friend,' said his Majesty. For a moment he seemed almost impressed.

'We are making progress.'

'So we have it on High Authority, the Bible and the Bard, no less, that the universe is running down according to the Second Law of Thermodynamics. Where do we go from there? What's it got to do with day to day life?'

'Living systems are made of ordered matter and highly complex ones at that. Life sustains an ordered living room as it were by continuously going against the Second Law. To do this it must acquire and expend energy. If the energy supply ceases, disorder commences. We refer to this as decay and death.

Your core program delays this event by organising the acquisition of energy from outside and supervises its conversion into useful energy within your body to keep your systems from falling apart. It signals hunger and thirst. You have to eat and drink. You can't eat sand and gravel. So animals like us have to acquire energy from other living things by eating them. Living animals have to eat. It's all a bit sordid. Plants are a bit better; they can sustain themselves by using radiant energy directly from the sun.

He paused to brush away some annoying flies that were circling us in the noon-day heat before continuing.

'The curse that living things incur for breaking the Second Law is the need to consume energy; and worse still, to compete for it. Competition is the ineradicable root of all Evil, something we all have to live with.'

He suddenly lost interest and stood up in one easy movement.

'I think that is enough darkness. Let's go back to the here and now and enjoy this fine sunny day while summer's honey breath still holds out.'

'But what about all the other things you mentioned – the Fall from Grace, Original Sin, Death and Damnation and all that? I'd like to know more.'

'They're just metaphors, metaphors and still more metaphors extending over the far horizon for ever and forever when we think. It doesn't make any difference to them whether you spell them with Capital Letters or not. At any rate it would be an original sin to waste a day like this in the dark dungeons of dodgy theology. Look, man, we are on a hillside in the most beautiful country in the world on a fair day of high summer. Let's take the cash in hand. We can continue our discussion on these dismal subjects some other time.'

He held out his hand and pulled me to my feet.

'This is a day for activity. I'll race you back down to the road.'

'You're on', I replied.

We ran down through the heather, through the scent of honey, raising clouds of pollen with each bound. About half way down he stopped.

'This is hallowed ground.' He said, indicating a stone. 'This is where Chris Guthrie died. And the tumbled ruin just below there - that was her wee bit croft house.'

We stood for a moment in silence; then he meditated aloud:

'So this is why we talk back and forth in the Scots tongue and the standard English we learned at school. We straddle the two, speaking neither the one nor the other. Remember Chris's soliloquy in Sunset Song when she is thinking of the speech of her parents: *"...you wanted the words they'd known and used.... Scots words to tell to your heart ....and the next minute that passed from you, you were English, back in the English words so sharp and clean and true – for a while, for a while, till they slid so smooth from your throat you knew they could never say anything that was worth the saying at all."*

But cheer up. This is just another of the facts of life. Language is shifting sand. Every generation straddles two languages: the speech of their parents and the speech they acquire as adults. You have retained some of your mother's tongue and so still have access to a vocabulary and a rich heritage of meaning lost to contemporary monoglotts. But even you and I in our present conversation are changing. Our pure vowels are becoming stretched and the good hard consonants are softening. Your children have less of the old speech and their's will have even less. That is the way of it. Written English is becoming like Chinese logograms.'

'Eh? How do you explain that?' He had a habit of veering off in tangents like this.

'Written Chinese', he explained, 'is the same for the two mutually incomprehensible languages of Mandarin and Cantonese. The same ideograms are pronounced differently.'

So?

Well, take the simple word "now", you tend to say "noo" using your lips whereas someone from the Thames estuary would say neh-ow and send it backwards up through the nose achieving a remarkable nasal triphthong. Both are correct in the sense that they are considered normal on the banks of the Tay or the Thames and, after a bit of thought, can be mutually understood. The same could not be said for spoken Aberdonian and Afro-Caribbean; they might be written the same but the spoken versions would need the services of a translator just as monoglott speakers of Cantonese and Mandarin. This is why it is important to keep a standard spelling of English words so that in the future the increasingly different dialects of English can be understood at least at the written level.'

He paused and then said, 'according to the stories you hear about me, I am supposed to be leading you down the paths that lead to intellectual degradation. Instead, you keep making me explain fundamental truths and pushing you intellectually uphill. You are a bad influence on me rather than the other way about. Enough of this.' he concluded, 'I'll see you at the foot of the hill.'

He bounded off. I followed. I was determined to overtake him but he reached the car park several yards ahead of me.

When I recovered my breath, I offered him a lift.

'Na, na my trusty fiere, I hae my ain horse here'

Parked next to my car was a brightly painted Harley Davidson.

'That's yours?'

'Indeed it is', he said, tying a red silk bandana round his curly hair.

'But that's a terrible cliché for a man of your stature. It's so undignified after the deep things we have been talking about. Can't the Prince of Darkness manage a real horse?'

He gave me a heather-coloured look.

'We have been talking metaphors all day. This is just another, this is a metaphorse. This is a juvenile subroutine in your brain. It's what you would like to have had when you were young. You just didn't have the chance.'

I looked crestfallen.

I'll come with a real horse one day if that's what you'd prefer.'

'You're a hell of a man, Nicholas'

'You never said a truer word, my friend. Is there anything I can do for you before I leave?

He paused for a moment with a half smile on his lips.

'Seeing you like clichés, could I fix you up with a nymphette, a succubus, maybe? You could give your core program a little gallop.'

With a mischievous chuckle, he started his machine, did a wheelie – quite a trick on a Harley Davidson – and was off down the road with the tails of his red bandana streaming in the wind.

The rest of the people in the carpark were obviously impressed by all this. Some of them were attractive queans, all plump and strapping in their 'teens. I basked in the reflected glory of my friend's flamboyant departure. I am sure I was the focus of a few 'come hither' looks. Mindful of the Aston Martin episode I climbed into my unfashionable car, gave the temptresses a cheerful wave and departed decorously.

I was left with so many unanswered questions. He had opened up so many vistas.

I hoped he'd appear again; he did make a sort of half promise. However he was not infallible. Chris Guthrie died on the Barmekin of Echt and not on the Tap o' Noth. I was one up on him there.

A Note on the Icebergs of Scoresby Sound

Icebergs are architectural wonders, things of exquisite beauty that use up lots of photographic film. In inner Scoresby Sound, broad glaciers descending from the central icecap reach the sea where large areas of ice more than a kilometre square float off complete with crevasses and moraines, ancient wrinkled parts of the Inland Ice that have embarked on their retirement cruise. It can take a long time to travel past one in a small boat. Such deeply crevassed plateau bergs subdivide over the years, and each piece is in its turn sculpted by wave, wind and sun. Admiring an individual iceberg is one thing, but travelling through a spacious city of them forty miles across in a small boat is awe-inspiring, in the old meaning of that term. An iceberg city is best experienced in the silence and reflections of a flat calm and is different at each time of day: in the first light it is austere and sharp, at high noon its buildings shimmer and hover, in the evening its grand boulevards are magnificent in the rich light, and at mid-night its ghostly cathedrals brood over black water.

Although I have never experienced it, my friend Professor Malcolm Slesser assures me that the ultimate aesthetic experience is to drive your own dog team through the frozen streets of such a metropolis in winter when the moon is high in the sky and ice crystals are a-twinkle. It is a different experience in bad weather. To travel among icebergs the size of a house heaving up and down in a heavy swell in mist, drizzle and wind is intimidating, but not dangerous, unless like the Titanic, you are going at 30 knots in a white out. Generally, life among icebergs is a lot less perilous than driving up the A9, or along many a winding highland road on a Saturday night.

If you are travelling through a summer city of icebergs, however, there are practical things you should keep in mind. Most of an iceberg is underwater, like an ice cube in a glass of gin and tonic.

They are therefore more subject to the grip of the dense sea than the less substantial air. When wind and tide move in opposite directions, the grip of the sea pulls the iceberg through the wind. This configuration is intimidating, but it at least provides a lee in the berg's wake for a boat to shelter in. When both wind and tide are in the same direction the berg moves with the tide and the bow wave is small, being generated only by the forward motion provided by the wind. Nevertheless, the boatman must precede the berg's advance with equal step. Since a berg may not be going in the required direction, exposure to the wind when crossing a fjord can be minimised by dodging from the lee of one berg to that of the next. One of the more terrifying configurations is a mixture of close pack ice and icebergs, since they move at different rates. If the tidal current pulls the berg though the slower moving pack, its bow wave compresses the ice in front of it, causing floes to override each other while in its wake the pack swirls around, filling up the empty space. No one in their right mind would voluntarily get mixed up in a situation in which so many variables were operating. Once, we did enter a narrow band of icebergs and close pack in a running tide. We wanted to reach the shore. It didn't seem all that far away. We were tired, and that is, of course, when you make mistakes. We had enough judgment left to get out once we realised the moving geometry was too complex to predict. The forces involved were huge and intimidating. In real life, the shortest distance between two points is seldom a straight line. However these are worst case conditions, and easily avoided unless you are given to travelling in straight lines.

Because they have a deep keel, icebergs are inherently stable. Some of them have given good ice-climbs to those who require that extra frisson. However, they are subject to differential melting by the sun above and the sea below, and at the waterline they are deeply undercut by wave erosion. On a hot day, streams of meltwater hollow out lines of weakness. Thus, from time to time a berg may split, releasing energy commensurate with the mass falling off.

Thereafter there is a period of uncertainty as the berg readjusts to a new centre of buoyancy. It may elegantly lean over a few degrees so that its former undercut waterline now runs obliquely or, very occasionally, the whole edifice may turn turtle. Sometimes a capsize or disintegration is brought about when a tide-driven berg travelling at several knots hits a rock, or the sea bottom. Bergs have enormous mass, so even when moving slowly they have a lot of momentum. The sudden loss of even a little speed triggers a massive release of energy, which can damage the internal structure of the berg and cause it to disintegrate. Since many bergs are as big as Ailsa Craig or the Bass Rock, such a collision can be an impressive sight. On the other hand, I have seen a berg with an above-water part the size of a small house disintegrate into a pile of rubble without a collision. It happened in a little bay one warm afternoon. The berg must have built up complex internal tensions until no more could be accommodated, and this set off a train of collapses. It spent the afternoon leisurely cracking itself to bits in the sunshine. Since bergs are usually going in the same direction, they seldom collide. I have only once seen a collision between big bergs. On this occasion, the leading berg was halted by hitting the seabed, and the following one hit it amidships at three or four knots. Nothing much happened on that occasion except some turbulence and a lot of rocking around as the two bergs bowed apologetically to each other before floating off to their separate destinies. This is obviously the origin of the 'clashing rocks' of classical literature. Far-travelling Phoenician traders of the Bronze Age, if they did not actually get north into iceberg territory, must have picked up the story from the locals along the western seaboard of Europe. It is too good a story not to incorporate into the 'improved' version of any tale of derring-do. In the last ice age, one the most spectacular sights in Scotland must have been watching the big bergs spawned from the Great Glen Glacier twirling and waltzing through the Corrievrechan on a flood tide. There is no equivalent race in the present Arctic tidal system.

Although there are plenty of islands and a fair tidal range, nothing like the Corrievrechan has been reported in Greenland. Perhaps the suitable channels lack overfalls, or are too deep to impede the tidal flow.

A berg is most dangerous to the ordinary coastal traveller if it sheds a piece in a narrow fjord. In this configuration, the waves hit the shore before they have lost much energy. A wave can mount high up a cliff or spread inland on a low coast further than you would expect. In open water, the waves from an isolated berg travel a long distance without losing much energy. They are no problem if you meet them away from the shore. When they hit the land they are still travelling fast and rapidly lose momentum as they encounter friction from the shore. They then become disorganised and turbulent. Some of their energy may be dissipated in wrecking a camp or boat drawn up on the beach. It is a matter of indifference to the wave what it does since, like us, it is blindly obeying laws it does not really understand. On two occasions when an iceberg calved a couple of miles away, we have been surprised at the size of the wave that reached us.

If there are a lot of other icebergs around, they baffle the waves and the energy from even a massive collapse may not be propagated far. Pack ice is even better at damping waves. You are fairly safe if there is a lot of ice around, but protecting ice floes may drift away during the night and leave your campsite exposed. The rule is: choose a landing in unconstricted water, and haul the boat further up the shore than you think necessary on driftwood rollers if you can find them. This is hard work if there is only two of you. We found a light weight winch and pulley system helpful on these occasions. It is also wise to take as much of your gear even further up the shore than you think sensible. Once we were glad of being over-prudent when a wave came in much higher than we would ever have predicted. It was a worst case scenario: high spring tide, a strong onshore wind, and a solitary berg shedding a piece the size of a double garage. The danger lies, as always, in getting negligent. If, as is most likely, nothing happens for weeks, or even at all, you think, 'Why bother?' This is the time to remember the First Law of Statistics, namely that once you use up your good statistics, only the dud ones are left and therefore extra care is necessary. The dud statistics will get you in the end, but there is no point in making it easy for them.

Pack ice is frozen winter sea broken up by wind and tide during spring and summer, and is less dangerous than icebergs, but more of a navigational problem. The polar pack, formed over decades and centuries, is brought down from the northern ocean by the East Greenland Current that flows south all year long at up to eight knots. Polar ice floes even as far south as the southern tip of Greenland can be several acres in area, and can provide a temporary refuge for a boat small enough to be drawn up out of the water. The problem is that the floe may take you somewhere you do not wish to go, and if the pack closes in a stormy sea, one floe may over-ride another. All in all, the outer coast is no place for a small boat. Fjord pack is local ice; it is thinner and younger and can be intermixed with fragments of ruined icebergs. In the outer coast, the two mix and the tides can bring polar pack into the outer Fjords and create an interesting range of textures. In the inner coast, open pack damps down the waves and small boat navigation is safer. The lee sides of big floes provide sheltered harbours in their scalloped edges. Close pack, on the other hand, prevents small boat travel or makes it painfully slow. Yet it is surprising what can be done to open up channels. One man standing on a floe exerting continual pressure by leaning on an oar on another floe can cause two massive pieces of ice to move gradually apart. We have had to do this several times, mostly out of impatience, but once from necessity. We also used to have a theory that there would always be an open lead along the shore where it was too shallow for the ice to reach, but we found from experience with an on-shore wind, even a minimal ribbon of free water is eliminated.

The 'proper' way of travelling these coastal regions is by kayak. You may go slower, but you see and feel more and, most importantly, you travel silently and look 'right'. A kayak can be hauled onto an ice floe or carried up the shore. You sleep better at night when you know your boat is safe. A kayaking lifestyle is elegant, but not suited to carrying the amount of equipment required for mountaineering, which has different priorities. Greenland is still the equivalent of an uninhabited, barely discovered Chamonix., replete with first ascents and new routes. A practical expedition will cough up money and go in by air, either by ski plane or helicopter, and so avoid the time-consuming hazards of coastal travel.

If you must waste valuable time by going in by boat, and there are no local boats available, then the ideal craft for getting somewhere quickly with all your climbing gear is a rigid-hulled inflatable. They seem immune to ice damage, whereas a wooden boat needs to be protected by metal sheeting. The next essential is a motor powerful enough to get a boat loaded with two weeks food and fuel up on the plane. To be really comfortable travelling at this speed, you need a boat with a cockpit and windscreen as well as a decent survival suit. Slaloming among ice floes at 20 knots out in the wild blue yonder is very juvenile, but very enjoyable. More practically, speed means safety as it allows you to pass dangerous places quickly. It also gives more time ashore for exploring. The alternative is to chug along in a slow underpowered, but more fuel efficient boat which is cold and tedious, and you spend more time travelling and less among the mountains. The downside of fast travel is that a powerful motor drinks a lot of fuel. A RIB four metres long can only carry so much and still get up on the plane. Fuel, food, a spare engine, camping and mountaineering equipment for a two to three week trip allows only two of a crew. Two people travelling alone in one boat has little safety margin. A lot of muscle power is required to empty a boat and then haul it up on the beach particularly on a windy lee shore, and if you encounter some dud statistics and one man gets disabled, it may be impossible to get a boat back in the water. The safest and most versatile combination for a small party is two small rigid hull inflatables among a party of four. This provides four people for hauling boats up one at a time. Only one spare motor need be taken, and in these days of easy radio communication the two boats can separate without losing contact. The spare motor is essential; if the main motor fails, paddling a RIB for a hundred miles would be a weary exercise.

During the last few decades I have found the miles have become longer, the mountains higher and the force of gravity considerably greater. In a way this has been a liberation. Once you are freed from the categorical imperative of ascending some worthy peak, logistics are simpler and you are free to enjoy the unique feature of Greenland - its colourful coast with so many curious geological formations, broad valleys, flowery tundras, big skies, far horizons and, of course, icebergs of every shape and size all bright and glittering in the smokeless air.

Autumn Glory

I didn't expect to see my infernal friend for another couple of years, but he turned up again two months later. I had been for a walk through the woods of the Ballochbuie. On the way back to my car, I stopped on the Old Brig of Invercauld and lent on the parapet.

The autumn colours were in full splendour; fortunes in gold coin hung from the tresses of the pendular birch trees, standing out bright against the dark pines. The sunlight shimmered on the chuckling waters of the Dee. It was almost as good as a picture on broad screen, high definition TV with surround sound. The only things missing from this ideal in your living room would have been the hot sun and the scent of pine resin wafted on a gentle breeze, but these defects could have been remedied by a sun-lamp, an aerosol and a fan. However, on this occasion I had to make do with banal reality.

Then I saw him coming from the Invercauld side. He was dressed much as before, except he wore a broad blue bonnet. Neither of us spoke. We shook hands and lent companionably over the parapet together with the sun at our backs lighting up the waters and woodland.

Eventually I said 'I thought you couldn't cross running water?'

'Neither I can but I can win as far as the keystane o the brig. You'll note I'm still on the Invercauld side. It is important to observe the conventions.' he said with a smile.

'So what's the topic of our discussion today', I asked.

'You choose,'

'I'd like to know more about all that disintegration and death you were talking about last time; they were the penalties for breaking one of the fundamental laws of the Universe, I think you said.'

'You humans are strange cattle. Why on earth leave a Paradise like this?' He paused for a moment, indicating the surrounding autumn gold. 'Summer's lease hath all too short a date – it's already gone – and yet you want to enter the nether regions of disintegration and death?'

'You mean standing here on the old brig o Invercauld is Paradise?'

'Yes, you won't get much closer to it than this. Think about it for a moment. You are healthy and free and well-fed. Best of all, you are aware of your surroundings and able to generate and enjoy such an advanced concept as beauty.'

He paused, looking at me with what I thought was compassion.

'But I keep forgetting your superabundant circuitry generates complexities. It leads you to leave any Garden of Eden you happen to be in and seek to understand what is going on. For some reason you like to call this inherent curiosity the knowledge of Good and Evil.'

'Yes, but that's because you are here. It's your job isn't it to tempt me with the apple?'

'No, that is the fundamental dereliction of responsibility at the heart of all Abrahamic theology. It is not me or the serpent who tempts you. It is *you* humans who can't help asking, yea, actively demanding, the apple. No one is tempting you. It is a property of your superabundant circuitry that it demands knowledge. Saying you are being tempted by the devil is like a wee boy being caught with an apple he has stolen and saying, "Please sir, it wasnae me. It was a big boy who made me take it and then ran away."

I just wish you would grow up a bit and give up blaming us devils.'

Then after a pause he continued,

'However, as your Evil Genius,' he bowed courteously, if a little wearily, 'I suppose I must lead you on, since it is your wish. But I am only doing it reluctantly and at your direct request.'

'Yes, tell me more about our original sin of breaking the second law of thermodynamics. I'll try to be my age and accept that I am voluntarily requesting this knowledge. I understand it is a consequence of having too much brain.'

'Good, now we can make progress.'

We lent over the parapet of the old bridge, one of us on each side of the keystone and watched the Dee running eastwards to the sea. He took that as his theme,

'Imagine the universe as a great turbulent river of matter flowing down to a state of minimal order, a river with many back eddies where the current swirls from time to time and goes in the other direction generating order. Life arose in one these back eddies. The retrograde surge which produced life configured a chemistry that was capable of utilising energy to replicate itself.

Nicholas paused considerately while my mind grappled with the metaphor of a turbulent river of matter swirling down the time dimension to a sea of tranquillity where energy was uniform, matter evenly distributed, and molecular jiggling minimal. I imagined a back eddy maintaining its position relative to the downward surge of a mighty universe. Such back eddies were sites where energy was used to create order out of less organised matter.

Okay, please proceed. I said eventually.

'Life,' he continued, 'is a molecular configuration able to maintain itself by harnessing energy. It can even edge its way upstream against the river of increasing disorder that is the ambient universe. By "edging its way upstream" I mean it generates and replicates systems of increasing order and complexity. It is a retrograde energy wave with a ruffled crest like the subdividing margin of a Mandelbrot Set.

'What in the name of the wee man is a Mandelbrot Set? '

'It's only a metaphor', replied my friend. It's defined as a set of points on a complex plane that has a fractal boundary, and before you ask, a fractal boundary is a surface generated by some repeated process involving successive subdivisions. Life is such a "repeated process involving successive subdivisions". Life is a system in which some of the material of the universe is organised in such a way that it can extract energy from its surroundings and use it to replicate and diversify its original organisation. The fractal edge of the standing wave of life is the wild frontier of evolution; it's where all the action is. It is distinguished by each small part of the crest, before it dies, harnessing more energy from the ambient universe to generate and diversify replacement systems of increasing orders of complexity – evolution is, I think, the appropriate term. Like a standing wave, we living things remain in position while eroding time passes us by. It's quite an achievement!'

'Are you trying to say that the crest of the wave is the place where the "Word is made Flesh? "'

'Yes, you could put it that way.' Then he smiled and said,

'It's obviously not only the Devil who can cite scripture when it suits him'

"I do beg your pardon,' I apologised, 'I didn't mean to usurp your prerogative.'

'It's not my prerogative. Misuse of scripture is difficult to avoid. It's mostly metaphor, and consequently capable of several interpretations. It's easy to break the laws of religion – people kill each other every day - often for frankly religious reasons, but no one has yet broken any of the laws of thermodynamics. A successful perpetual motion machine has yet to be built.

But that is enough. The decision I am making for you here and now as your Evil Genius is to enjoy the present; I can't imagine things getting any better for you than just now.'

We returned from the interior of our heads to the banks of Dee, to the sound waves generated by waves of water flowing over the bright stones of its irregular bed and the light waves reflected from the multifaceted trees, boulders, and waters of the ambient world through which the silver Dee flowed to the sea. Our superabundant circuitry, without being asked, converted all these signals into a coherent pattern and generated the curious state of being aware. I was about to ask him about this when he raised his arms to embrace the autumn glory that surrounded us. I was expecting some important revelatory announcement but all he said was,

'Time to adjourn!'

We walked back towards the parking place provided by Invercauld Estate at the reasonable rate of £2 a time.

The tension had relaxed, and I felt free to be a little flippant.

'Is it your Harley Davidson again?

'Aye, my conveyance is there. I've even bought a parking ticket.'

Conveyance? You mean you have something different? What kind of eccentric steed have you got to impress me this time? A chariot of fire?'

'Wait and see.'

The park was quite full. Next to my car was one of these three-wheeled motor bikes with the raked front wheel and handlebars. It was floridly coloured in sinuous red, yellow and black stripes simulating flames; this chariot of fire was attracting quite a bit of attention.

'You do overdo things', I chided him.

'Och man, remember I'm just your wish fulfilment.'

He unlocked a box at the back and took out what looked like a winged Darth Vader helmet and black cloak.

He doffed his blue bonnet and handed it to me with a bow

'We'll meet again my friend. We get on well; we can travel a lang gait together. Maybe next time I'll come for you on a horse. Just now my insurance doesn't cover a passenger, so I can't offer you a lift.'

We shook hands; he donned his winged helmet and mounted his machine.

'Aren't you offering me the usual farewell temptation?'

Och man, I thought you and I were getting beyond sic theatricals, but if you wish I could arrange for a bag of gold or a million or two in banknotes to appear in the boot of your car.'

'No, no', I said hurriedly. I don't have money-laundering skills. I would have to open a Fish and Chip Restaurant to recycle all that wealth. No thank you, I have more to do with my time than cope with unexplained wealth.'

He gave me an approving big-brotherly look.

'You are a gleg loon right enough. You are becoming a worthy companion. We shall meet again - unless you have some unexpected encounter with the Second Law and undergo terminal disintegration.'

He started his far-out machine, and left in a cloud of stoor with his cloak billowing behind him. I could hear him stop at the main road – he had already said how important it was to observe the conventions. He must have turned east because the sound of his engine died away in the direction of Ballater.

The people standing around were obviously mightily impressed, and once again I basked in the reflected glory while wearing his blue bonnet.

I checked the boot of my car to see if he had double-crossed me, and sure enough there was a pile of bright gold coins there. They weren't of metal; they were autumn birch leaves. I didn't put them there. My friend Nicholas obviously had a sense of humour, the devil.

So that was that. However, when they emptied the money from the parking ticket machine the next day, they found two solid gold merks from the reign of James IV accurately adjusted to the size of one pound coins. It was all a big mystery. There were a few learned letters about it in the Aberdeen Press and Journal.

I.H.M. Smart

Back Where we Came From

Okay, so this is not mountaineering but it is the origin of our climbing skills and is thus of some antiquarian interest even to modern climbers. Tree climbing can be regarded as a refresher course in what life was like in the good old days before the trendy smart Alecs (who are always with us) started to walk about on the ground. As if that wasn't enough they evolved bigger brains and we, their descendants, became more and more sophisticated and forgetful of our origins.

The trees are still there and we have retained a lot of the original adaptations still lodged dormant in our deep programming. We can still climb trees quite well. If I had anything to do with it, it would be a condition of Club membership for applicants to have climbed at least one tree of an acceptable standard in the year prior to their application to show their versatility and sense of historical continuity. Alas, if I ever brought up such a proposal at the AGM everyone would think I'd lost my marbles. Be all that as it may, I have had some interesting experiences among the branches of our arboreal homeland; here are a few of them.

Avenue of Beeches

The drive up to the Big Hoose has ten copper beech trees along its north side. They are very special beeches in that they have produced a profusion of branches radiating from a short central trunk. Not for them the conventional straight pillar and huge canopy of the majestic classic giants; these eccentrics have explored the format of a giant bush

My favourite in the row is the second one. Struggle through the first branches then you lose sight of the ground and become a denizen of the tree.

In the spring of the year the leaves are soft and bright green and the tree's interior is filled with a green glow. It is a bit like the Mallorm trees that Tolkien describes in the land of the Elves. A climb of maybe thirty feet of moderate standard takes you to the crown. It is an agreeable experience to emerge from the summit of its canopy of whispering leaves into the blue dome of heaven.

In summer when the leaves turn copper the mood is different. The mature leaves are paper hard and flutter rather than whisper in the wind and the contrast between the dark copper-green shades of the inner tree and the heaven above is even more dramatic.

Best of all is to climb it on a starry winter's night after the leaves have been blown away in the autumn gales. At such a time the wild wind sings in her bare branches and her dark tresses are full of diamonds. It's quite an experience.

Swinging Birches

Robert Frost has a poem that begins:

> *When I see birches bend to left and right*
>
> *Across the lines of straighter, darker trees*
>
> *I like to think some boy's been swinging them.*

Until I read this poem I had never thought of swinging a birch tree. One day on a visit from my friend Stewart McGavin, a fellow Frost aficionado, we decided to do some research on the topic. As explained in the poem the technique is to select a sapling with a single trunk sturdy enough to bear your weight almost to the top. When it starts to bend maybe twenty feet above the ground, you grip the narrow stem with both hands and launch yourself into space. After a moment of free flight, the good birch tree lowers you gently to the ground and on release springs back up again. At the time of this research project there were a number of suitable saplings near our house, We spent a happy morning swinging from heaven to earth from a couple of dozen youthful birches. We found this experience in practical poetry, exhilarating and very satisfying. It didn't seem to do the supple birches any harm. Fifty years on they are still straight and graceful whereas Stewart and I are bent and painfully stiff.

In and out the dusky bluebells

According to Katherine Briggs in her "Dictionary of Fairies" you have to be careful travelling through woods at night. Oak and willow woods are particularly dangerous. Oaks, as befits their ancient, god-like status, bitterly resent being cut and an oak coppice springing from the roots of a felled oak wood is malevolent and dangerous to travel through at night , "*more especially if it is a blue bell wood.*"

I have never traversed a coppiced oak wood in the dark but I have walked through an un-coppiced wood carpeted with bluebells in the dusk; there is one quite near us.

I have a form of colour vision deficiency in which in poor light, I lose the low energy radiations of the greens and reds so that in the gloaming only the high energy blue radiations trigger the cones in my retina, In fading daylight blues continue to glow in the gathering dusk; it is quite an eerie effect. People with normal vision retain greens and reds for longer and have a more balanced rendering of colour even in poor light. They must miss the spooky effect of blue lamps glowing in the dusk.

D.H. Lawrence probably had a similarly diminished ability to transduce the lower energy light waves to judge from his poem 'Bavarian Gentians'. In this well-known poem he goes on about gentians being:

> *Torch flowers of the blue smoking darkness, Pluto's dark-blue haze*
>
> *black lamps from the halls of Dis, burning dark blue*
>
> *giving off darkness, blue darkness……*

He was obviously highly strung and blue gentians in the dusk must have spooked him mightily. At the end of the poem he wanders off with one in his hand down the path into Pluto's dark kingdom in search of Persephone, a metaphor for his lost youth and innocence.

In the wood I am talking about, however, the mood was soft and gentle, under the benediction of subtle Aphrodite, goddess of immanent beauty, rather than Pluto, king of the dread dungeons of lost time.

Creepy willows muttering in the darkness

Willows, according to Katherine Briggs, are even more sinister. These trees, it is said, have a habit of uprooting themselves on a dark night and following a solitary traveller, muttering. The fact that they 'mutter' gives the story a hint of authenticity – who would invent the idea of a willow tree following behind you 'muttering' unless they had actually heard one do it?.

I once encountered a willow wood in the deep dusk when we were late off the hill and lost the path. There was, indeed a lot of malevolent muttering following behind me and the noise of something that could have been roots being withdrawn from mud. It was of course, my companion whose progress was impeded by bog and wilfully obstructive willow scrub. The trees didn't have to bother doing anything, except get in the way.

Lonesome Larch in the Moonlight

About a mile from our house high on a bare hillside there is an isolated larch tree. It is a lucky tree to have survived on a heathery hill patrolled by sheep cattle, deer, rabbits and sundry small rodents - or else it enjoys some sort of protection. It must have been a sapling when the great gale that demolished the Tay Bridge felled the rest of Persey Wood. It is not one of those straight up and down things, that have grown up imprisoned in a plantation, nor is it a bush, like the beeches lower down near the house. It is a free tree that has made it on its own, surviving for more than a hundred years, full half a mile from its nearest neighbour. It is now about fifty feet tall and has many branches, supporting a spreading canopy; its sturdy roots grip the solid bedrock of its homeland - a sound survival strategy for both man and tree.

To get onto its lowest branch is a severe move. From there on the route is moderate; its branches toughened by many winter storms are robust enough to take you to the very top and give you a panoramic view from the Cairnwell at the top of Glenshee to the Sidlaws on the other side of fair Strathmore. I have climbed it in all seasons of the year and times of day. Most memorably I was up there one midnight, under the light of a Hunter's Moon, shining high in a clear sky. The air was still and frost crystals were a-twinkle in the silence. Scarves of mist wound among the dark evergreens surrounding the hidden loch a hundred feet below. Then, three swans glided in from the north like ghosts and disappeared among the trees, presumably to land on the loch. It is possible that I was the only person in all the broad lands of the fair Kingdom of Scotland who was thirty feet up a tree on that particular night appreciating a very 'Private Viewing' – not in an oversophisticated Art Gallery but at a True Showing of the Real Thing. Any attempt to record it in pigment or pixels would have caused the equivalent of a collapse of the wave function: it would have changed from direct sensual magic to Gothic bathos.

The anatomy of brachiation

After all that it would be best to end up on a practical note of some relevance to modern climbing to which this Journal is dedicated. Tree climbing offers all the usual rock-climbing moves of traverse, mantelshelf and overhang.. In some trees you can actually brachiate. I don't know if you have ever looked at the anatomy of the shoulder girdle but if you raise your arm above your head and observe the muscular configuration in a mirror you will see your muscles converge around your oxter as a hollow half cone with its base attached to your trunk and its apex around the shoulder joint. The original function of our upper limb in this position was to provide a dynamic pendulum for swinging from branch to branch. It's a very efficient means of locomotion as you use the momentum of the gravity-assisted downward swing to propel you on the upswing. It is only a few million years since we were really good at brachiating. We have almost lost the knack after so many generations spent running along the ground. Were it not so our corridors would have bars along the ceiling and we would swing along with a fraction of the effort of walking; even better if we had retained a prehensile tail. Nevertheless, the ancestral memories are still there somewhere in our deep programming. Modern gymnasts have retrieved these old routines and by constant practice have taken them to fantoush lengths of ballet-like precision. An intellectual ape would be astonished at the extraordinary routines performed at the Olympics, but would be dismayed by the pointlessness of their predictability and the amount of repetitive practice required for their perfection. Conversely gymnasts wouldn't be much good at traversing the variability of the holds on offer in the jungle.

Principles and practice of brachiation in rock climbing

Brachiation hasn't much of a role in rock climbing, since to brachiate successfully the next hold must be visible and sufficient to provide a fulcrum for the next swing and once embarked on, the move cannot be cancelled. Also you are more or less compelled to swing with your body facing the rock and your head turned to identify the hold you are hoping to grip in the very near future. I am sure I remember doing a manoeuvre like that once or twice somewhere or other. A special application of the brachiation principle is the pendulum at the end of a rope, like the famous King Swing on the nose of El Cap in Yosemite. In this case you build up momentum gradually by adding velocity as you run up and down the increasing segment of a circle whose radius is the length of the rope. With persistence you reach a hold high on the far side of a smooth slab. The trick is to reverse quickly at the end of each run when your momentum is momentarily zero. At this crucial point it is necessary to keep tension on the rope and start running back down to build up momentum again; otherwise you will enter free fall and be struck like a match against sand paper. There is a possibility of transferring this technique to tree climbing à la Tarzan. Lianas, as used by our hero, are not features of Scottish woodlands but could be replaced by a doubled rope looped over a branch sticking out towards the next tree, near enough to reach it when you swing. It's unlikely to catch on if you will forgive the pun. But no doubt if it does, the first tree crossing of Scotland without touching the ground will be a notable achievement.

Keeping in the swing

There is a tree near our house where you can do simple brachiation relatively safely because the suitable branches are near the ground.. Starting high up you can jump for a lower branch and swing onwards to catch another at the same height and swing onwards to do it once again. In this case it is easy because the elastic recoil of each branch helps you on your way and gives you a moment of free floating 'air time' and a brief sensation of what life was like in the good old days. On one occasion when I was sure no one was looking or within earshot I beat my chest and gave a Tarzan call before swinging on my way. But all that was long ago when I was emotionally immature and as elastic as the branches. Even then I couldn't have gone on for very long. The arms get tired of living in the past.

I.H.M. Smart

By the Way

One fine day in June 2003 I was walking through the oak woods on the lower slopes of Ben Airidh Charr. My intention was to trace the old postman's path that ran along the lochside in the elder days from Ardlair to Letterewe. It was warm work travelling across the grain of the country. About noon I stopped for a rest under a spreading oak shading a pleasant patch of greensward. In the restful shade, I set out my lunch of bread, cheese and honey – a meal of ancient simplicity still on sale in village shops. After half an hour I started reluctantly to get ready to go on. On a hot day like this it would have made more sense to drowse away the afternoon in the dappled shade playing with the tangles of Neaera's hair. In spite of this sensible call to sun-dappled slumber, I continued to put the remnants of lunch back into my rucksack. The Protestant Work Ethic is strong. Unless you are actually doing something all the time, preferably something difficult, you feel you are failing in some way. It's a terrible curse; I have been fighting it all my life. Suddenly over a few seconds the air became colder and I felt a friendly presence. I looked up and there was a twelve-year old sitting on a branch swinging her legs in the air. She was dressed in some sort of mossy green gossamer.

'Hello,' she said, 'why are you in such a hurry?'

I thought she must be some child playing at make believe. How did she get to this remote place all by herself? I decided to make a run for it. It doesn't do for an old man to be alone in a wood with a twelve year old. I could already see the newspaper headlines: "Elderly beast molests child in lonely wood."

I looked at my watch. 'I'm late.' I said, 'I must get going.' I started to hurry, stuffing things willy-nilly into my rucksack.

'Don't go', she said 'I haven't talked to anyone for years and years.'

She seemed older, more serious than a romantic child, consequently probably more, rather than less, dangerous. She might be a professional nymphette with her lawyer hidden in a nearby bush. We live in terrible times. Nevertheless, I don't like being rude, so rather than get my things together in silence I asked, 'Where did you come from?'

'Nowhere, I live here.'

'Where? Up there in that tree? Do you have a house or a nest up there?'

'No I live right here within the tree, you daftie.'

I ransacked my mind for something else to say while I put more things in my pack. I decided to play along.

'You must be a tree spirit – a dryad, perhaps?'

'No, as it happens I'm a hamadryad'

'Is there a difference?'

'Yes, I am part of the tree. I live in this tree all the time.' She patted the branch affectionately. 'Dryads are free to wander around. We hamadryads are stuck in one tree for its life span.

I was silent; I am quite out of my depth with loonies, particularly loony children.

'Well say something' she said. 'Tell me your name?'

I wasn't going to fall for that one. Once they had your name you were done for. If she was real her lawyer would use it to identify me and if she was a genuine tree spirit she would have power over me. The latter is a well-known fact. I have read about it in books.

I changed the subject. 'Aren't you lonely up there all by yourself?'

'No, the trees are good company and I chat to the other hamadryads. We network through the interlocking root systems of our trees. We are always in touch. We often have parties and when there is a wind we sing together.'

I didn't reply

'What's wrong with you people,' she asked, 'haven't you anything interesting to say?'

'I am sorry', I replied 'I'm just not used to chatting with supernatural beings.'

'I am not supernatural. I am entirely natural. I am made from the same material as the tree and the same material as you. We're all based on carbon chemistry. It's not too difficult for me to emerge from my tree from time to time. I just re-configure some of the material of the tree to clothe my spirit and use some of its moss for a dress. All hamadryads can do it. I have forgotten the details of the theory behind it but I know it's something to do with managing probability.'

'Probability is something that can be managed?' I queried in some surprise.

'Yes, didn't' you know that? You must have heard of quantum tunnelling, surely? You know an electron has only a probability of being at any particular place.'

'Well yes, but that only applies to electrons in the subatomic world - not to big molecules out here in the real macro world.'

'Well put it this way: from your point of view it is very improbable that part of a tree can come out and re-assemble itself into a likeness of a hamadryad.'

'The likelihood is vanishingly small', I agreed. It was getting very wearing having this heavy conversation with a ken-it-all *enfant savant.* It was a ridiculous scene. There I was on my knees with my half-packed rucksack before me being lectured on nuclear physics and probability theory by a hamadryad sitting airily on a branch of her oak tree.

'Well,' she continued, 'if you know how to manage probability it's easy to make what you would call improbable things happen. I am using the technique we were all taught when we became hamadryads. Like everything else manipulating probability needs energy. You must have noticed that before I came out the tree the atmosphere was quite sultry and now it is cool and fresh. The cooling results from my mobilisation of energy from our surroundings to configure my present form. It's easier to do on hot windless days like this: there is more ambient heat energy around. Even so, I can't keep up maintaining this improbable state for long. So let's get on with our conversation. How old are you?'

'Almost eighty.'

'Almost eighty! Gosh, you humans don't wear very well. I'm over twice your age. It's a hundred and sixty years since my tree and I were an acorn. My tree can probably do the same again before old age really sets in. I don't age fortunately. I'll just get another acorn from somewhere when my tree's time comes.'

'Does every tree have a hamadryad?'

'I think so, all the trees in this wood do, at any rate.'

'Where are they?'

'They're still in their trees. No point in them coming out. You are under my tree. You belong to me for the moment! But they are listening to us.'

'What puzzles me I said is how a hamadryad speaks Academic Scots with an Edinburgh accent?'

'Because that's the way you speak. Before you noticed me I tested you for Gaelic but without sufficient response so I had to lapse into your speech.'

This child seemed to have all the answers. I changed tack again.

'You say you all can sing when the wind blows?'

'Yes we just adjust the angles of incidence our leaves make with the wind.'

'You mean you can control the leaves like reeds in a wind instrument?'

'Yes, why not? We are the original woodwinds, after all. What's more, our singing doesn't have stupid arrangements like beats to the bar. Millions of leaves precisely adjusted to the wind generate complex harmonics. Our melodies are huge and our rhythms immense. Your music by comparison is like a bird fluttering in a cage. It can't escape for the bars. "Beats to the bar" is a terrible concept; it is equivalent to corporal punishment. I think it comes from the way you have of writing music down. Before that your music was free. The pipers, in the old days knew how to play in the free way. That was when tunes were passed on from piper to piper by ear and each tune had its genealogy. Traditional pipers still say, " I got this tune from . . . . and he got it from . . . ." and so on back to the tune's origin. The old music was much more sensitive to the great natural rhythms of wind, sea and running water. If music is to respond to these elemental forces it can't be imprisoned in a cage, however golden. Such sophistication leads to deafness and too much sophistication to stone deafness. Everyone knows that.'

Then changing to something less intellectually demanding (I think she noticed I was struggling), she said.

'But usually we only sing at night.'

'Only at night? Why?'

'Because during the day the leaves are adjusted to catch the radiant energy from sunbeams. This has priority. The trees need energy to grow. But on a good sunny day there are plenty of spare leaves and we do a bit of daylight singing. But at night we have all the leaves to play with; we are a massed choir. Well worth hearing. If we get a decent wind at the next full moon we are having a big concert. We have been rehearsing for months. We expect a lot of dryads will visit us. As I explained they are free to move around. I am on the waiting list to become a dryad', she added.

'What do you sing about?'

'Different things, it depends on the wind and the mood we are in. In gentle breezes we do lovely sussurating lullabies, in boisterous weather we do the equivalent of strathspeys and reels and in a full gale we do jigs and headlong gallops. We also do serious stuff, praising whoever it is who runs the universe – equivalent to your hymns and oratorios - during storms we usually do a paean. In winter when our leaves have fallen our bare branches are more like a stringed instrument. We can't adjust them so the wind plays its own music. We learn some interesting things from the wind when the breezes whisper through our branches.'

'You know, I have always suspected something like this was going on', I said. 'I will listen more carefully in future. Tell me do you appear to everyone who rests beneath your tree?'

'No, of course not. As I have explained it takes a lot of energy to come out and talk. Usually it's not worth the effort. You just looked less dozy than most humans so I decided to give you a whirl.'

'Have I been a disappointment?'

'So-so. At least you haven't run away screaming like some of them and you seem to be interested in our singing, which is something. Now look, I can't keep this up any longer. I see my leaves are beginning to droop. I have only a minute or two left. Tell me something interesting. Quick.'

'All I can say is I find the world a much better place now that I know for sure that hamadryads actually exist and trees can sing and some pipers are still playing the real un-caged music. I will listen more carefully in future'

'Well, if I've managed to pass on that message, the effort of materialising has been worth it. Goodbye now.'

She faded and a couple of handfuls of moss floated down from where she had been sitting. I carefully replaced the moss on the branch in case she needed it again sometime.

But that is all by the way. What I am really trying to tell you about is the postman's path form Kinlochewe to Letterewe along the side of Loch Maree. The ground is steep and rough and at times precipitous right down to the waterside. The path is not obvious; it offers multiple choices with unavoidable detours both up and down. By mid-afternoon I had drifted fairly high on an intermediary ridge. I was probably sitting at the very place where on another June day exactly 200years ago the writer, poet and shepherd James Hogg of Ettrick paused on his journey in the opposite direction. His party had been driven similarly high by the lie of the land. He looked back towards Letterewe and saw

'. . . . a lady of most delicate form and elegantly dressed . . . . climbing over the dizzy precipices in a retrograde direction, and after fixing one foot, hanging by both hands until she could find a small hold for the other.'

This spirited lady who understood the elements of rockclimbing, was a Miss Jane Downie, daughter of the Manse of Urray near Dingwall. She was on her way to the Lewes to visit relatives. She, Hogg and two locals had tried to row down the loch from Letterewe but had to give up because of the head wind. Leaving the boat they had continued on foot into the teeth of the wind. Hogg goes on,

'[Her] clothes were partly torn and otherwise abused, and the wind had carried off her kerchief altogether. For upwards of a mile we were forced to scramble in this manner, making use of all fours . . . '

He continues,

'I was in the greatest distress on account of the lady. The wind which had grown extremely rough took such impression on her clothes, that I was really apprehensive that it would carry her off, and looked back several times with terror for fear that I should see her flying headlong toward the lake like a swan.'

Miss Downie was an accomplished lady.

'Being the daughter of a respected clergyman, she had received a genteel education, a circumstance to which the utmost attention is paid by all families of rank in the north. To this she added a extensive knowledge of the world, of which she had seen a considerable part for one of her age and sex, for besides her acquaintance with both the Highlands and the Lowlands, she had resided some years in St. Petersburgh with a sister, who was there distinguished by royal favour and protection.'

After this 200 year old, wind-buffeted foursome had passed by I felt a sense of anticlimax. I could see the rest of the route to Letterewe - miles and miles of repetitive, tree-clad ups and downs. On a day like this when the sky was blue and visibility only limited by the curve of the earth's surface, it would be more interesting to wander among the breezes of the upper air exploring the summit ridges of sunlit Beinn Airidh Charr.

It was the right choice. What a view point! Don't take fright – I am not going to describe it to you as it deserves, but I must record the blue of the lochs in the brown heathlands and away to the west the blue-grey patterned sea edged by the Long Island and leaving Gairloch was a boat with a brown sail – probably bound for the Lewes with Miss Jane Downie aboard.

The day was still young so I descended into the complicated territory on the north side and identified the main feature, a steep buttress rising to the summit where Glover and Ling had made a Diff route in 1910. In that year Osgood Mackemzie must have been an active stripling of sixty six busily engaged in building the celebrated garden on the once barren peninsula next to Inverewe. The Ling-Glover duo were not the first to climb these rocks. Osgood mentions that when he was '*not more than seven or eight years old*' the sea eagles nested on

'*that stupendous precipice at the back of Beinn Airidh Charr just above Carn nan Uamhag (the Cairn of the small Caves) – that wonderful cairn and stronghold of foxes and wildcats where the last of our marten's was killed.*

He continues on his deplorable expedition to raid the sea eagle's nest,

'*. . away we went on pony back with an expert rockclimber and ropes etc.*' So rock climbing using a ropes etc has a long history in the Gairloch area. For a minute or two I watched the young master and his retinue of family retainers on their shaggy ponies picking their way along the path to the bottom of the crag. I could see the gillie reaching the nest of the distraught sea eagle and removing the eggs to gratify the eight year old son of the laird.

I also tried to find the site of the first recorded traverse of the summit crag. It was made long ago by a shepherdess looking for the spindle she had let fall from the summit. She fell to her death, alas. I didn't investigate too closely; she might still have been there and in a chatty mood. I had had enough epiphanies for one day.

I.H.M. Smart

Red Fly the Banners Oh!

We climb in the spirit of our times. At present we live in a Golden Age. Climbing shops are Aladdin's Caves full of shining metal and brightly coloured nylon. Climbing gear, camping gear, and clothing are wonders of intelligent design. Climbing standards have reached stratospheric heights of excellence. The whole world is accessible to people of modest incomes. I once heard some of our members discussing the possibility of climbing Mount Kenya in a long weekend from Edinburgh. I remember leaving my home in Glen Shee about lunchtime and the next evening standing on a remote peak in East Greenland watching the sun set briefly behind a jagged row of northern peaks with my ski tracks leading to a comfortable camp on a snowfield far below. My friend Phil Todd standing beside me had also flown over the day before from his home in Oregon on the far Pacific shore. Nearer home, my granddaughter has to have all her gear; ropes, slings, karabiners etc in matching colours.

It was not always so. I write of the years of the mid forties spanning the last years of WW2 and the beginning of the Cold War. During this time, Russia became morally dominant and the extension of Communism seemed imminent. Russia and its leader Stalin were idolised and idealised by many in the industrialised West and in the emerging post-colonial countries of Asia and Africa. The great fear was that the Americans might use 'The Bomb' if Russia attempted to overthrow Capitalism in the small part of Europe west of the Iron Curtain. I remember people saying with fearful awe that the Communists had learned how to 'change human nature'. Top of the Pops was the Red Army Choir singing loud and vigorous renderings of stirring songs. In comparison, the Rolling Stones would register less than the half droop on the virility indicator and the Beatles would seem soft and self-indulgent and ideologically immature, if not, frankly decadent. It is only against this backdrop that the events described below are plausible.

Glencoe by lamplight

This episode must have taken place in the middle of the war. We were in Glencoe Youth Hostel. It was a winter night. About a dozen and a half young boys were in the common room; we were all below military age. The smell of beans and dried egg still lingered after the frugal supper. The room was lit by tilley lamps; electric light was not yet with us. A group of seven or eight lads sat together at one end. They were engaged in serious talk. The rest of the room gradually fell silent as the group broadcast their earnest conversation to engage our attention. They told of the new world to come after the war. They were members of a Young Workers Mountaineering Club from somewhere in the Glasgow area. I remember watching with the fearful awe of an outsider in the presence of dedicated believers. They had hope and a frightening idealism. They talked of the dictatorship of the proletariat that would be established after the war, and how the working class would be released from bondage; their vision was of education, intellectual advance and high endeavour, not booze and free-loading on the broo. They were not unfriendly, far from it. But they did glance at the rest of us, implying that this was the new reality; it was coming and we had better adapt to it. Stalin and the USSR were models of a workers' republic. They would liberate the whole of Europe, and after the war there would be a Soviet world of working class unity in which the nation state would wither away.

They sang a lot of songs. One I can still remember. Instead of 'Green Grow the Rashes' it was a rousing, 'Red Fly the Banners-oh'

Five for the years of the five-year plan

And four for the four years taken,

Three, three the rights of man,

Two, two a mans own hands,

Working for his living-oh,

One is workers' unity

And ever more shall be so.

Another had the chorus line:

With every propeller

Roarrrring "Red Front!"

In defence of the USSR!

We crouched behind our paper-thin copies of RLS and Frank Smythe as these songs were followed by the inspiring sound of the Internationale and the Red Flag passing over our heads. I knew that if the workers' republic ever came to pass I was doomed. Not because I was against a fair society – an educated population was what civilization was all about - but in the one they offered there would be no room for solitary seekers; individualism would be classified as deviationism, and suppressed for the good of the community. It was this need to conform that struck an icicle into the heart.

The next morning we climbed up the path to Binnein nam Bian in shabby clothes and sub-standard hobnailed boots. We clumped through the snow on the final slope without rope or ice axe. At one time, we saw the vanguard of the proletariat silhouetted against the skyline of the Aonach Eagach on the opposite side of the glen. As far as dress and equipment were concerned, we and they were indistinguishable. We were all shabby, under-equipped mountaineers. They were, if anything, more affluent than we were; they had jobs and an income however small; we were still at school, and dependent on our cash-strapped parents. Even so, between us there was a deep glen of incompatibility. If only we could have suppressed our desire to explore by ourselves, we could have joined their band of hope and marched in the vanguard of a reforming movement singing rousing songs. People who won't follow a leader have always been a problem.

Ben Alder Cottage

In Ben Alder cottage, I encountered intellectually tougher Communists as reported above ("An Encounter with Gramsci"). They had guns, and one had fought in the Spanish Civil War. In their conversation, there were quotes from Marx and Lenin and it was there I first heard the word 'dialectic' used in argument. I never understood what it meant. At any rate I felt an empathy with these robust exponents of the great ideal; they were worldly wise and serious but this was tempered by humour and an agreeable gallusness. I felt at home with them, perhaps because they went out on the hill in ones and twos and fished by the lochside alone. Their type of Soviet Scotland might not have been at all bad.

Playboy of the Western World

My first visit to the Alps was with early versions of Malcolm Slesser and Geoff Dutton. It was just after the war, probably in the summer of 1947. We were inexperienced and overawed by the scale of the Swiss Alps. It was quite a challenge even to get to Switzerland. Money was short, tickets were hard to get; they had to be bought in advance in London. Malcolm's sister, who lived there, queued for them. They were the size of a pamphlet, printed on low quality brown paper. After the dinginess and frugality of war-ravaged Britain and France we entered undamaged Switzerland where food was abundant – except we didn't have money to buy much of it. We climbed the Fiescherhorn and the Wetterhorn and then ran out of Swiss francs and we had to return.

I stopped off in Paris and stayed at something called a Camp Volant - about a dozen old army tents pitched on a bombed site. The address I remember was 8, rue Barbet de Jouy, somewhere near the Musée Rodin. For a small sum you got a camp bed, a well used blanket and breakfast of a single tin cup of curious flat coffee and a piece of dry bread. In the evening, a simple one-plate meal was served. We sat around trestle tables lit by hanging kerosene lanterns and ate beans and bread and cheese. I think you could buy 'coffee' as an extra.

The other people at my table that night were young intellectual communists; they were students; none were working class. They, too, assumed that Capitalism was doomed; it was just a matter of knocking away a few rotting props and the whole shoddy edifice would come tumbling down and socialist republics modelled on the Soviet Union would bring, justice, education, self-respect and honourable employment to all.

The man opposite me was a young Englishman complete with beard and spectacles who exuded moral superiority with a quiet matter-of-fact scholarliness. He had practical experience; he had spent the summer working on the Yugoslav Youth Railway. In this project, young idealists from all over Europe had assembled to help build a rail track somewhere in Bosnia. Each morning they marched off to work singing rousing songs. (Those members old enough to remember Len Lovat singing 'La Bandiera Rossa' will recall how rousing these songs were.) From such seeds a new socialist Europe would grow, the man opposite me declared. I kept quiet. I felt like a spoilt brat, a playboy who had been scrambling in the Alps while European youth were resisting the re-establishment of the yolk of monopoly capitalism and the tyranny of the military-industrial complex. The group of left wing intellectuals at the table came from half a dozen countries. They seemed less abrasive, less aggressive than the bright-eyed singers in Glencoe; they were intellectual by-standers who were witnessing the inevitable; they felt no need to man the barricades. But once again I felt out of it. I could have climbed the Fiescherhorn any old year, but the Yugoslav Youth Railway was an unrepeatable moment in history. A few years ago, I met by chance in a bothy, someone who had actually worked on the railway. He had shared a barrack with Austrians and Palestinians. On the wall he distinctly remembered a slogan reading: 'Long Live Arab-Jewish Anti-Imperialist Unity.'

The spirit didn't last. The professional priests and politicians couldn't allow power to slip out of their hands and they had to re-exert religious and political differences; their futures depended on exploiting these divisions. The politicians were on a loser since they promised heaven on earth. The religious authoritarians won because they were more astute; they very sensibly promised heaven after death and, unlike the politicians, have yet to be proved wrong.

The sunny side of the street

About the same time, I encountered idealists working from the other side of the social order. I was an instructor one Easter in one of the first mountaineering courses run by the Central Council of Physical Recreation. Its acronym CCPR was not too different from USSR in Cyrillic lettering, but there the similarity ended. We were based in the luxury of the Cairngorm Hotel in Aviemore – war-worn Glenmore Lodge had yet to be renovated. We went by lorry each morning along the dirt road from Coylum Bridge to Loch Morlich, then by footpath to Coire an t-Sneachda or Craig Calaman. Many luminaries graced the course. Frank Spencer Chapman of Arctic and Malayan war fame spoke of facing down adversity by sheer force of character. Prunella Stack an attractive, athletic, up-market lady who was a leader in the Health and Beauty movement spoke of a healthy mind in a healthy body; I have experienced this combination myself from time to time for short periods and she was quite right, it really is a very agreeable state. Noel Odell, the last man to see Mallory and Irvine on their way up Everest, was there, and I had the honour of climbing a route in a Coire of Braeriach with him. He cut the most enormous steps even on relatively easy ground, obviously mindful of the train of porters coming up behind. One day I went out with Lord Malcolm Douglas Hamilton. He feared Britain was in imminent danger of becoming a left wing dictatorship. As we trudged up the path through the old Caledonian forest, he explained how it was quite likely that within the next few weeks, Aneurin Bevin would mastermind a coup, seize parliament and the radio stations, and declare a Socialist Republic. The Daily Worker would replace the Times and public schooling would mean just that. It was all maybe a little paranoid but in the context of the time, not entirely implausible.

Epilogue

In the event, it was the Sun and the Mail that replaced the Daily Worker and the Times as the most widely read and influential papers in the land. The Internationale that united the human race and caused the nation state to wither away was a global market in which everything was for sale and international boundaries were archaic impediments to maximising profit. Nevertheless, feral Capitalism, for all its faults, encouraged inventiveness and individuality. Inventiveness in the mountaineering market has generated affordable equipment of astonishing ingenuity and sophistication beyond the wildest dreams of the gas-cape-clad denizens of the mid forties, carrying their cotton tents with separate groundsheets in heavy ex-army Bergen rucksacks. Individualism has flourished as never before, as is evident in the pages of our Journal.

Under a Soviet system an off-beat organization like the SMC, full of difficult people who won't do what they are told and don't like being led, would not have been allowed; the present membership would have been sent off to the Gulag for re-education as a job lot. Ironically we would probably have found the Creagh Dhu already there, as even worse examples of incorrigible individualism. Unless, of course, as is not unlikely, they had finessed the situation and were actually running the place, in which case they might extend a kindly tolerance to those of us who could climb above hard VS.

One day, runaway Capitalism will collapse under the weight of its internal contradictions and drown in its own excrement. Before this unhappy terminal event, we have great opportunities for travel to all the world's mountain ranges. We can catch the night train from Beijing to the Forbidden City of Lhasa where we can erect our tent in the municipal campsite. We can also do it all in greater safety than before. With our GPS's we can now find out exactly where we are and, if we do get into difficulties, we can use our mobile phones to summon a helicopter. If we ever get lost, now we can be found. Truly an Amazing Grace! It's all too good to miss. Let's get on with surfing the present wave of prosperity with all the originality we can muster .... before it hits the beach, that is.

Crossroads at Midnight

I was driving to my home in darkest Perthshire from Glasgow late at night after a social evening that had gone well. The conversation had been good and I had left my friend's house too late. Once the bright lights of the energy expensive towns lay behind me, life became restful. I discovered it was a fine frosty night - no wind, with a waning moon making the hoary fields glow silver grey; an occasional wreath of mist drifted here and there shepherded by the prevailing variations of temperature and humidity. I turned off the A9 at Bankfoot and just after Stewart Towers my headlights started to dim and the engine suffered the equivalent of a massive stroke. The alternator had failed. The sparkplugs no longer fired and the refined fossil fuel in the cylinders no longer ignited. The half ton of sophisticated engineering I was driving became a slowing lump of metal I had enough momentum to reach a place where I could come to rest on a grassy patch just off the road.

So that was that. This was in the days before I had a mobile phone, so the only thing to do was to walk to the nearest phone box, which, I guessed, would be at Meikleour, some ten miles away. Breakdowns like this occur from time to time and have to be coped with…

It was a fine night for a walk and I had a pair of boots in the back. So, I decided I would go cross country to Meikelour. The ground was crisp with hoar frost and easy to walk over. At one stage I followed a forestry track and came to a crossroads where I tried to work out the optimum route. I could see the North Star and the Great Bear, so I was sure of my bearings. None of the roads, however, seemed to be going in the right direction. I was trying to come to a decision when I heard hoof beats in the distance. Who on earth was out and about on a spooky night like this? Usually horses are confined to fields with dominant women making them jump over obstacles. This rider must be some oddball romantic whose vision went beyond dressage and rosettes. I waited expectantly. In a few minutes, a horse approached at a canter from the south. It resolved itself into a big black beast with a man on its back. It slowed when he saw me and I recognized the rider as my old friend: the Prince of Darkness. The horse snorted impressively, and its breath steamed in the frosty air.

'Its you again,' I exclaimed.

'Yes , indeed. Why are you surprised? It's midnight at a lonely crossroads under a waning moon. Who did you expect? A bossy girl from the riding stables?'

'Well, this is all a bit of a cliché.', I said indicating the black horse and the silver studded harness gleaming in the moonlight. 'You haven't missed a detail.'

'Yes, of course I knew you would see through it, but I thought you'd appreciate the effort I've made.'

'I do indeed. I have always wanted to meet the devil at a crossroads at midnight. I never thought it would actually happen.'

'Well it has now, so make the most of it. I'll give you a hand up behind.'

'You're sure you won't gallop off to the nether regions with me?'

'Oh grow up, man. Dinna be sae blate. I'm a figment of your imagination, remember.'

'Maybe so, but that horse looks solid enough and I can see it has left real hoof prints in the frost.'

'Aye, of course. You did hear hoof beats did you not? If my horse's hooves hadn't been solid and hit the ground, the air wouldn't have vibrated and sent sound waves ahead of me. I would have been a ghostly apparition and frightened you out of your wits.'

'Well, you are not doing badly as it is. Okay, man, I'll tak a chance.'

'Good for you. When we met last summer we had a metaphorical gallop through the underworld. This is the real thing I promised you. Gie's your hand, man, and I'll heist ye up ahint me. We'll hae a grand gallop through time and tide. The hour approaches we maun ride!'

And so we set off through a world of shades of silver and black like a photographic negative - now there's a good metaphor for reversal of the perceived world. We galloped under the starlight through dark-dappled woods and over silver fields. We skelpit on through dub and mire in the howe dumb deid o' the cauld hairst nicht, louping easily over fences, stanks and logs fallen tapselteerie across our path. The horse knew what it was doing but was yet responsive to the directions of my friend. At one stage His Majesty turned and remarked,

'Now this is what our superabundant circuitry can do when we learn to control the wild horse of our core program. Our superabundant circuitry can make all the radiations we receive from the world around us into something original and exciting.'

We continued at speed until we reached the old brig of Kinclaven. He pulled up at the threshold and we both dismounted.

'As we agreed last time on the Brig o Invercauld, I canna cross running water, so I'll hae to leave you here. You'll manage fine fae here; it's only a mile and a bittock tae Meikleour, where you'll find a phonebox.'

'Well., thank you, Your Majesty, that was quite an experience. I wouldn't have missed it for anything.'

He replied that it was an excercise in what you can do if you keep things under control. We shook hands

'Fare ye well for now. Here is a wee present for you.'

He withdrew a three foot long box like a rifle case from a saddlebag

'Dinna worry it's quite safe. You may even find it useful.'

I opened it. Reclining in a bed of black velvet was an inordinately long silver spoon.'

'Man, ye ken a' the caintrips in the book.' I said smiling.

'Aye I'm a real de'il. Fare thee weel '

He remounted, gave a salute, wheeled the black power in the form of a horse on which he sat and galloped back to the west. When the hoof beats had died away I was left alone in moonlight and silence. I crossed the silver river, shuffled along by the beech hedge kicking up the autumnal leaves stiff with frost, and fifteen minutes later arrived at a phone box. After another fifteen minutes, a taxi arrived. It slowed and I could see the driver looking at me carefully; he drove past and then returned. Fortunately it was a driver who knew me. He said, 'When I saw you with that gun under your arm I thought you were a terrorist. Just as well I recognized you.'

'Och, its just my clarinet case,' I explained.

I couldn't have told the truth. After that we had a pleasant chat about cattle and sheep and the incompetence of the local council.

Camped Out There in the Cold

The temperature was below zero. Near enough, for the purposes of this story, to the 50 below when the man from the creeks stumbled into the din and the glare of the Malemute Saloon prior to the shooting of Dangerous Dan McGrew. We were 15 degrees further south in the rain shadow of the Coast Range of British Columbia somewhere between Lytton and Lillooet. I write of an event that took place some sixty years ago when this area was still fairly empty and a faint whiff of the old frontier lingered on; the people of the First Nation still retained a presence in this backwater.

We left the car at the end of a long dirt road and started off through the cactus and sagebrush that lined the valley bottoms where the rain shadow was deepest. This gave way to a pleasant forest of Ponderosa pine. A few hundred feet higher up the open pine forest turned to increasingly dense spruce plugged with deep dry unconsolidated snow. After a few hours of struggle we reached our first flowery alpine pasture, at this time of year covered by a couple of feet of floury snow. We could see our ridge leaving the trees a few hundred feet above the thinning trees leading to a shapely summit.

By now the sun was sinking over the western peaks; the temperature started to fall; things were about to get serious. Under these conditions it is wise to bivouac early so you can see what you are doing. We headed for a thick island of spruce, one of several dotting the ragged edge of the tree line, here to make a des. res. for the night. The islet was particularly well favoured; it had three taller trees at its centre and the space around them was protected by a dense hedge of smaller trees. The central space was snow free and level. Once we had got our sleeping bags out and a candle burning on a knife stuck in a tree trunk and the primus roaring, we had a sheltered home and dined in comfort. Outside our nook the silence was deep and the stars glittered in a black, black sky.

Something – hopefully a coyote or a wolf, rather than something less tangible – howled from time to time from different locations in the surrounding forest primeval.

It was the first time we had tried out this type of bivouac. We were following the advice of a patient of mine, a Red Indian, by the name of Murdo MacDonald who had explained that this was standard practice among his people when out on a winter hunting expedition. He also gave me the helpful advice that if attacked by a bear you should get your back against a tree, hold your knife in your right hand point upwards and throw your left arm across your throat to protect your windpipe and great vessels. When the bear embraces you its claws dig into the tree rather than you. Before its teeth can do too much damage to your left arm, you stab upwards with the knife under its rib cage into its heart. This is anatomically a plausible procedure and may even work. His camping advice was certainly sound but, thankfully, I never had the chance to test his technique with an uppity bear.

The next morning we started late. It was cold outside and a strong wind was blowing. Our refuge remained sheltered, a warm microclimate filled with the comforting aroma of coffee and pine resin. We lay in our sleeping bags listening to the wind in the branches until the sun was well up in a bright blue sky. When we eventually did get going the wind cut to the bone and travel through the spindrift and deep unconsolidated powder was slow and painful. We could see long plumes of silver dust streaming from our ridge all the way to the summit. It must at least be snow free up there and we prepared for a battle along a windy corridor. To get shelter from the wind for as long as possible we returned to the trees and gained the lee side of the shoulder leading to our ridge. The price of the lee was deeper snow and denser forest as we were crossing into the climatically different Pacific slope.

I emerged from a dense thicket into a clearing. A few seconds later I was facing an Indian pointing a rifle at me. Then two other

Indians materialized also with rifles. They seemed vastly relieved at something. But not half as relieved as we were when we learned they were on the point of shooting us as deer. However, something about our progress was un-deer-like and had made them pause. They spoke little English but the message was the same as you get for spoiling the sport of a stalking party anywhere in the world.

We pointed uphill and asked 'Okay?' They gestures us on and we continued our struggle. The incident had been a close call. A lot of people get shot by mistake in the hunting season. In some areas farmers have been known to put white smocks on their animals with 'COW' or 'HORSE', as appropriate, written on the side in large black letters. We were lucky to encounter experienced hunters on their native heath. Townie palefaces tend to shoot anything that moves or even rustles. All this showed our double inexperience: the woods are dangerous in the hunting season and the new unconsolidated snow of November is best avoided.

We continued on to the foot of the ridge but after leaving the trees we were into wearing wind and waste-high spindrift. The ridge was longer than it looked from below and after a hundred feet or so of exposure to the wind hypothermia set in; it would be easy to die pointlessly in this unforgiving land. We wisely retreated to descend a couple of thousand feet through the spruce to the kindly belt of whispering Ponderosa pine.

Here we found a sheltered spot floored with pine needles instead of snow. We made a modest campfire and after our bacon and beans, mandatory fare in this context, reclined in happy comfort beneath bright stars twinkling in a black sky undiminished by the glow of urban electricity. My companion was moved to quote from the Shooting of Dan McGrew:

'Were you ever out in the Great Alone when the moon was awful clear,

And the icy mountains hemmed you in with a silence you most could hear,

With only the howl of the timber wolf as you camped out there in the cold

While high overhead, green, yellow and red the North Lights hunt in bars?-

Then you've a hunch what the music meant… hunger and night and the stars.'

Okay, so we weren't hungry, there was no music, no moon, no aurora and the wandering thing that had howled in the darkness the night before seemed to be elsewhere, but the rest of the *mise en scène* was there: the icy mountains hemmed us in and there was silence….. and night…. and the stars.

Sociological Note

The above episode happened almost sixty years ago. We were young and romantic at the time and much given to reading Robert Service; we saw the West through his eyes; we were very immature. To be fair in the early fifties of last century, there was still a faint sense of the old frontier in British Columbia, outside the towns at any rate. There were still prospectors left over from the gold rush days living in shacks up Tranquille Creek near where we lived and they would tell tales of the wild times in the old days when the west was predominantly a footloose male society. For example, the first time we went into a pub in BC we walked up to the bar, lent on it and asked for two beers. Everybody laughed and someone said, 'You guys must have been fresh off the train this morning.' At that time in a bar in BC you couldn't drink standing up. You had to order while sitting at a table; you were limited to two glasses of beer at a time; the glasses were small, less than half a pint if I remember correctly and they were brought to you at your table. So we sat down at a table and we each raised two fingers to indicate we were hard drinkers and wanted the maximum.

In remoter parts of the Province virgin land was still on offer from the Government at 25 cents an acre, provided you lived on it and cleared an acre a year; after five years it became yours. I forget the various obligations but they weren't onerous for a young man to fulfill. We thought seriously of combining homesteading with prospecting. Surely in a few years up some remote creek in the interior ranges of British Columbia we would strike it rich, find a mother lode and remedy our lack of wealth. I had taken instruction in prospecting procedures and had actually acquired a Free Miner's License that gave me the right to stake a claim and affix my own numbered 'claim plates' to mark it and later register it at the appropriate government office; it would then be mine for five years.

A technique Murdo MacDonald had told me about sounded interesting; it was to wait until a likely river froze and dig out the ice at the bottom of the waterfalls and then mine the gravel at the foot. This is where the heavy gold would have accumulated over the years. Come the spring the, stockpiled gravel could be washed at leisure and the nuggets recovered.

Alas, that is as far as it went; you need real courage to take wing and leave the cage. I was at the time a employed ingloriously as a civil servant by the BC Department of Health. We worked a five and a half day week with two weeks holiday a year. After fifteen years service you qualified for an extra week of annual leave; this in an area of spectacular unclimbed mountains!!! - all far too big for a day and a half expedition. The dimensions of Scotland are more suited to someone who needs the belay of secure employment.

I.H.M. Smart

Ariel

There are many kinds of artificial aids for arriving over the top of a mountain. One no more disreputable than any other is by light aircraft. True, unless things go badly wrong, your feet do not actually touch the summit, but then what is the difference between a few hundred feet of air and the hightech bootsole of the conventional climber? The number of intervening molecules is probably about the same. This analogy is not entirely convincing, and so the following accounts of airborne munrobagging are given with a feeling of guilt. Ringing the quiet hills with so many decibels wrung out of the blue belfry of a peaceful sky is, I suppose, the auditory equivalent of discarded orange peel.

The flights described here were made in a Cessna 152 out of Riverside Airfield, Dundee. This aircraft is a highwing monoplane with two seats and a cruising speed of about ninety knots. Real airmen consider it a very boring aircraft, and refer to it as a 'spam can', but to an inexperienced pilot like myself it feels like being at the controls of a Sopwith Camel heading into peril. This feeling, however, sharpens up the senses; the familiar hills beneath gain a new magic as the vertical dimension is suddenly enlarged, made mobile and put under your own personal control. The accounts below are not given in the spirit of Biggles nor with the gravid introspection of St Exupery, but are responses to the high aesthetics of soaring above the fair land of Scotland in its different moods, to the privilege of travel in four dimensions with all senses heavily engaged in responding to the total ambience yet with the practical need to keep one's hands on the control systems connecting the appreciative brain with the uncompromising reality of aerodynamics.

Spring Song

This flight was made on a fine day in May. I flew north over fertile Strathmore, parquet-floored with fields of winter brown and the fresh green of brairding crops. Then up to eight thousand feet above the scattering of fair-weather cumulus clouds of the type that angels recline upon with their harps. (You occasionally see them in the passing; many are clearly recognisable as former members of the Club and give you a friendly wave as you fly by). Far below were the sun-dappled moorlands of Strathardle and bonnie Glenshee and there, by the silver river, was my house. Over the Ben Iutharns, the clouds ended and the captured Feshie could be seen hair-pin bending into the Spey instead of the Dee. Above the Garbh Coire Mor I throttled back, put down half flap and commenced a lazy circling descent in a clockwise direction over the snow-wreathed hills. The old familiar landmarks appeared on the horizon one after the other: the Monadhliath, the great forests of Rothiemurchus and Nethy, Ben Avon and Ben a Chie and the plains of Aberdeenshire beyond, then the Dee and dark Lochnagar, Glen Clunie with its rolling green slopes, Ben y Gloe of the many corrries, the Drumochter hills of the many horizons and back to the Monadhliath. The Lairig Ghru, meanwhile, spiralled up from below growing in texture and detail with each circle. At five grand, I levelled out and made a turn round Braeriach, wing tip pointed at the cairn, and eyes checking the dials for slip, bank, height and speed - you can't be too careful. Nevertheless, there was enough cerebral capacity left over to appreciate the total situation. You could see into sunlit Coire Bhrochain where we had camped in deep snow on Hogmanay 1948 when the hills were empty. There was the little lochan below Cairn Toul and now the textured floor of the Garbh Coire Mor itself sparking the memory of that winter day when the great quilt of cloud cascaded off the edge of the plateau into the gloom of the coire, then the Wells of Dee of the memorable June bivouac in perfect weather and now Rothiemurchus, once wild and lonely with only a rutted track to Glenmore Lodge which lay on the edge of the then known world. I am telling you all this to illustrate how much parallel processing the creatively stressed brain can accomplish as it wheels about in time and space above a landscape heavily associated with the brain's own formative experiences. Then on over the trackless plateau of Ben Macdhui, now well and truly tracked, a look into Loch Avon where Broon kept a lonely Hogmanay long ago when there actually were deep midwinters, over barnacled Ben Mheadhain where I once drowsed fawnlike one youthful summer afternoon, past Ben a' Bhuird of the frost-bitten toe and the Mitre Ridge of high ecstasy, then back south by dark Lochnagar and many-branched Glen Clova, an eastward curve over the Howe of the Mearns to the silvery Tay and a near-perfect landing at Dundee. I walked away from the plane six inches above the ground having lived a full three weeks in an hour and a quarter of elapsed real time.

High Summer

This was a windless day, slightly overcast with a thin layer of high cloud and enough sunshine to give a hint of shadow. Below the cloud, the air was clear to the sharp horizon as it often is after rain. The first leg to Inverness lay over the detailed landscape of the rolling eastern Grampians. Loch Builg, Tomintoul, Loch Garten, the Spey and the Findhorn all appeared below uncannily in the order predicted by the map. After a coffee in the International Lounge and an altercation with the security guards who wanted to see documents we didn't have, we were escorted back to the plane by an embarrassed local who apologised for the extraterrestrials who seemed to be running the place. Then the flight to the rough bounds of Wester Ross and Sutherland began. First direct to Loch Maree at four grand. Between us and the far horizon lay the fabled lands of the West from the Skerries to the Lewes. To the left, the textured lands of Torridon, and to our right the wilderness of Sutherland whither we were bound. It is good to be lucky, but magnitudes better to actually know you are lucky; aware of my doubly privileged situation, I tried to respond to everything that was going on. The maximum amount of brain was dedicated to appreciating the fleeting complexity of all that was happening, yet retaining enough reserve capacity to cope with flying the machine and with emergencies, such as the engine stopping or the propeller falling off. This total commitment of the mind at so many levels is for me the greatest exhilaration of flying. I thought I would mention this because if you have actually read this far into the Journal, you will be people of discrimination, and I would not like you to think I was being thoughtlessly self-indulgent or, worse still, trying to solicit admiration.

We made a descending circle over the shaggy islands of the reflection-filled loch with Sliochd as a backdrop, then over by Beinn Airidh Charr to the Fionn Loch with herons circling the only wooded island. Over Strath na Seallag you could make out Sheneval and the Larach an Tigh Mhor before passing by mighty, many-summitted An Teallach and crossing the Loch Brooms to Coigach.

From this vantage you could see that the north-west was the ragged fringe of Scotland, the rocky edge of Europe, the end of the road for folk migrations from the Eurasian hinterland. Below us, the present day Gaels were being displaced by poor souls from England and elsewhere driven out of their ruined homelands in the overpopulated twilight of the Anglo-Saxon fringe. At the end of the Achiltibuie road I could see the croft of Cul na Creag where in the late forties of last century I had stayed in a Gaelic-speaking household, still rich in song and story; probably they speak some form of broad Cockney there now. In another hundred years maybe the Gaelo-cockney tongue will be replaced by Urdu and Wee Shias may reign in Coigach with all the benevolence once exercised by the Wee Frees before them. From up here, you gain a detached perspective on these transient human population movements.

The flight continued with a low circle round Stac Pollaidh then round mighty, gloomy Suilven with its head moodily in a cloud. Back in Inverness, we refueled, flew down the Great Glen, turned left up Glen Coe flying below the summits - that was exciting -

then hung a louie over Kingshouse to take us along Loch Laidon where the super camping island is, then by Rannoch and Tummel to Pitlochry, grabbed a roger here and so back to Dundee. The four hours in the air now required as many weeks to think out. The soul, as is well known, travels at walking pace and requires frequent rests. Go any faster and it gets left far behind; bits of mine are in fact still to this day wandering around the rough bounds of Wester Ross.

Autumn over Schiehallion

This was as fine an autumn day as you could wish. There was a bit of a temperature inversion. A big glacier of cloud filled the upper Tay from Pitlochry to fair Strathmore and over towards Perth. Elsewhere the glens were clear, the sun was brightly shining and the highland summits stretched away to the horizon dusted with early snow. The autumn colours were aglow - russet bracken, yellow-gold birch and yellow-ochre larch. The great Schiehallion from which Fujiyama was copied lay ahead, and beyond it the long view over Loch Tummel and Loch Rannoch and Lochaber to the clichés of the Isles. A wide climbing turn over the sacred mountain took us to twelve grand. Scotland lay below from the Scuir of Eigg to the Bass Rock looking like a brighter version of a Bartholomew's map. At times like this it would be possible to exclaim, 'Oh, joy, oh, rapture!' and get away with it. I wish I had had the nerve to try on this occasion. Alas, I flew stolidly homeward, frightened of committing a solecism; it would be nice to be a tearaway once in a while and really let yourself go. An hour later I was sitting at my desk wondering if it had all happened.

Darkness and Light

I flew towards Ben y Gloe late on a sombre February day. The sky was overcast with layers of blues, greys and gunmetals leading into the cave of the advancing night. The snows of the Grampians, backlit in the dim light, glowed above the dark glens. Gloom and mystery reigned over familiar country. Heading into desolation and winter darkness grips you with apprehension and exhilaration. Maybe this desire to put yourself to the test, to explore the unknown and actually enjoy hovering at the boundary of your ability in a demanding situation reflects the way our nervous system is organised. Such willingness to probe the edges of the physical and intellectual world, the fearful delight of putting your head beyond the perceived envelope of safety is the brain function that carries us beyond ourselves. Were it not so, we would still be living happily in the trees of Africa. In the somewhat overcivilised situation I am describing now, the subconscious, perhaps, saw the flight as a metaphor for death, a sort of training run, a reconnaissance into the ultimate extinction from which this time you could return if you found it all more than you could handle. North, by the way, is a metaphorically safe direction to explore because, as everybody knows, come summer the darkness will turn into brilliant continuous daylight, everything will be young again and spring will return to the step. Be such speculation as it may, the little plane with its navigation lights twinkling flew into the intimidating gloom. I circled Ben y Gloe about half a grand above the soft glow of the summit snow, acutely aware of being alive and in a state of high exhilaration in the closing mouth of the winter night.

Stylistically, the story should end on this eirenic note of contemplation of the final things, but real life doesn't seem to be much interested in style which is a grammatical conceit, a sort of retrospective tense applied in the reflective mood. In the real life aspect of this story, there was a lot more hard reality to be handled before a safe touch down allowed the luxury of literary style to emerge.

I came back the long way round using the dark gothic tooth of Broughty Castle silhouetted against the sea as a landmark. Over the

Tay, the setting sun had broken through a complicated cloud system. We have all seen memorable winter sunsets; this one was as complex and colourful as they come, doubled in the reflections of the mirror smooth river, and enhanced by the spectacular glooms that surrounded it; like an impressionist painting, it was full of bits of light and dark; you were aware that there were complementary colours resonating in the shadows. An imaginative man would not have been surprised to crash suddenly into a giant Monet hung on the wall of the western sky. Blessed with a dour, unexcitable disposition, no such wild thoughts went through my mind; I boringly lined up the plane on long finals for a straight-in approach to runway two eight zero, carried out my down-wind checks (brakes off, under carriage down, pitch fine, carburettor heat on, mixture rich, engine dials reading okay and seat belt tight), lowered twenty degrees of flap, trimmed for an approach speed of sixty five knots, reported short finals on the radio on 122 decimal 9 kilocycles and made a passable landing with knuckles maybe slightly white on the control column.

Above the Clouds

This flight to the west was made part of the way above the clouds. This is perfectly legal provided you remain within sight of the ground and a certain distance from the cloud. Within these constraints, you can explore the great bens and glens of the upper air, the great one-off cloudscapes that will never be repeated. You can frolic around in complete privacy in this constantly moving country of beauty and mystery. I have never seen anybody else up there, although doubtless there are marauding military jets, setting an objective danger like avalanches or collapsing seracs. This high territory is one of the last great wilderness areas. It is like the mountains below used to be before the industrial age of mountaineering, before our bizarre activity became just another sector of the market economy. It's like sailing still is, once you get to the western coasts of the Outer Isles and keep away from the St Kilda run.

This time we were on our way to Mull. There were glimpses of Ben Lui and Ben Cruachan below the surface of the high cloud fields. At Taynuilt, the cloud ended and in calm sunny weather we landed at Glenforsa on the meadow that serves as the airport. The skylarks were singing; lunch was out of doors. An hour later, we flew over Ardnamurchan, to the beaches at Arisaig of the islets and Morar of the silver sands (but at a discreet height and distance), half way up Loch Morar a turn south over the rough bounds of Moidart to the Ben, a circle here for admiration and homage, then back over Luibelt, Staoineag, Loch Ossian Youth Hostel, Ben Alder cottage and other important centres before turning south east to eventually leave the rugged terrain and enter the contrasting lowlands of far eastern Scotland.

Envoi

This flight will never take place. Nevertheless, I am going to tell you about it. It would be made on a clear, windless winter night with a full moon. The lochs will be frozen, and there will have been a heavy snowfall. I have made a training flight under these conditions and it was indeed an exhilarating experience with Strathmore and its surrounding mountains all a-glimmer below, and town, village and even individual farmhouse lights twinkling and identifiable. Circling the aircraft in level flight at a 45 degree angle of bank from pole star back to pole star while the well-known constellations pass in procession before the windscreen is an exacting test, particularly when you are asked to continue for a second round to make sure the first time wasn't a fluke.

On this final flight, I'll fly north over Braemar, then low between Cairngorm of Derry and Ben MacDhui. By Carn Etchachan, I'll put down full flap and descend into the head of Loch Avon with a glance from the corner of the eye at the Shelter Stone and its crag, then fly low over the twinkling snow on the loch and through the bealach to the Nethy, then climb high over Strath Spey and continue north again. Maybe keep on going over the Monadhliath and the Great Glen to Stac Pollaidh and Suilven, ghostly in the moonlight. Maybe keep on going over the sea until summer.

9255281R00149

Printed in Great Britain
by Amazon.co.uk, Ltd.,
Marston Gate.